Isabel of Castile, the august queen that united a fractured, war-ridden land into a unified country under a single religion and language after seven hundred years of war and domination, is the same sovereign who made it possible for discoveries as prodigious as the Americas, the matchless regent whose rule led to the ushering in of the Renaissance into Spain. And yet, her journey to the throne was far from likely.

Torn away from her childhood home, the pious and observant young Isabel is brought to the debauched Court of her brother, King Enrique. But when political strife leads to civil war between her two brothers, the young princess must defy the tyrannical control of the king, escape manipulative noblemen, and save herself from being used as a pawn in an arranged marriage, in order to protect the future of her kingdom and marry the man she believes she is destined for.

In *Isabel of Castile: Making of a Monarch*, the woman that would be hailed by the Vatican as "the Catholic Queen" maneuvers her way through the social, political and cultural milieu of patriarchal 15th century Spain, and establishes an era of justice, faith, and unity.

"A remarkable novel based on an intimacy with historical context, Nichole Christakes Dapelo offers a dazzling fictional account of Isabel's long journey to womanhood and queenship."
>—Dr. Teofilo Ruiz, Chair and distinguished professor of UCLA's Department of Spanish and Portuguese History

"*Isabel of Castile: Making of a Monarch* is a well-written historical novel based on the adolescence and coming of age of one of the leading figures of the Spanish Renaissance. The author captures the essence and uncertainties of this turbulent transitional period in time, and recreates the key events and figures of this pivotal moment in Spanish history."
>—Fernando Dameto Zaforteza, Director and Professor of Humanities at Instituto de Empresa, Madrid

ISABEL OF CASTILE
Making of a Monarch

Nichole Christakes Dapelo

Moonshine Cove Publishing, LLC
Abbeville, South Carolina U.S.A.
First Moonshine Cove edition November 2019

This book is a work of fiction. Names, characters, places and incidents are products of the author's imagination or are used fictitiously. Any resemblance to actual events, locales or persons, living or dead, is entirely coincidental.

ISBN: 978-1-945181-733
Library of Congress PCN: 2019918308
© Copyright 2019 by Nicole Christakes Dapelo

All rights reserved. No part of this book may be reproduced in whole or in part without written permission from the publisher except by reviewers who may quote brief excerpts in connection with a review in a newspaper, magazine or electronic publication; nor may any part of this book be reproduced, stored in a retrieval system or transmitted in any form or by any means electronic, mechanical, photocopying, recording or any other means, without written permission from the publisher.

Cover photograph provided by the author, cover and interior design by Moonshine Cove staff.

About the Author

Nichole Christakes Dapelo is an author and scholar of Medieval and Early Modern History, with a focus on women's role in society. Her first novel, *Madame de Pompadour: Making of a Mistress*, was published in 2017. Her books are available on Amazon, Barnes & Nobles, and bookshops and boutiques in California and Florida.

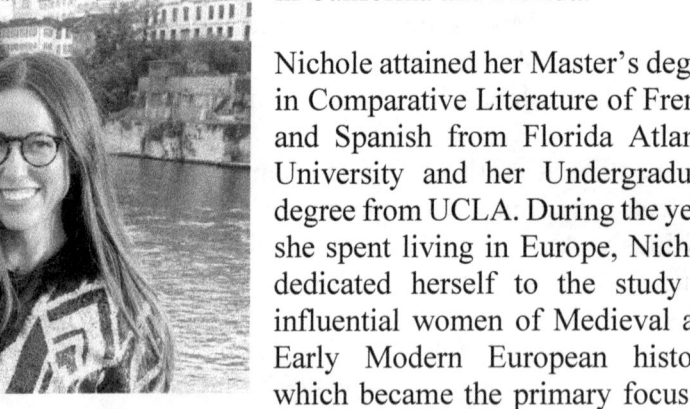

Nichole attained her Master's degree in Comparative Literature of French and Spanish from Florida Atlantic University and her Undergraduate degree from UCLA. During the years she spent living in Europe, Nichole dedicated herself to the study of influential women of Medieval and Early Modern European history, which became the primary focus of her Graduate degree. Nichole C. Dapelo is a native Californian and currently resides with her husband and toddler in Vero Beach, Florida.

For Gabriel and Coco Isabel. Your make our world complete.

Acknowledgment

Firstly, I would like to express my warmest gratitude to Dr. Teofilo Ruiz. Dr. Ruiz not only took a great deal of time to review the historical accuracy of this project, but has been a continuous source of encouragement of my writing since my days at UCLA.

I would like to thank Dr. Horswell, Dr. Gamboa, and Dr. Gosser-Esquilín for allowing me to tailor my graduate studies around the social and political milieu of Isabel la Católica, the forces leading to her rise in power, and the developments and transformation of Western Europe as a direct result of her life.

To Dr. Petersen Cruz, your passion for the life experiences of the Early Modern Woman are infectious and elating. Thank you for your mentorship.

I would also like to express my thanks to the mentor that has most profoundly shaped my life since my earliest memories, Dirk Anderson. A great deal of my sense of independence and value of female autonomy, my willingness to explore the unfamiliar and to challenge perceived limitations, is because of you.

To my husband and life-long partner, Brian, you are the rich color to the canvas of my life and the weight of my world. I couldn't have completed this project without your patience and steady encouragement, especially as a young mother.

Finally, my deepest gratitude to my mother, Dana, and mother-in-law, Charlene. Your grace, compassionate heart, daily grit, extraordinary resilience and willingness to love exemplify what I hope to evoke in my characters, as well as myself, and weave you together with the fabric of the strong women that have impacted history.

Author's Note

One of history's most fascinating protagonists, the woman remembered as Isabel la Católica, Queen of Castile, has provoked and inspired for over five centuries. She is often remembered for her role in the European discovery of the Americas, the conquest of the Moorish empire after seven hundred years of Islamic rule, and the ushering in of the Renaissance to Spain, as well as atrocities, such as the expulsion of the Jews and the Spanish Inquisition. Even to this day, her influence is evident. Timeless texts of the Early Modern era are a product of her impact. Niccolò Machiavelli's *The Prince* and Miguel de Cervantes' *Don Quijote de la Mancha*, literary works whose words still reverberate in our world today, would not have been possible without these author's observations of this formidable lady. Another example of Isabel's fingerprint on society, the University of Salamanca still bears the words, "los reyes a la Universidad, y la Universidad a los reyes" on the façade that she, herself, brought to the institution after her conquest of Granada.

Many historians regard her as the most important woman of her era. And yet, like many powerful female leaders of the past, history often degrades her for her achievements, categorically undermining her by labeling her as what Dr. Helen Castor would call a "she-wolf." These "she-wolves" are precisely the characters I find most intriguing.

However, what I found particularly engrossing about Isabel was not so much the grand triumphs she achieved later in life, but instead her unlikely journey to the Crown and the riveting vicissitudes of her life that led to her acquisition of power…

With a half-brother as king who already had a daughter and heir, as well as a second brother before Isabel in the line of succession, it would have been quite unimaginable for her contemporaries to have considered Isabel as a likely claimant to the throne of Castilla y León. And yet, how differently the world would be if the crown should have fallen onto the head of another.

My intention in writing this novel is two-fold. First, basing my writing on documented events, research of the individuals surrounding her life, and historical episodes, I hope to depict Isabel, the intensely pious, fearless, loyal, wise, insightful, ambitious, and passionate individual that she was. Secondly, I hope to portray the incredible agency of the dual identity of Isabel, as both young woman and princess, maneuvering her way through the tangles of 15th century patriarchal Spain. Thus, my intention is to represent who Isabel was, while simultaneously revealing the development of the self-fashioning of Isabel, the sovereign.

As a student of women in historical fiction, what I find most interesting is the way history casts its female protagonists, often relegating them to the role of virgin or whore, saint or she-wolf, and how these women overcome patriarchal limitations. Despite societal obligations, there are those spectacular few who dare to defy tradition and undermine convention, those who take advantage of patriarchal norms, treating them as a stepping stool to find their own voice and carve out their own road to authority, autonomy, and influence. This, in essence, is the story of Isabel.

Historical Note

As an author of women's historical fiction, I endeavor to present my reader with a story that is based entirely on real characters and events in history, as well as real historical facts, representations of locations, and recorded reactions and quotes. In consideration of this endeavor, I have detailed several points that will be of interest to the reader of history.

In creating the scenes of medieval entertainment and the power and authority that is rooted in such events, one of my most indispensable resources has been *A King's Travels: Festive Traditions in Late Medieval and Early Modern Spain*, by Dr. Teofilo Ruiz.

On a similar note, one of the predominant themes to be found in this novel is "self-fashioning" and legitimization of authority. The self-fashioning of Isabel into a Marian figure was one of Isabel's most useful tools in asserting and maintaining her legitimacy as a female sovereign. For more insight into this subject, see Barbara Weissberger's book, *Isabel Rules: Constructing Queenship, Wielding Power*.

A further example of "self-fashioning" and authority can be found in Isabel's use of symbols and devices, as is evident in the ubiquitous objects of the coin and the coat of arms of Isabel and Fernando. Aware of the societal requirement to abide by patriarchal traditions, Isabel used objects such as these to evoke a public image of unity and equality, while privately maintaining her rights as queen regent. For example, as opposed to previous rulers, in which the king's image enjoyed the predominate space on the coin, Isabel ensured that the coin displayed an image of herself and her husband facing one another. Secondly, Isabel implemented the symbol of Alexander the Great's Gordian Knot into imagery throughout her reign, including the coat of arms designed for her marriage, which was featured in the architecture of colleges, churches and hospitals throughout the kingdom. The importance of the symbol is its message that the "ends justify the means," as well as linking the Reyes Católicos with Alexander the Great, which further legitimized their authority by connecting them with great leaders of history.

One of my favorite "fun facts" to be found in the novel regards the game of chess. Prior to Isabel's reign, the rules of chess were different than how they are practiced today, particularly the freedom of movement of the queen chess piece. It was during the later years of Isabel's rule that the chess piece of the queen enjoyed more agency, and many historians attribute the change in rules for this single chess piece to be a result of the power and agency exercised by Queen Isabel.

The poem found on page 65 was written by Isabel herself (excepting the first two stanzas, which were written by Nichole C. Dapelo) and was recited for her brother Alfonso for his birthday, as is found in *Isabel la Católica: vida y reinado* by Tarsicio de Azcona, pg. 113. All translations from the original Spanish to English are my own.

As an author, I chose to use the Spanish translation of names, titles, locations, etc., as opposed to an anglicized version. This choice was made as an effort to preserve the essence of the story as belonging to Spanish history.

The vase described on page 69 was once a gift given to William IX of Aquitaine by a Muslim king of Zaragoza during a brief period of peace, as is told by historian María Rosa Menocal. After the fall of their capital to the Almorávides, the Muslim king partnered with the Christian Spaniards, including William IX, Duke of Aquitaine. As a show of his gratitude, the Muslim king gave the French duke a jar that is, to this day, preserved at the Louvre in Paris. Regarding the origin of the tradition of the troubadour, William IX's father's vassal delivered a thousand Arabic female slaves to the Court of Aquitaine, thereby creating an environment in which, since his earliest memories, William would be exposed to the songs and poetry of the Arabic tradition. Here, the Arabic poetic "jarcas" mixed with French influence, evolving into what became the art of the troubadour. Therefore, the origin of the troubadour tradition is a hybrid of Arabic and French.

In certain moments of the novel, Isabel speaks of her maternal grandmother, as can be found on page 71, etc. Isabel was very close to her Portuguese grandmother, Isabel de Barcelos, whom she spent much time with during her childhood in Arévalo with her mother and younger brother. She was an exemplary influence on Isabel during her formative years, and I argue that history can see the result of Isabel's grandmother's influence by Isabel's choice to patronize Columbus' maritime expeditions.

Isabel's statement that "a man that is willing to betray you once must never be trusted again," as is found on page 174, is inspired by lessons taught by Niccolò Machiavelli's *The Prince*. Written a generation later, Machiavelli's work was most likely influenced by his observations of rulers such as Queen Isabel of Castile, and certainly by her husband, Fernando. Thus, one can better imagine Medieval ruler's perspective and behavior through the works they inspired.

Finally, I would like to briefly touch on the subject of slavery. Isabel was deeply opposed to the enslavement of the indigenous tribes whom she desired to convert to Catholicism. Upon the discovery of the Americas, Christopher Columbus saw the value of enslaving the Indians, as is evident in his first post-discovery letter sent to Isabel. But Isabel would not have it. Instead, she emphasized the discovery as an opportunity to evangelize. As opposed to others, Isabel was very protective of the Indians and commanded that they be treated with respect. It wasn't until her later years, as she grew frailer, that she lacked the strength to act in their defense. Towards the end of her life and thereafter, without the protection of the queen, the treatment of the indigenous grew shamefully worse.

ISABEL OF CASTILE: Making of a Monarch

Christina
Enjoy the read!
xox,
Michele C Naylor

Chapter I
February 1462

There, in the shadowy corner of the room, I stood with eyes wide open. The humidity in the room was nearly palpable, despite the bitingly cold February day. The queen's ladies-in-waiting rushed back and forth, bringing water, fresh cloths to replace the blood-soaked ones, scurrying to deliver whatever the queen demanded. My half-brother, King Enrique IV, anxiously paced back and forth, while the midwife took charge and instructed Queen Juana. To his right stood Beltrán de la Cueva, Enrique's favorite, and notably one of the most handsome of his courtiers, within but an arm's reach of the queen.

"Now hold your breath, and push as hard as you can," the midwife instructed, her voice firm, calm and steady, as if she had complete control over the healthy birth of the royal heir.

The king would have preferred his physician perform the birth instead of a midwife, but Queen Juana de Avís refused, saying that she had endured enough quackery at the hands of his Jewish doctor and his sordid instruments, and she wouldn't allow his hands to touch her again. Besides, the midwife had been bringing children into this world for decades. Beltrán de la Cueva supported the queen's wishes, and the king gave no further argument.

Juan Pacheco, the Marqués de Villena, leaned almost imperceptively towards his uncle, Alfonso Carrillo, the Archbishop of Toledo and whispered discreetly in his ear. With eyes cast downward, I strained my ears to hear his words. Though I was a child and unfamiliar to the life of a king's Court, I knew well enough the value in an exchange between two powerful men at an event as pivotal as the birth of the king's child. But their words were too faint and my ears failed to hear.

"Water!" shouted the queen. I rushed to her Majesty's side and put the goblet of cold water to her lips, then returned to my corner. Somehow it felt safer there, as if the shadows hid my frail frame from view and no one would take notice of me. I wondered if my entire life would be spent in a shadow, a small figure lost in the cracks of a royal Court.

Soon, things will get better, I reassured myself. Today is the day that the queen will bear a son, a child for her husband and for the realm. And when the heir is born, her Grace will no longer treat me so harshly. When the heir is born, I will no longer be treated as a threat to my brother's throne. My brother will no longer be plagued by the insults of being labeled as "Enrique, the Impotent," an emasculating moniker for any man, and even more so for the ruler of a kingdom that demands dominance and masculine leadership. The failure of his first marriage to the princess of the neighboring kingdom of Aragón, coupled with his failure to produce a child after so many years of marriage to Queen Juana de Avís, will disappear today, with the birth of his heir, *el infante.*

Queen Juana's face clenched in pain as she bit down on a folded cloth to keep her teeth from grinding together, and her voice groaned as she willed the child to come out from inside of her.

Even now, as she endured the horrors of childbearing, the queen was still undeniably one of the most remarkably beautiful women in all Castilla, certainly the most beautiful woman I'd ever seen.

"He is beginning to crown, just one last good push, my lady," the midwife exclaimed enthusiastically. Then she pushed her thick, pale hands inside of the queen and pulled the child out.

Immediately, the room went quiet. The light in the midwife's face disappeared, and she looked from the queen to the king, then to Juan Pacheco, the Marqués de Villena. Finally, her eyes dropped to the floor, exaggerating the drooping skin beneath them. A heavy silence hung in the air.

"Go on," the marqués de Villena impatiently demanded the answer that every one of us wondered: had the king secured the future of the Crown? Had he delivered the kingdom a son?

"A girl," she answered through terse lips. Then, exhaling deeply, she corrected herself. "A healthy princess."

The king stared out the window, as if refusing to acknowledge his wife and newborn daughter.

"Isabel," he called out softly.

A wave of distrust washed over me. Turning away from the window, he walked towards me, positioning himself directly in front of me, making me feel small enough to crush. The blood drained from my face as I looked up at my half-brother, who, at over six feet tall, towered over me. His golden hair and deformed nose made him look like a lion, not a powerful and regal beast, but instead like a lion that had been defeated and now lived in a cage, controlled by his handlers. I watched as his emotions shifted. He was not angry, only sad. Just like everyone else in the room, the king realized that the birth of a daughter would reflect on his own inability to secure the throne.

"Sister," he said to me, making me realize that the wave of simmering anger had washed away, and was followed by the shadow of disappointment that seemed to haunt him. "I name you as godmother to the *infanta*. You will oversee all the details to the princess's christening."

"As you wish, your Highness. I welcome the honor you bestow upon me," I answered, bowing my head with gravity and respect.

Queen Juana de Avís held the small child against her bare skin, cooing to her lovingly, not bothering to pay any mind to her husband and his disappointment of not having a son, and I found myself smiling as I watched her relishing the moment she had finally become a mother. This was the most tender I had ever seen the queen behave. Perhaps she would grow softer now that she was a mother. At least, one could hope.

"Madam," said the wet nurse, reaching out her hands to take the child. A queen never breastfed her own child, instead, the responsibility went to a wet nurse.

"No!" the queen retorted with defiance, slapping the woman's hands away. "Remove your hands from my child and return to wherever you came from. Your assistance is not welcome here." Her words were harsh, authoritative. Then, turning to the king with glaring eyes, "I will feed my daughter myself. She is, after all, *only* a girl."

The wet nurse looked to the king, unsure of how to respond. But my half-brother didn't bother to reply; it was not worth the fight with his wife. Better to just let her have her way.

"As the queen wills it," he answered, and left the room.

I stood there, in shock at the queen's behavior, and the king's submission. Yet, despite my sentiments, my face revealed nothing of what I felt. Despite all the corruption and debauchery I witnessed in the Court of Enrique IV and his queen, my involvement would be nothing more than to serve and observe.

Chapter II
Baptism

The little *Infanta* Juana lay coddled in my arms, warmly wrapped in her white silk and lace christening gown draped luxuriously to the floor, as I solemnly stood before the assembly. Her face was serene, almost angelic. She was a peaceful child, hardly ever fussing. I gently rocked her back and forth, and waited for Archbishop Carrillo to perform the religious duty and to dip his finger in the holy water.

"Receive the sign of the cross on your brow and on your heart," he said, his cold fingers gently touching her forehead. Still, she did not wake, so soundly was she resting in my arms. But as soon as the salt was placed in her mouth by the archbishop she began to whimper, a cry that only grew louder. I did my best to rock her, but I knew well enough that she wouldn't be contented until she was in her mother's arms.

"I know, sweet princess, I know," I whispered to her. And I did. No one more than my younger brother, Alfonso, and I could feel more empathy for this precious child who would find no solace until she was reunited with her mother. Little over a year ago, her Grace had deemed it necessary that Alfonso and I be ripped out of our mother's arms and brought to this Court. All we wanted was to return home to our simple life in Arévalo.

Little by little, my niece, Princess Juana, drifted back to sleep, and I took the opportunity to peak out at the crowd standing witness. All the most honored families of the kingdom were in attendance, as was the clergy. All were present to witness the long-awaited moment of the baptism of the firstborn child of Enrique IV, King of Castilla and León.

Certainly, the baptism of a royal child was an event to be celebrated. But as I looked around, it was obvious that abnormally great lengths had been taken to honor the birth of *this* child. Clearly, a small fortune had been poured into the trappings of this baptism, especially considering that the baptism was for a girl. In the streets, the fountains would spout red and white wine, and after the ceremony, twenty different types of birds would be released. The people, after all, must have their entertainment.

I was no fool; I understood my brother's intentions. Later today, while the nobles were still gathering in the presence of the king, all would be required to come before the Princess Juana and swear their fealty to her as heir to the throne. Enrique expected that his unruly nobles would be disinclined to break with the tradition of a male heir. Therefore, measures were taken. Pledges must be made; the baptismal ceremony must be magnificent. It must impress the audience, and leave all with an impression of the profound power and undeniable legitimacy of little Juana as the future heir to the throne.

The nobles all stood tall, their legs most likely growing as weary as mine were after so long on my feet. I ignored the aching in my knees and turned my attention to the crowd before me. All were proudly dressed in elegant headdresses and the finest clothes they owned to celebrate the monumental occasion. Yet, despite the appearance of sophistication and dignity, it was evident that too many members of the king's Court were seething at what they were required to proclaim.

And at the head of the aristocracy's discontent stood Juan Pacheco, Marqués de Villena. His stare was sharp, almost violent, as he looked on at Beltrán de la Cueva, the king's favorite, the one that had taken Pacheco's place as the man closest to the king. But this was not merely an issue of jealousy. Nearly all the nobles hated de la Cueva, a man that came from nothing, who was, little by little, attaining the highest honors of the kingdom. Just recently, he was granted the distinguished title of Count of Ledesma, and as no one could figure out what right he had, or what he had done to earn the promotion, it left much speculation to the imagination. Tongues wagged.

And now here they stood, one next to another, all expected to swear loyalty to a princess, a female heir to the Castilian throne. Perhaps it wouldn't have upset them quite so much if there could be the hope that more children would soon follow little Juana, but no one was foolish enough to think *that* a possibility. Two wives and too many years without producing a royal babe in the nursery waved away any illusion for more offspring.

This was not what our father, King Juan II, would have wanted. Everyone knew that, most of all Enrique. Everyone knew that the entire reason our father felt compelled to remarry, choosing my mother for a bride, was because of his disappointment in Enrique, the son of his first marriage. Our father had lost faith in him. After failing to consummate his first marriage to Blanca, the Princess of Navarra, on their wedding night, he then failed to consummate their marital bed every night after. That failure would never do in Castilla. The Castilian expected their king to be powerful, virile. A man that couldn't consummate his marriage, that couldn't produce an heir, and ended up sending back his wife "as much a virgin as she was the day they married," that was a man emasculated in the eyes of his countrymen. If he couldn't perform his duty in the bedchamber... It didn't take long before the unforgiving noblemen labeled him as "Enrique the Impotent."

The ceremony ended and Pacheco gave the slightest bow before being the first to exit, his face still filled with disgust.

I looked down at the *infanta*, searching the baby's face, trying to find any characteristic of my half-brother or from my side of the family. The ladies-in-waiting all said that newborns almost always look like their fathers. But there was nothing in her countenance that resembled the Trastámara family. The child looked nothing like the king. And I couldn't help but worry that the whispers were true, that this child had been sired by another.

How different my grandmother's expectations were when she assisted my father, King Juan II, in selecting Juana de Avís as a bride to my older brother, Enrique. After all, my grandmother was also from Portugal, and encouraged my father to strengthen the ties of kinship through marriage between Castilla and the ever-expanding international power of Portugal.

I closed my eyes and tried to remember my grandmother, how she smiled, the softness of her skin. My grandmother, Isabel of Barcelos, was the wisest woman I had ever met. *Composure, child. Observe first, and let your reactions come from a place of control*, she often reminded me. It was one of the greatest lessons I would ever learn.

My grandmother had served on the privy counsel to my father. And she had indeed been of great service in arranging the marriage between Portugal and Castilla. But if my grandmother were to witness what I was exposed to, the decadence of the Court, she would have never had made the match.

I cringed to think of this little girl, the future queen of Castilla y León, growing up in the depraved environment of Queen Juana's Court. As godmother, I had a responsibility both to the child and to God to encourage the princess in her spiritual journey. But what power did I have to combat the lasciviousness of the queen's ladies she had brought with her from her Court in Portugal?! Every one of them was a woman without decency. They went about, with their low-cut dresses, never bothering to conceal their bodice, and the queen turned a blind eye to their wonton affairs. Even she, herself, flirted shamelessly with other men.

Meanwhile, the king blatantly dishonored the Castilian tradition. Instead of presenting himself as a *cristiano viejo*, a descendant of a long line of Christians, he favored the Moorish style in both dress and behavior. My brother and his wife failed to fulfill their duty to serve as an example to their countrymen. Such behavior made a mockery of the Crown, dangerously so.

More and more, the nobles showed little fear in airing their complaints to my brother. Meanwhile he did little more than vacillate between paranoia over his inability to satisfy their demands that some days left him paralyzed with fear, while other days he appeared distant, distracted, and unfazed by the grumblings of an aristocracy that held growing power over him.

Castilla was disillusioned. I was just as aware of it as every other courtier. And the only ones to blame were my brother and his foolish wife, whose behavior had put the future of the Trastámara family at risk. The throne had belonged to our family since the mid-1300s, but I was beginning to fear my brother's incompetence would put us all in danger. I feared to ask: would his weakness lead to the end of the Trastámara reign?

Chapter III
1463

"My lords! Please!" came the panicked cry of a courtier, his belly protruding robustly before him as his feet frantically shuffled towards Enrique and his entourage. The cavalier laugh of Beltrán de la Cueva, Count of Ledesma, resonated through the air as he rode just next to King Enrique, but as soon as he spotted the man approaching, de la Cueva jerked the reigns and positioned his horse protectively in front of the king, all the while keeping his hand steadily on the hilt of his sword.

"Forgive us, we were expecting you a week ago," the courtier said, making his best effort to sound dignified, despite the heavy panting of his labored breath. "If it hadn't been for the clouds of dust, we would have no idea of your arrival."

"A king's travels always take longer than expected," my brother replied, unperturbed by the servant's anxious reaction. "Let his Grace know that we have arrived. His sister, Queen Juana, is eager to see him."

Enrique had invited my little brother, Alfonso, and me to join his entourage for a visit to El Puente de Arzobispo to meet the queen's brother, King Afonso of Portugal. My younger brother was surprised that we would be included, but I knew such a gesture was strategic, it was a means for the queen to keep us closer at hand.

"Isabel," Alfonso softly whispered to me, "do you think Enrique will let me ride with him and the other men?" The queen shot him a seething look, but Alfonso didn't notice. Ever the distrustful sister-in-law, Juana always kept an ear out to listen to any exchange between my little brother and me.

"His Majesty isn't to be disturbed," the queen interjected in a voice so harsh, I feared my brother's eyes would well with tears.

"Once we get there, I'll take you riding, I promise," I said, and patted his hand.

I too would have preferred to have ridden on horseback, and poor little Alfonso was not happy about being cooped up inside with the queen's litter. He wanted to ride alongside our half-brother and join the other men, not be stuck with the ladies.

But we had little choice. Her Grace insisted we stay by her side. She reasoned that, as we were so young and had only been outside the protective walls of Arévalo just a handful of times, it was best to stay close to her. And there was no doubt that she was right in the fact that neither of us had been exposed to very much outside of our childhood home. Fearing the dangers of the outside world, our mother thought it best to keep us indoors, away from the public eye. "No need to bring unwanted attention," she would often warn. "The world can be a dangerous place, especially for children of the late king."

My mother wanted to shield us, hide us from the eyes of anyone that might want to do us harm. And Queen Juana, too, intended to hide us, but not from harm. No, her prerogative was far different from that of my mother's.

Juana secretly feared us, though she would never deign to admit as much. As the only other male member in our family, my little brother was a living, breathing threat to the crown that the queen expected to one day rest on her own daughter's head. What other excuse was needed to explain her every effort in keeping us so terribly close at hand.

"Brother," King Afonso of Portugal exclaimed in a jovial voice, walking towards Enrique with arms spread wide. The Portuguese king's burly chest swayed back and forth as he walked, and his legs arched like bows from all the years he spent on horseback. My half-brother gracefully dismounted from his horse and the two men embraced.

"My goodness, Enrique, it is good to see you. You had me worried that I was going to have to send out a search party for you." He let out a hearty chuckle.

"I would have come sooner, but the hunting in Segovia was too great a temptation. I couldn't help myself. Nevertheless, I come bearing gifts. Tonight, we feast on deer."

"Stag?" the King of Portugal asked, and Enrique nodded. "Good man." Afonso gave him a sturdy pat on the back. "Now, where is that beautiful sister of mine?"

"I'm sure not far. Beautiful she is, but that woman has been nagging me since the day we left."

Just for a moment, Enrique looked off in the distance and sighed. A few steps away, the servant reached out his hand to assist the queen out of the carriage, and my little brother and I lined up, waiting to be introduced to the king of Portugal.

"Afonso," the queen sang out in a sonorous tone, nearly jumping into her brother's arms and he spun her around. I couldn't help but let out a gasp. Juana's behavior normally shifted between bitterness towards her husband to unrestrained flirtation with other courtiers, but never had I seen her behave with such innocent elation. I wondered if she had been happier in Portugal, before her marriage to my brother. "I do hope my husband apologized. I tried rushing him, but he hasn't a care in the world for my nerves. He spent days doing nothing more than wandering about, plucking up plants and studying animals."

Enrique was visibly embarrassed by his wife's dismissive attitude of his interests and her open criticism of him, but he refused to reprimand her, especially in front of her doting brother.

"Anyway," the queen went on, negligently waving her hand as if shooing away a fly, "we are here now."

Afonso grinned. "Yes, you are. And the entertainment awaits."

"You'd never dream of the beauty that is to be beheld in Africa," King Afonso declared, turning his corpulent body towards Enrique, who appeared especially sinewy when placed next to the Portuguese king.

The dining hall was packed with nobles and courtiers, all here to partake in the week of festivities in celebration of the royal visit. The queen sat on the other side of Enrique, though she rarely turned towards him. It was not her habit to pay her husband any mind. Instead, she seemed distracted by the gossip being shared from the Portuguese noblewoman she sat with. My little brother, Alfonso and I, sat apart. To be sure, our place was not alongside the royal table, Juana had always made that quite evident, and Enrique never resisted her harshness towards us. Instead we sat directly in front of her, where Juana could keep her eye on us.

"Traveling aboard the fleet with my men, the fresh salt air, waking with the coming of the rising sun to see the sky change from the deep blue darkness of the early morning to vibrant colors of the sunrise, why, there is nothing like it," the queen's brother went on, leaning on his elbow towards Enrique.

It was obvious that he enjoyed talking for his own pleasure as much a he enjoyed entertaining others. No doubt, his favorite subject was his adventures and exploits.

"I can only imagine," King Enrique replied. "You do have a reputation that proceeds you. I've heard it said that you've earned yourself the nickname 'the African.'"

His words were proper, respectful even, as befitted a king, but his tone revealed a secret wish for the life like that of this man, his brother-in-law, a life of exploration and discovery of the exotic and foreign, and the honor it had earned him. Two kings from neighboring kingdoms, and yet they were so very different.

"El Africano," Afonso repeated, as if to savor the title bestowed on him. The king of Portugal gave a light chuckle. "Indeed, sir. Indeed, I have. And it's a name I'm fond of. Sailing the vast blue sea, exploring new territory, it's what a man lives for. And the profit that is to be had…" he emphasized, shaking his head and widening his eyes, "the kingdom grows richer still!"

"I have no doubt. Particularly now, I imagine, since the pope in Rome provided dispensation to enslave the African pagans," Enrique suggested, not without a touch of provocation.

Quietly, unnoticeably, I had been paying careful attention to the conversation between the two kings. It was my habit to listen with intent, while simultaneously appearing to be engaged in other matters. *Your ears are a tool, a weapon*, my grandmother frequently taught. *Information is a key that unlocks many doors, one never knows when it will be of use.*

But when King Afonso said that he had been enslaving the Africans, my eyes betrayed me, and I couldn't help but look up at him. He felt my stare and gazed back at me with a smile, completely unaware of the disgust I felt at what I had just overheard.

How could a king, a man placed by God Almighty into a position of authority and stewardship, misuse his power and enslave those he was meant to protect? Providence brought him to these pagan lands, delivering their inhabitants into the hands of this Christian king. This could have been used as an opportunity to evangelize and civilize. King Afonso seemed so proud of himself, but I was less than impressed with him.

The King of Portugal held his stare, as if he were contemplating me, and I quickly dropped my eyes, unwelcome to his royal attention.

"I imagine you have rooms filled with prizes you've brought back from your journeys," King Enrique continued, bringing Afonso's attention back to him.

"Filled!" he exclaimed, waving his hand as if to show just how high his treasures reached. "In fact, before you leave, you must see it for yourself." King Afonso picked up his goblet of wine and drank heartily, and the well-trained servant was quick to refill the glass. "Brother," he went on. "I applaud you on taking your time to journey here. There are few greater duties for a king than to travel through his kingdom and visit his subjects."

"Your sister was less than thrilled at the delay," Enrique replied with petulance.

King Afonso waved his hand as if he were swatting a fly. "Nonsense. What does a wife know about ruling? That's a man's job. My sister has but one duty, to produce heirs. A woman's battle is in the birthing room. But a ruler understands the love between a king and his subjects, like a father with his beloved children. Your citizens must see you. They must know that their king is still young and healthy and active. There is no better way to stir up loyalty. Trust me in this, brother, I've been ruling since I was only six years of age."

Enrique sat, a pensive look on his face. "Loyalty seems to evade me, despite my best efforts. If I'm not enduring the nagging of my wife, I'm listening to the complaints of the Castilians."

"Be mindful of that," Afonso warned. "Your subjects must be made to understand that their place is to serve. I hear you are letting your nobles run wild," the King of Portugal stated bluntly, and Enrique shifted uncomfortably in his seat. "There was a time, when I was just a child, when others thought they could rule me as well. I put a quick stop to that. Listen to me, Enrique, you are too passive. None must be made to think they can control you. None must believe you submit to the will of others. A king must rule with an iron fist. And above all, keep the power secured in your hands alone."

The King of Portugal had made grand arrangements to celebrate his time with his sister and brother-in-law, and every day seemed more dazzling than the last. The nights were spent with elaborate feasts and dancing in rooms filled with flags and banners and bright colors. Musicians played their instruments to perfection, and *juglares* performed their most renowned ballads.

The days were spent enjoying the entertainment of tournaments and jousts, where men proved their bravery by riding on horseback, carrying lances in their hands — playing at war. Both Enrique and

Afonso partook in the events, but the queen refused to let them joust against one another; one of them was bound to get hurt, and that would ruin everything, she warned. Enrique acquiesced, as was usual. Nevertheless, King Afonso rode, and another man mounted his horse to joust against him.

"My lady," the Portuguese king approached, presenting me with a gold and navy handkerchief on the tip of his lance.

Heat rose into my cheeks and my entire face flushed red with embarrassment. Never, in all my thirteen years, had I received this type of attention before. Though, I well knew that once I had flowered, I was to be wed. The arrangements had been made, my brother had secured the negotiation of my marriage with Edward IV of England, the Plantagenet king. Still, I was not accustomed to receiving gestures of courtly love.

"Isabel," the queen snapped, annoyed at my lack of a reaction to her brother's overtures as the chivalrous knight to a fair maiden. "His Grace is paying you a compliment."

"Thank you, your Highness," I answered, my voice meek as a mouse's.

King Afonso of Portugal smiled warmly and gave a slight bow of his head, then turned and prepared to joust.

I found the queen's eyes fixated on me, her fingers tapping against the wooden armchair, as if she were plotting. "If you are to receive the attentions of a king, we will need to make sure you are dressed better. I will not have you wandering around looking a step up from a milk maid, like your mother dressed you," the queen said to me. "Remember your place, you are a princess of Castilla y León, even if you are nothing more than half-sister to the king."

My eyes stared down at the delicate satin slippers with pointed toes, made with the same canary-yellow fabric to match my skirt and the false sleeves tied to my dress. With each step, I did my best to walk gracefully, as I had seen the other ladies do. King Afonso of Portugal was just a step behind me as we meandered at a slow pace through the garden paths, his arms clasped casually behind his back, and although he seemed entirely at his leisure, I couldn't help but feel the nerves in my tummy.

"Let us rest a moment. I have a gift for you, my lady," announced the King of Portugal, then he gestured towards a bench for us to sit. Gently arranging the folds of fabric of my skirt, I obediently sat down and folded my hands in my lap. Afonso placed a small square object wrapped in silk into my hands, with a single rose tied to the top. As carefully as I could, I untied it.

"Your brother said you are a woman of great piety. I knew you would appreciate this."

Gently, I opened the front cover, turned the pages and gasped. The craftsmanship of the Bible was exquisite. Each page, more beautiful than the last, had hand-painted lettering in gold leaf, and in shades of reds and blues.

"It was made using Johannes Gutenberg's printing press," he explained, knowing I would be impressed with such a valuable gift.

"This... this is a treasure I will forever cherish, my lord. I don't know how to thank you, Sire."

"Your company is all I ask," he replied, pleased at receiving such admiration for the gift he had given. A smile rested on his face, and for the first time he seemed more approachable than I previously thought "el Africano" could ever be.

"Did you know," I said, venturing to begin a conversation with him, "my grandmother grew up within your Court. Her name was Isabel de Barcelos. Did you know of her?"

"Of course. Barcelos," said the king of Portugal, squinting his eyes. "They are among the most distinguished of noble houses. You come from good stock."

"When I was a child, I loved hearing tales of her life at Court as a little girl, of the conquests and travels made by the Portuguese throughout the sea."

"Very good indeed." Afonso nodded his head, contented by the fact that Portugal had been venerated in my life since my earliest memories. "How delighted I am to hear you have an appreciation for your ancestral home," he answered, pleased.

"You have traveled much, as well," I said, leading him to carry on the rest of the conversation. I well knew Afonso enjoyed talking, especially about himself, and there was much to be learned through remaining silent.

"It is the Portuguese way. We are voyageurs. And there is too much of the world to see and discover for me to be trapped inside."

"And you are good at it, are you not?"

"The best. The land grows richer with each new expedition."

I ran my fingers along the edge of the Bible he had just gifted me with.

"And it is an excellent means of evangelizing," I noted, insisting on using this opportunity to make a point. "My grandmother always emphasized the importance of the naval missions to Africa and throughout the unchartered territories. She said that these voyages were more than excitement and wealth. She said they brought a sense of identity to the Portuguese. I could only wish the same for the future of Castilla y León."

"A naval expedition would be quite a feat for Castilla," the king said, then took my hands into his and looked boldly, deeply into my eyes, as if he were trying to read the secrets I hid inside. "Though, if you are determined to bring the wealth of expedition to your land, perhaps, *princesa*, you, yourself will carry on the lessons taught to you by your grandmother. If this is truly your wish, fair Isabel, I could give you everything you've ever dreamed of. You need only be willing."

Days later, I left with King Enrique and his entourage.

Again, the journey took longer than expected. Enrique insisted that the ladies have time to rest, but really he was only concerned with securing ample time to hunt or explore nature. My brother Enrique had a predilection for all things exotic — plants, animals, cultures, people — and I couldn't help but fear that King Afonso looked at me with the same eagerness for ownership of something unique.

After hearing morning Mass, Archbishop Carrillo and I explored the grounds of the Monastery of Santa María de Guadalupe. The monastery was founded nearly a century ago, and was an example of architecture at its finest, with the craftsmanship of its bronze doors on the Basilica, the intimacy of its little chapel, and endless views of valleys and high reaching mountains surrounding the land.

I inhaled deeply, breathing in the freshness of the chilly morning air.

"It's beautiful here," I stated, and it was. Truly, the monastery was one of the most breath-taking constructions I'd ever beheld.

"Hmm," he agreed. "That was the intention. The monastery's construction is, of course, meant to leave an impression. Building works made to honor God must evoke an image of power in its splendor."

"His Grace, my lord brother, seems happier here," I added.

"Naturally, his Highness enjoys his visits here," the archbishop replied. "His mother is buried here. You must remember how close they were."

How could I forget? For most of Enrique's life, his mother was all he had, the only love he knew. Sadly, there was a coldness in our father's interactions with his first-born son, and he often treated my half-brother like a disappointment. Our father, King Juan had such high expectations for his son and heir, his legacy, the future ruler of Castilla y León. And my half-brother had done nothing but earn a reputation as a man that could be easily dominated by others, a man who couldn't make a decision without vacillating on his word. As my half-brother passed from childhood to adolescence, the relationship grew more strained. Father wanted nothing to do with him, so great was his regret and disillusion with his heir, and instead of bothering to discipline Enrique, he ignored him. It was little wonder that Enrique clung to his mother.

"Have you enjoyed the journey, *princesa*?"

"More than I can say," I smiled. "Never have I seen so much of the world."

He walked alongside me, his fingers interlaced in the way he liked to walk, and listened patiently.

"My childhood years were spent sheltered inside, where it was safe," I continued. "And my mother hardly had the resources to afford provisions and manage the small staff we had, let alone entertainments as elaborate as what I saw these past weeks."

"It appeared that King Afonso took an interest in you," the archbishop noted, and it was clear he meant to discuss my feelings on the matter.

"He seemed more interested in regaling us with his achievements than beginning a courtship with me." I scoffed, waving away the notion. "Anyway, I am promised to the king of England. It is a good match and I am contented with the thought of Edward, just as I am with myself as his future queen."

The archbishop nodded and listened. "Ah, the York king. King Edward IV is a desirable mate for a young lady. Handsome, youthful, and known as a man of great chivalry, you must be overjoyed," Carrillo replied. "But should you ever feel that you need someone to share your thoughts or feelings with, do know that I am always here for you, as I am for your little brother, Alfonso. I promise I will always do everything I can to protect you both."

I looked at the archbishop in the eyes, hoping to read what I could. He was a man of the cloth, yet his reputation of breaking his sacred vow of celibacy was only too well known. Still, my intuition promised me I could trust him.

"Thank you, father. For this, I am grateful."

"And now," he went on, "after a week of seeing how royalty amuses themselves, what are your thoughts?"

Silently, I thought about all I saw and felt that week.

"That spectacles and pleasures such as these serve a purpose," I finally answered.

Archbishop Carrillo raised his eyebrows. "Well done, child. Your wisdom surpasses my expectations."

The exciting jousts, the elaborate feasts, the poetry in remembrance of grand patriotic events and great love, it had a purpose: to instruct and impress. There was no doubt that the king of Portugal, Afonso V, "*el Africano*," was a wealthy and powerful ruler. But he was pouring a small fortune into these entertainments, and to what end? What purpose did such ostentatious displays serve?

The more I watched, the more I realized that these events were political. Just as King Afonso had encouraged my brother Enrique to travel his kingdom in order to keep himself in the forefront of his subject's minds, he, too was displaying his own power, and it served as a means for him to further validate and uphold his right to rule his kingdom. The king was playing his part just as much as the dancers and actors and jousters played theirs.

But what was my part? I was a princess, the sister of the king of Castilla.

But soon that, too, would change.

I would no longer be the forgotten little princess that the queen couldn't wait to get rid of. Soon I would be married to Europe's most desirable king, Edward IV. Soon I would be queen of England.

Chapter IV
April 1464

"Where have you been? The queen is looking for you!" Beatriz de Bobadilla whispered harshly, then tilted her head and looked at me like a mother scolding her favorite child. "Come quickly."

The color dropped from my face and my heart began to beat harder. Without saying a word, I rose to follow behind Beatriz and hurried to the queen's royal chambers.

The queen stood in front of the large oval mirror recently arrived from Bavaria, absent-mindedly petting the little dog she held in her arms, then dropped her gaze to compare the rolls of luxurious shades of purple silk stretched out before her that were to be used for the dresses she was to have made.

I came before her and bowed.

"Ah, finally, the princess deems to grace us with her presence," she said, not even bothering to look up at me.

"Forgive me, your Grace. I was praying and did not realize how quickly time had passed."

"What a fascinating life you do lead," she said mockingly, and the other ladies giggled.

"Do share, what is it that you were praying for?" one of the ladies teased. But I paid her no mind. I had no illusions of being treated with kindness from this Court, filled with courtiers who reveled in their immorality. My piety was nothing but a joke to them, and my conservative manners did not fit. To them, I would forever be the outsider.

"The king received news that regards you," the queen continued.

"News from my lady mother?" I asked, my words spilling out quick with anxiety, betraying my worry. "Is she well?"

"Your mother? Well? Certainly not. The whole Court knows she is mad and claims she speaks with the ghost of Álvaro de Luna." The queen laughed. Clearly, she enjoyed mocking my mother and insulting me. "But no. Alas, this news has nothing to do with that poor woman, really I do pity her. It has to do with a much more important matter. News has arrived from England."

"Edward," I said, my voice a whisper. My heart began to beat harder, and I felt my chest fill with the excitement of anticipation. Soon, I would be removed from this Court. I would be a queen, married to Edward, the most dashing king in the whole world.

"Precisely. King Edward. Your engagement is off," she announced coolly, scanning my face for a reaction and letting the disappointment sink in. "Apparently the idea of marrying you was not enticing enough for him. He prefers to instead wed a widow who has already birthed a handful of brats."

"But that's impossible," I argued, shaking my head in disbelief. "We have been promised to one another. We are to be married. King Enrique gave me his word, I am to be the queen of England."

Juana sighed, tilting her head as she stared back at me.

"Men break promises all the time, you will grow more used to it, just like I did. Anyway," she asserted, stopping herself from revealing too much of her own disappointments in life, "King Edward is a fool. He met this widow, whoever she is, somewhere along a town road. Some say it was an enchantment, a bewitching, perhaps. The two married in secret, without bothering to receive any counsel from his advisors, the fools. It's a decision he will come to regret."

I stood aghast, speechless, but no one took any notice of me.

"I have heard that the king of England is desperately in love," one of the queen's ladies carried on, eager to gossip, and entirely unaware of the fact that my hopes for my future had been completely dashed.

"Surely it's a poor match. There was no benefit to England in his marrying her," Beatriz de Bobadilla argued, trying to stop the gossip that treated me as if I hadn't been personally affected. "King Enrique will not accept such a dishonor as a broken vow made to his sister." Out of all the women at Court, Beatriz was the only one that befriended me. "He could have married Isabel, as your husband arranged, and their marriage would have created ties between England and Spain. And Edward has only so recently taken the crown, a crown he had to fight for, and still fights for. Mark my words, that man will regret his rash action."

The women continued discussing, but I heard nothing of what they said. Silently, I walked to the window. It was the closest thing I had to a moment alone, while forced to stay inside the confines of the queen's quarters.

My Edward, he had abandoned me. And with him went my hope of escaping this prison and beginning a new life with a new sense of identity. I squeezed my eyes closed, willing myself to not shed a tear for a man that could dismiss his promise to me so easily. I would have been a true companion for him, and yet, he cast me aside for the youth and beauty of another.

"Many are saying he was bewitched," gossiped one of Queen Juana's ladies, interrupting my stream of thought. "They say his wife and her mother practice all sorts of magic."

"You sound a fool. The king of England wasn't bewitched," Juana maintained, noticeably irritated. "Passion is more potent than magic. There was an attraction between them and he couldn't resist taking what he wanted. Marriage was his means of satisfying his carnal desire."

The queen's voice betrayed her cynicism. She looked at me, standing alone in the corner. "No need to be quite so disheartened, Isabel. Enrique has had the foresight to make other arrangements. You will have the great honor to marry my brother, Afonso. No need to fret, you will still be a queen, of Portugal."

"No," I declared defiantly, surprising myself at my own boldness. "I don't want to marry your brother. I don't love your brother."

Her eyes narrowed, and her eyebrow raised. "Little girl, no one asks what you want, and certainly no one expects you to be in love, whatever that is. You are a princess. Marriage to you has a value, and as my ward, I plan to make use of it."

Quickly, I gathered my composure. I had insulted the queen by my outright rejection of her brother.

"Forgive me, your Majesty. All I meant was that King Afonso already has children. If I were to marry him it would be of no benefit to the Trastámara dynasty. His first-born son will be heir, and the children I bare him will only be contenders for the throne of Portugal."

"That is correct, contenders for the throne. Just like you and your little brother."

There it was. Therein lay the reason the queen hated my little brother and me so much. After Enrique, Alfonso was the only male heir to the throne of Castilla, and the queen feared for the inheritance of her only child. Queen Juana's daughter was her one joy, and she would do anything to protect her claim to the Crown.

"You need not concern yourself with political matters," she went on. "Leave the art of governing to the king. You have but one purpose, to obey the wishes of your sovereign master, King Enrique. And if his Grace wills that you marry the king of Portugal, you will accept with the deepest gratitude for a great honor that you, frankly, are not deserving of. I advise you, have no concern for bearing Trastámarian heirs. No one expects that of you. They only expect that of me, and of my daughter, the *infanta*."

But she was wrong. For Enrique to arrange a marriage between me and the king of Portugal, it was required that he first attain my consent, a consent that I refused to grant.

The queen could rule my brother, but come what may, she would find that she could not rule me.

Chapter V
1464

"Good, you're improving," the boy encouraged, a mop of shaggy chestnut hair falling lazily over his eyes. He was dressed simply, wearing a loose white linen tunic and leather boots, marking a distinct difference between himself and the pretentious gowns and capes worn by the other courtiers.

"Again," he commanded my little brother, Alfonso, then he lifted his wooden sword and took a step towards my brother. Seeing me approach, the boy brushed his wavy hair out of his eyes, lowered his wooden sword and bowed.

For several moments I had been watching from a distance, observing the interaction between Alfonso and the handsome and agile young swordsmanship instructor.

"Isabel," Alfonso gleefully called out to me. "Come watch! Once more, Gonzálo. I want my sister to see what I've learned," he said. The shaggy haired boy named Gonzálo bowed his head and the two boys began practicing their fighting again. Alfonso did his best in his attack, but Gonzálo's swift reaction blocked his every stroke."

"You look as if you are dancing," I said to the instructor.

"Swordplay is somewhat like a dance. A dance between two partners reaction to one another. Well done, sir," he said, turning back to Alfonso and performing a respectful bow to indicate the conclusion of their lesson. "We will practice more tomorrow." Then, he turned and left us to ourselves. I watched him walk away.

Alfonso and I sat under the heavy shade of the oak trees, their large beautiful branches protecting us. The breeze rustled the branches and leaves went swirling in the air.

"Who is that boy?" I asked.

"Gonzálo Fernández de Córdoba. He is a gift from Pacheco."

"A gift? Why is the marqués de Villena presenting you with gifts?"

"Because," he answered, obviously not happy that I was questioning Pacheco's motives. "I am the son of Juan II of Castilla. The son of a king should be educated in the art of warfare. And if King Enrique is not going to properly administer my education, the marqués promised he would oversee it himself."

"Did he also give you those clothes?" I asked, touching the new velvet doublet and jacket my brother wore.

"Yes, of course. The son of a king must be dressed as such," he replied, repeating the importance of his position as the son of our father. "Señor Pacheco promised to make sure that I live as I was meant to live. He even gave me an allowance. He said it was criminal that King Enrique has withheld the funds that father left us in his will, and he feels it is his duty to make sure that I live like a proper prince. He promised to look after me, just as he looked after Enrique when he was a boy."

Instinctively I knew something was not as it seemed.

"And what does he get from it?"

"Nothing, just to help guide me as I grow up. He means to be a mentor to me, just as any young man that is born of the stock of kings would need."

My brother sounded even more a child as he repeated the words that surely were told to him by Pacheco. Recognizing the defensiveness in his own voice, the resonance of his tone changed before he continued.

"Father died when I was only a baby, and I don't remember him at all. But Señor Pacheco said he will look after me as if I were his own."

Immediately I grew suspicious. Juan Pacheco, the Marqués de Villena had been the favorite of my brother, King Enrique, since his adolescence and for most of his reign, until his position as favorite had been unseated by Beltrán de la Cueva. Naturally, the marqués had benefitted enormously from such close contact with Enrique.

Proximity to royalty delivered wealth and power into Pacheco's greedy hands. So, what could he want with an eleven-year-old boy, a child that Enrique had always treated with little regard? Why would Juan Pacheco, the most powerful man in Castilla, take any interest in my little brother?

"I've come to say goodbye, sister. But don't worry, I will come for you soon," Alfonso announced.

"So then, King Enrique agreed to Señor Pacheco's terms at the Representation of Burgos." I felt the uneasy feeling of tightening in my stomach, a feeling that was becoming only too familiar.

"Entirely! He agreed to everything! Beltrán de la Cueva and his filthy Moorish guards are most probably already sent away! Though the king had little choice. Pacheco and his uncle, the Archbishop Carrillo, sent the open letter through the whole kingdom, confronting Enrique for poor leadership and misrule. Once the king realized he could not count on the support of his nobles, he submitted like a dog to his master."

My brother's disrespectful manner underlined the change that had taken place in him since he came under the supervision of Pacheco.

"And the *Infanta* Juana? What of the king's daughter?"

"The queen's daughter, not the king's," he corrected. "She is the *infanta* no longer. The king openly declared her to be a bastard. Everyone calls her "la Betraneja," the illegitimate daughter of Beltrán de la Cueva. Still, I feel sorry for her. After all, it's not her fault she is a bastard. Anyway, the king has declared me as his sole heir. He has made me the master of the Order of Santiago and declared me as the prince of Asturias. Isabel! Do you know what that means? I am to be king of Castilla!"

His voice was full of exuberance and elation, the words spilling out of his mouth, one after another. But each word only caused me to feel more fear for what this all meant. The nobles were tearing the crown from one brother to put onto the childlike head of another, and, innocent as he was, I knew Alfonso had no idea how great the price of the crown was.

"Congratulations, dear brother," I said with little enthusiasm in my voice.

I tried to clear my mind and consider the motives of the nobles. Pacheco was one of the most powerful men in the kingdom, primarily because of his grip over Enrique. But now, the same man that had overseen the maturity into manhood of King Enrique, the king he now unseated, was to have custody over my little brother. This all sounded dangerously confusing.

"Why aren't you happy for me?" Alfonso asked, furrowing his eyebrows.

I knew something wasn't right, but Alfonso wanted approval. He wanted me to share in the excitement of his future.

"I don't know if it's wise to trust Pacheco," I said, carefully choosing my words.

"But you're wrong, Isabel. Pacheco is my greatest supporter. He has made arrangements for a ceremony to take place immediately in Cabezón, for all the nobility to swear an oath of fealty to me. He will secure my position. I've never had a secure position, not since Father died. Pacheco will do more for me than anyone else ever has."

"And how does Pacheco benefit from this?"

My brother stared at me with his big, gentle brown eyes, reminding me that he was still just a child.

"Pacheco's loyalty is to the Crown. He wants what is best for the kingdom. I am the future of Castilla, and so that makes it his duty to look after me. He knows I am not safe with King Enrique and Queen Juana, and he can help me prepare to rule."

But he could see that I wasn't convinced.

"Sister, believe me. Señor Pacheco, all the nobles, are fed up with the lawlessness that is destroying the country. No one feels safe, and the king is too weak to fix it."

Again, I could hear the words of Pacheco already coming out of my brother's mouth.

"But when I rule, it will be different. Pacheco will prepare me to be a strong leader, just like Father was. He will make me into a man. He will be like a father to me."

His words broke my heart.

Never had I wished more that I could turn back time and bring my father back. My little brother needed a father, and now he was going to be instructed in the lessons of manhood and the art of governing by the same man that had overseen the most formative years of my older brother's youth — the older brother who he now betrayed.

Pacheco was a manipulative man and had always gotten what he wanted from Enrique, the same way that Pacheco's predecessor, Álvaro de Luna, manipulated my father.

It was a vicious, unforgiving cycle. Throughout his entire reign, Enrique had been treated as though he were little more than a figurehead, a puppet whose strings were controlled by the king's favorite, and now Pacheco meant to get his claws firmly into my little brother while he was young, so that he could control him once he began to rule. I had always been the one to protect my little brother, but now? What could I do? Now, I was defenseless.

I sat in the chair, along with the queen's other ladies-in-waiting, and carefully pulled the thread with the needlepoint. My neck ached from looking down at my work, and my palms felt clammy from the dry heat of the summer, a heat even more crushing inside the walls of the palace at Segovia.

Stretching and straightening my back, I finally made eye contact with Queen Juana. Her eyes had been searing into me for some time, but I could no longer ignore the stare.

"Are you not feeling well, your Highness?" I asked.

"On the contrary. *I* am feeling quite well. Though I doubt your brother, little Alfonso, will be feeling well once the king gets a hold of him."

My stomach twisted inside of me, but I refused to show any reaction.

"Forgive me, madam. I don't know what you're speaking of."

"Haven't you heard? Oh, no, of course you haven't. You spend all your time kneeling before your crucifix in prayers, your little white knuckles clenching those rosary beads. Well, you have good reason to pray now."

"The king finally came to his senses," interjected the soft voice of Beatriz. "The news reached Court yesterday that he has reinstated princess Juana as heir. And now many of the noble houses are in open revolt."

"Enrique broke his agreement?" Though, I shouldn't have been surprised. My half-brother could rarely be counted on to make a decision, and once made, he hardly ever kept his word.

"Agreement? I would hardly venture to call it *that*. The nobles strong-armed my husband, they forced his hand. He would never have agreed to hand the crown over to your little traitor of a brother otherwise."

I felt my belly fill with fire and my jaw tighten. No one, not even the queen herself, would insult Alfonso.

Unclenching my teeth, I forced myself to speak calmly and firmly. "Alfonso is innocent. He is only ten-years-old."

"Innocent or not, he was the crown jewel of that shameless… that sacrilegious ceremony," the queen said, spitting out the words.

"Sacrilegious?" I almost laughed out loud. A queen who had no qualms about her reputation as a notorious coquette, whose ladies basked in the delights of seduction and excess, dared to call a ceremony naming my brother as king sacrilegious.

"How dare you question her Majesty! The ceremony your brother played puppet to lacked all decency. Starting with Archbishop Carrillo, one by one, the nobles proceeded to strip an effigy, a doll they made of Enrique, tearing away every regal object, starting with his crown, then his scepter, then his sword. Finally, they cast the doll representing the *true king* from the stage onto the ground, kicking it and cursing it," one of the ladies recounted, excited by being the one to share such scandalous gossip. "Yes," she emphasized, "I would call that sacrilegious."

The account was jarring, and I placed two fingers over my mouth to hide my reaction. I pictured the effigy doll of my half-brother, sitting on a pretend throne before the nobles that had shared Enrique's dining halls for decades.

Beginning with the archbishop of Toledo, a man dedicated to God, the doll-king was deprived of each object that separated him from his subjects — his crown and scepter, signifying his distinction as ruler, then his sword, the weapon of justice and leadership. And finally, casting him on the ground, they called him "*puta*," "whore," going so far as to deprive Enrique of his manhood. Never had I heard of an act so degrading.

"Have no fear, Isabel. King Enrique knows you are here, safe in my keeping," she said with a sinister smile. "Despite the machinations of Alfonso, our king is magnanimous, he considers you to not be a party to all this. But mark my words, all those nobles that now claim your little traitorous brother as Alfonso XII, King of Castilla, will pay dearly. And do you know how I can guarantee that Enrique will win? Because Alfonso is too new to this game. He doesn't know who to trust, and what he will have to sacrifice to play. He plays king, and the nobles may indeed even call him king, but he is no more than a child, a political play thing in the hands of thieves."

"How can you be sure?" I made my voice flat and steady, revealing nothing of the fear I felt for my little brother.

"Because I know what our enemy wants, and I know how to give it to them without it costing me a thing."

"And what's that?"

"You."

"Me?"

Queen Juana de Avís nodded her head once.

"Should you be punished for having a traitorous brother?" she asked.

"But I have two brothers. And I love them both."

"Yes, two brothers at war. But to whom is your loyalty?... Little matter," she concluded, not allowing me to answer. "Your allegiance is of no consequence, but *you* are. Congratulations, you are to be married, and the honorable Pedro Girón will be your spouse. He is headed here at full speed to marry you immediately."

I let out a gasp, and the queen made no further action but to stare at me, her hands serenely clasped in her lap, a mocking smile slowly spreading wider across her porcelain skin.

My lower lip started to tremble, and I wiped away a tear that had escaped my eyes and now ran down my cheek.

"No!" I cried, my voice cracking. "Pedro Girón is a monster. He is evil. I'll never marry him. Tell my brother, tell Enrique that he can't make me do it."

She tilted her head. "I will tell the king nothing of the sort. It was at my suggestion. Be honored, little princess. You have the great privilege of being betrothed to the Master of Calatrava." She knew well enough it would enrage me that Enrique had given away the prestigious title that rightfully belonged to Alfonso to that monstrous brother of Pacheco, and still the queen was eager to twist the dagger in my side. "And he is rather impatient to marry a girl as beautiful as our little Isabel," she said in a calm, patronizing voice. "You may be a prude now, but Girón has quite the reputation, he will strip you of any of your silly prim, moralistic airs as quickly as he will strip off your underclothes, just as he has a hundred maidens before you."

"Master of Calatrava? To hold such an honor as to be master of the religious order of Calatrava requires chastity."

"An honor he gladly relinquishes at the prospect of marrying into our family. Anyway, the matter has been arranged. I'll hear no more about it."

There were few people I loathed more than Pedro Girón, and few I was more frightened of. To call him a brute was an understatement – he was cruel, a fiend. Despite his vows of chastity taken in order to attain the mastership of Calatrava, he proceeded to rape and pillage at will; no farmer's daughter was safe.

Girón had even attempted to dishonor my own mother. It wasn't until then that she developed her mental condition, a condition that had only spiraled since that day. And as he was the brother of Juan Pacheco, the Marqués de Villena, he had no fear of retribution, but instead only felt more entitled to ravage at his leisure. The man deserved to have his head on the edge of a pole before he deserved to be wed to royalty.

The queen, I decided, was as much of a monster as Pedro Girón. I needed to get myself away from all of them.

"Excuse me, madam."

But when I tried to stand up, I felt my legs shaking beneath me. My hand reached out to grab anything to steady myself.

Composure, Isabel. Don't you dare show weakness, not to her.

I rushed to my quarters and threw myself on my bed. Finally, in the privacy of my room, with no one else watching, I could release my emotions. I covered my face in my hands and hot tears streamed down my cheeks and onto my pillow.

Why would she do this to me? Why would she force me to marry the most villainous man in all of Castilla? This was all a disgusting, violent game to her — a woman so unhappy in her life that she took pleasure in destroying mine. Again and again her words repeated themselves in my mind, until I boxed up my ears and screamed into the pillow.

I needed to calm down and think clearly. What did this all mean? The queen said she knew she would win because she was willing to give the enemy what they wanted most, but what they wanted most was... me? What could that mean! My head ached. All I wanted was to close my eyes, to fall asleep, and to wake up once again in my home, with Mother and Alfonso. That life was a dream gone by, a dream whose life was slowly bleeding away, a slow death for the joys of an innocent childhood.

And then it occurred to me. Enrique wanted Juan Pacheco back on his side, whatever it cost him. That was why the king was willing to let Pacheco's brother marry me, so that, through sacred union, Pacheco would be married into the royal family. And if Pacheco was able to remove my little brother, Alfonso, from the line of succession, then that would put Pedro Girón dangerously close to taking the throne for himself.

My heart dropped and I felt overcome with fear. Alfonso was in the custody of Juan Pacheco, a man that had already betrayed him only weeks after declaring him king. My little brother wasn't a king, he was as much a hostage as me. And I could do nothing to warn Alfonso. Nothing.

I was trapped. The walls of Enrique and Juana's Court were my cage, my quarters were litter more than a sepulcher.

My bed could bring me no comfort. Instead, I knelt before my prie-dieu. My hand fell to the Bible, my refuge. I held it close to my chest and opened to Psalms 44, whispering the words of David over and over again until they became my own.

The Lord is my refuge, my strength and my song.

The Lord is my refuge. My hiding place. Lord, hide me. Deliver me. Protect me from this man. I cannot marry him. I'd rather die than marry him. I'd rather die than let him touch me.

My God, save my brother. Don't let anything happen to him. He is all I have.

Father, save Castilla, save our home, our ancestral land.

Saying those last words, having to pray for the life of Alfonso, and knowing how close he was to danger, made me sick to my stomach. Fear overcame me, tears streamed down my face and my dress. My fists tightened, and I gripped the object in my hand. It was the cross from the rosary.

Again, I repeated Psalms 44.

God is my refuge. God is my strength. God is my song.

My heart turned from fear to determined faith. My God *would* rescue my little brother and me. Yes, my God *would* protect my little brother. Come what may, even to the point of death, I would never marry Pedro Girón.

A hand gently stroked my face, jolting me from my sleep.

"Don't touch me!" I cried out frantically.

"Hush, sweet princess. No need to be afraid. It's only me," came the reassuring voice of Beatriz de Bobadilla.

My eyes were nearly swollen shut from tears. I ran my fingers over my ribs and felt the aching pain caused from falling asleep on the knotted wood floor in front of the prie-dieu.

My chest ached with anxiety where my heart still beat hard and fast inside my chest.

"I thought it was Pedro Girón, that he was already here."

Beatriz took my hand and squeezed it between her own.

"You must eat," she said. She dipped the spoon into the bowl and fed me by hand, like a mother feeding her sick child. "Very good. Now, let's get you ready. We must be getting to the queen's rooms soon."

"I'm not going there. I will not pay court to that woman. No, Beatriz," my words coming out faster and more panicked. "I have to get out of here. I need to get to my little brother and warn him."

"It's too dangerous," she answered in her calm, controlled voice. "You must stay here."

"You think it's safer here? The queen keeps me trapped. It's nothing short of a prison, and I'm being held captive until she can hand me over to the most degenerate man I've ever met." Tears started to well up in my eyes. "And Alfonso..." my voice broke off just saying his name. "My brother... what will they do to him?"

Beatriz shook her head in disapproval and whispered, "This would never have happened if King Enrique had a shred of authority. His wife is out of control as much as his nobles, and he does nothing to check their transgressions."

"She's allied with Juan Pacheco. She means to have my little brother killed. I know it. She will do anything to push me and Alfonso out of the line of succession."

"Pacheco. The country grows more fractured by the day because of his scheming. He forces every noble family of Castilla to choose a side, and just when he brainwashes Alfonso, a child, into believing he should be king, he turns his back on him."

I sat in silence, watching the concerned thoughts shift through my friend's mind. "My husband's fears are true," she went on. "The king's greatest mistake was ever allowing Juan Pacheco to wield such unbridled power."

Juan Pacheco, Marqués de Villena, had been the king's favorite since Enrique was a child, and now the king had grown accustomed to him, so much so that the very keys to the kingdom lay firmly in Pacheco's hands. Now, two brothers looked at one another like enemies, and Castilla was about to plunge into civil war.

"Enrique should have learned from the mistakes of our father. He saw with his own eyes the control Álvaro de Luna had over Father, and how it hurt the kingdom, as well as his own marriage. Pacheco is nothing but an overly ambitious nobleman. And he has my brother in the palm of his hand. Beatriz," I pleaded, "please, I need to get to my brother. I can help him. I will fight alongside him," I said, and for the briefest moment, the image of Joan of Arc flashed before my eyes.

Ever since I was a little girl, I idolized Joan of Arc, the heroic French teenager, a vassal sent by God to save her kingdom from the hands of the English. I still had the letter she sent to my father, King Juan II, when I was just a little girl.

"Impossible. Every one of your movements is watched. Every word you say is monitored. There are spies constantly reporting anything you say, any letter you write, to Juana. She knows when you go to Mass, what you eat, when you last bled. Her eye is sharp and it is turned against you. There is no way you can escape the walls of the castle. The queen is sure of it. Make no mistake; she intends to keeps you here."

"Pedro Girón is coming for me. And I swear, Beatriz. I swear I will die before I let him touch me!" I said through gritted teeth, my voice as resolute as my will.

Our eyes locked, and I knew she finally realized just how serious I was when I said I would welcome death before I welcomed Pedro Girón to my marital bed. She stood up and began to rapidly pace the room.

"I'll never let him get to you. I will kill him before he lays a finger on you."

She gently patted a fold in her dress, as if to confirm that an object held there was still in place. I looked harder, trying to make out its form, then suddenly realized. Beatriz had secretly stashed a knife inside her garments.

"My husband," she whispered to herself. She stopped and turned to me. "Doña Isabel," she said, her voice growing firm. "You can be sure that no one will infringe upon your honor. If my husband loves me as much as he says he does, and if he is as devoted to the future of Castilla y León as much as I know Don Andrés de Cabrera to be, then I swear by the Virgin Mother, you have no reason to fear Pedro Girón."

CHAPTER VI

During the days that followed, I kept to my chamber. The queen made no request of me to join her ladies, and was just as happy to leave me forgotten in the solitary confinement of my room. At least in here, I didn't have to endure having to watch the flagrant behavior of her ladies, and the constant reminder that I was not welcome.

In the little wooden chair next to the hearth, I sat and read. Before me rested my small private collection of books that I was allowed to take with me from my mother's home. The collection had been carefully curated: Aristotle, Cicero, Virgil, and my father's old copy of *El Libro de buen amor*.

But as much as I tried to concentrate, my mind would not allow itself to be distracted. The arrival of Pedro Girón was imminent. There was no way I could escape him alive. In my prayers, I pleaded with God to save me. I was entirely helpless, there was nothing I could do to protect myself.

My only hope rested in God. One way or another, I knew my God would rescue me, even if it meant my end.

The words on the page stared back at me, but in my mind's eye, all I could see was the image of Pedro Girón. Over and over ran the memory of my mother, cornered by Girón, as he towered menacingly over her. I could still hear the words. *Your husband is dead. And it's your hands with blood on 'em. Whisperin' in his ear against Álvaro de Luna. Plotting you were, to bring about de Luna's end. But he was the wrong man to kill, he was. That ghost'll follow you to your own grave, aye. You are no queen, now. You are nothing but a common woman. Scream as loud as you like, anyone that dare come to your defense will meet a swift end at the tip of my blade.*

I remembered seeing his hand resting on the crook of her neck, that intimate place on a woman's body. He sensually ran his fingertips along her collarbone. I shouted for him to remove himself, and as my mother's scared eyes looked at me, I could see there were red marks left on her neck where he had gripped her moments before.

After that day, my mother was never the same. Little by little, her mental condition grew more worrisome. She started to complain that the ghost of Don Álvaro de Luna was haunting her, and soon after we often found her in a room, by herself, talking to Don Álvaro as if he were there in the flesh.

And now Pedro Girón was after me.

I knew his intentions of marriage had but one purpose: to be the father of King Juan II of Castilla's grandchildren. He would force himself on me, just as he had forced himself onto countless young girls across the kingdom. Once I bore him children, it mattered little whether I lived or died. And if he and his brother, Juan Pacheco, could find a way of ridding themselves of my little brother, Alfonso, then the children I bore him could be heir to the throne of the realm.

I was nothing more than a pawn to them — all of them — not just Pedro Girón, but also to the queen, and even to my own brother, Enrique.

"Isabel," came the sharp whisper of a voice at the door, a voice I immediately recognized as Beatriz's. "Isabel, quickly, let me in."

The bolt of the door creaked as I pulled it back and opened it. Beatriz looked both ways to make sure no one saw her before closing it behind her.

She pulled me away from the door to the corner of the room. Beatriz knew as well as I did, in a Court like this one, even the walls have ears.

"Here," she said, "read this."

She handed me a paper that had been folded small enough to easily hide.

My eyes quickly scanned the paper, and my mouth dropped. I stood there speechless, staring blankly at her.

"He is dead! Isabel, he is dead!" she whispered, leaning towards me and pointing to the words on the paper.

She stared into my eyes, waiting for a reaction. But I could not move.

"Isabel, did you hear me? You are safe." She reached for my hands and gripped them between her own, as if to wake me up.

Finally her words sunk in. I leaned forward and hugged her, and hot tears ran down my cheeks.

"Thank you, Father," I prayed aloud. "Thank you, my God."

"Indeed," she said, and crossed herself.

"When did this come?" I asked, careful to bring my voice down to a whisper.

"Just now. Delivered by my lord husband's most reliable page. We are the first to know."

"How is it that Don Cabrera knows this before anyone else?"

"What does it matter how my husband knows?" she answered, protecting her husband's secret. It was best, I realized, not to ask if her husband had a hand in Girón's sudden death. "You are safe from Girón, that's all I care about," she said, gently wiping the tears from my cheek.

"Do you know what caused his death? Was he poisoned?"

"Whatever happened to him was well-justified."

I understood. It made little difference how the deed was accomplished. Pedro Girón was a soulless man, a tyrant, and it mattered not what happened, just so long as he was no longer a threat to me or to the rest of the country.

"In a few days time, my husband will send me a formal letter announcing Girón's death in more detail. I am sure the letter will show his sorrow for the loss of the life of a servant to King Enrique. It is only a cover. The letter is to arrive after everyone else knows of his death, and his sorrowful words will serve to prove his innocence and ours. But I must warn you," her voice grew nearly imperceptible, "now more than ever, you must take care. Act no differently than before. Everyone knows you have strong connections, and the queen will find any excuse to link you to Girón's death, even if she names you a witch."

"A witch?" my voice shuddered. "But I am innocent! I haven't left this room. I haven't had contact with anyone."

"It matters little if you are secured within the king's Court or anywhere else. You are not above suspicion and may even be a target. They have accused women of witchcraft and the use of magic to exercise their will over the life of a man for lesser causes than the death of a nobleman," she warned, reminding me of the unjust trial of Joan of Arc.

My breath abandoned me at the threat — a threat that was entirely too real for many women. From failed crops and diseased flocks of goats to enchantments and poisons, women had been held responsible for all types of crimes, persecuted and burned as heretics and witches. Even Joan of Arc was accused of witchcraft.

"And everyone knows you were capable of doing anything to avoid marrying Pedro Girón."

"But I've done nothing other than stay here and pray."

"Good. Let them see that," she replied in a low, calm voice that reminded me to remain calm as well. "Let everyone see that you are innocent. Most importantly, let them see that you prayed, and God heard your voice. God answered you, Isabel."

"Beatriz, I did not mean for you to get tangled in this." I dropped my eyes. "This was supposed to be my problem, I'm sorry to have you and your husband implicated."

She placed her hand under my chin and smiled at me warmly.

"You are my best friend, my sister. Always know that I will do whatever it takes to protect you."

"If…" my voice said shakily, then, correcting myself, "when my brother wins this war, when I have power, I can promise you that your loyalty will be remembered."

News of Pedro Girón's death was quick to reach Court. I awaited Juana's reaction, but refused to let my face reveal any elation, uncertainty or fear. If I had, surely it would be a means of condemning me as guilty.

The queen might have hoped that such news would have kept me even more isolated than before, but no accusations were ever declared against me. Perhaps she feared that if she claimed I had a hand in his death, then she would be publicly acknowledging that I had more influence than she would like to admit.

Surprisingly, with the news of Pedro Girón's death, my entire existence began to shift. Before, because of my resistance to the immoral behavior of the queen and her ladies, I was treated like an outsider. And now, because of this same piety and purity, I was not treated like an outcast, but as a woman set apart, unique and separate from the rest. Courtiers and nobles alike bowed their head respectfully to me and looked at me with reverence in their eyes as I passed by them in the hallways of the palace.

No longer was my life lived in the shadows. *And never again will it*, I swore to myself.

From that moment on, for the rest of my life, people looked at me differently, treated me differently. Whispers began to spread that I was chosen by God, set apart by the Lord Almighty. I had the Lord's favor; He answered my prayers. I had an anointing on my life.

Chapter VII
August 1467

It was still morning, and yet the heat of the August day was already suffocating. The ladies fanned themselves with their carefully painted *ibánico* fans, but nothing could distract any of us from what was happening, and we all feared what news the end of the day would bring.

"How much longer 'til the Court comes back?" complained Doña María.

One of the biggest flirts of all the ladies I'd met at Court, Doña María was a rosy-cheeked woman with a large bosom that she shamelessly set on display. "With all the men away, it's too quiet here."

The one-time boisterous Court of King Enrique and Queen Juana de Avís now experienced a marked difference. No longer was the air filled with giggles and whispers between courtiers. There now reigned a silent, undeniable tension in the atmosphere. Everyone was aware of the battle taking place that would soon decide the fate of the entire kingdom — a battle that affected no one in this room more than the queen and myself.

"I agree," came the voice of another of the queen's ladies. "The Alcázar is far too boring. Why couldn't we have joined the king, like when he fights against the Moors?"

"You sound like whiny little children, and I am not in the mood to listen to your complaints," said the queen. "Stop fumbling," she snapped to the servant that was fixing her hair, her voice as cutting as ice. "Your hands are as clumsy as a stable boy's. Isabel, you may finish my hair."

The servant curtsied and turned to hand me the comb. It was obvious that the queen intended to make me feel as if I were nothing more than a servant. Gently, I brushed Juana's hair, careful not to pull. Her hair was thick and blonde, exaggerating the pureness of her pale skin and rosy lips. I would have thought her quite breathtaking, if her beauty hadn't been overshadowed by her wickedness.

Satisfied with my brushstrokes, Juana continued. "You all should be grateful to be here. I can promise you there is nowhere safer than the Alcázar while my husband is at war. Anyway, the battle he faces today is far too dangerous for us to be there. He isn't fighting the Christian enemy. He is fighting his own brother, a traitor who is even worse than a Moor."

I knew her words were aimed at insulting me. But I refused to look at her. Juana's slights held little sting for me, and I was unperturbed by what she or any of the other ladies thought about me. Theirs was not a tribe I wanted to join. Let them treat me like an outcast, what did their opinion matter anymore. It didn't. No longer did any of it matter.

Their insulated world of superiority and power was slowly crumbling out of their hands — and they knew it. Suddenly, their world was shifting upside down, a shift that became only more apparent with the recent whispers on the lips of the courtiers. Whispers of me, Isabel, a woman favored by God Himself. Whispers that passed through the halls of the palace, gaining momentum with every breath. And now these same women that one time ignored and mocked me began to revere me, to perhaps even feel a sense of fear towards me, for with each passing day, more and more nobles declared their loyalty to my little brother, naming him as king of Castilla.

The floor was cracking beneath their feet while it was consolidating beneath my own.

And yet... and yet I was overcome with fear. My brother, my sweet Alfonso, was still only a child. No sooner was he hoisted onto the stage at Ávila and declared king of Castilla, than he was sent off to battle.

My stomach twisted inside of me. Come what may, I must get to him. I needed to warn him of Juan Pacheco. But how? It would be impossible to send a message to him, not with Juana's eyes watching my every move, waiting for any reason to accuse me. Even if I tried, I knew that there would be no hope of it reaching him. Surely it would be intercepted. But there had to be a way to help him.

Gonzálo.

The image of the handsome young swordsman in the loose cotton shirt practicing in the fields with Alfonso emerged to the surface of my mind. He was an exceptional swordsman, the greatest I had ever seen, and before we parted, he swore to me that he would protect my brother with his very life. Gonzálo Fernández de Córdoba, my one hope. He would find a way. If anyone could, he could, I knew it. Gonzálo, I knew, would never fail my brother. Something inside of me swore with even more confidence that he would never fail me.

Gonzálo was like no one I'd ever met. Chivalrous and wise beyond his years, he was a prince among gentlemen. During those months we all spent together, he pledged himself to me more than once, swearing that he would honor and defend me with his life, and his love. He well knew that the best way to serve me was to protect my Alfonso. Once he was sent on this mission, there was little doubt that he would keep my brother safe, whatever the risk.

My thoughts lingered on the boy, a young man, really. I didn't think him so very handsome at first, not from a distance. It was only upon coming closer that his beauty struck me, then seemed to have a way of sinking in deeper once he spoke. It was odd, really, when I came to think of it, how much time we three had spent together, a commoner and the children of a king. But there was something about him so familiar, it almost felt like home. It seemed like I had known him all my life.

So strange was it to think that we had known each other for less than a year. When he first came into our lives, he was meant to merely serve as a page to Alfonso, and in exchange, such closeness to the royal family would most certainly enrich his future. But in truth, it was us whose lives were enriched. No one, except perhaps Beatriz, understood me the way Gonzálo did.

Just thinking of him made me smile to myself, with his chivalrous ideals of duty and honor. We had so much in common. The time we were together was spent talking and debating about Greek philosophies and faith. He loved Aristotle and could use his reasoning to defend any argument, and I loved to debate him, pointing out some of the more ridiculous theories of Aristotle, coupled, of course, with theology to support my argument.

I exhaled slowly and closed my eyes, trying to remember that day, watching my brother and Gonzálo practicing their swordsmanship together.

"Are we safer here?" probed the doubtful voice of Doña María, breaking me away from my memories.

"Naturally," answered the queen, refusing to allow any shred of fear from her ladies. "You must know that the Alcázar was originally a Roman fortress. Now it serves us well as a palace. Just look," she gestured towards the window. "Before you stand the protective walls surrounding the Alcázar, stone covered cliffs and mountains, and two flowing rivers that separate Segovia from the rest of the world. We are untouchable. Have no fear, the usurper will soon be handled." Yet, despite her confident words, her voice echoed a thinly veiled uncertainty.

I looked out the small rectangular window of the tower at the countryside, a tower built by my father, King Juan II, all those years ago. His work was meant to be an example of architectural excellence, its aesthetic would serve to enhance the grandeur of the palace. If only he knew that now it served to cage in his only daughter like a prisoner, while his two sons were at war against one another. And should the worst happen, should something happen to my Alfonso, I knew that I would suffer a far worse fate.

"Isabel, what are you doing?" Juana snapped, disrupting my thoughts. "Praying again, I suspect. Well, I can only hope that you are praying for your lord and king, Enrique." She patted the beads of sweat off her forehead. "Do something useful and bring me my water."

Obediently, I stood and poured water from the pitcher.

"But war is breaking out everywhere, not just on the battlefield!" cried another of the queen's ladies. Then turning to me, "and it's Alfonso's fault. Noble houses are breaking with the king and shifting to Alfonso's camp, and it is only causing more skirmishes. Your traitorous brother is razing the entire kingdom. Homes in every town and city are raided, farm stock burnt to the ground, and good men killed. The nation is being destroyed, and all because of your little brother."

My eyes narrowed into a sharp glare. I had had enough. No longer would my tongue rest at such flagrant insolence.

"Fool," I said through clenched teeth, steadying my glare on the Portuguese woman who served the queen. "Have you no mind of your own? Are all your opinions spoon-fed to you? Castilla is not split because of Alfonso, but because of poor government, poor leadership, and Alfonso would never be at war and never be in danger if Castilla didn't need him to lead. If Enrique could execute the task he had been given by God, to create a stable kingdom, and to produce heirs of his own, then Alfonso would never have been placed in harm's way."

"Heirs of his own?!" shouted the queen, her words spitting out. "Heirs of his own?! Our daughter is the true heir to the king of Castilla y León. You would like nothing more than for your pretender of a brother to wear the crown. Well, he has cast the dice, as have you. Once the king has won this war, I will make it my mission to see your dear little Alfonso's head on a spike."

My chest filled with rage. I would permit no one to threaten Alfonso. At this moment, I knew that the queen was, from this point forward, forever my enemy, and come what may, I knew she would do her best to ensure my end. There was no turning back. Now was the moment for me to declare my position against Queen Juana de Avís.

"The daughter of the queen is a bastard," I growled through gritted teeth, "the illegitimate child of Beltrán de la Cueva and the queen's illicit and scandalous union. Your debauched affairs, your Majesty, have earned your daughter a future of scorn. Everywhere, she is mocked as 'la Beltraneja.' No one believes she is of the Trastámara seed. Your own flesh and blood is condemned, and you have no one to blame but yourself."

My heart beat hard inside of my chest with each violent word. My lungs filled with air, but my words were spoken with a controlled, steady, condemning calm. "Our family, the Trastámara line, descends from the greatest of Spanish heroes, and before them, the Visigoths, and before them, Hercules, even back to the sons of Noah. That line will not be corrupted by you and your devious ambitions. God is on our side. Mark my words, the future of the Trastámara dynasty will be protected."

Chapter VIII
August 1467
Segovia

Twice a day without fail, a servant came in, delivered a piece of stale bread and hard-boiled eggs, and left. Everyday I pressed her for news of the battle raging between the two brother-kings, but the maid kept her eyes lowered, not daring speak a word to me.

It was the only interaction I had all day, and soon the days began to blend, one after another, and another. On and on it went until it no longer mattered what day it was. No one bothered me now. They let me alone, waiting in the silence of my chambers for the news of the outcome of the battle between Enrique and Alfonso. But no one disturbed me.

The whispers and muffled feet shuffling past my door grew louder.

"Make haste, we haven't much time," I heard one courtier shout out to another from just down the hall. "They are nearly here."

After spending so much time locked in my quarters, my ears had seemed to grow deaf to the outside world, taking no notice of the sounds of voices and feet outside my door. But the commotion took hold of my attention, distracting me from the pages of Scripture I was studying. Holding my breath, I noticed the sounds of the shouting, as if hearing them for the first time. The citizens of Segovia were cheering, their voices growing louder and louder.

My heart sank in fear. Segovia was Enrique's treasure, his most beloved city in all of Spain. I knew that the cheers coming from the Segovians could only be to honor the return of the king that loved them so well. I tried to pray, but no words would come. All I could think of was of Alfonso, my innocent young brother.

The cheers grew louder, so I squeezed close my eyes and prayed out loud. As the voices outside grew stronger, so did my own, so desperate was I to drown out their words. The beads of the rosary passed through my fingers, and I realized my hand was shaking.

Shouts of *"viva el rey,* long live the king," grew bolder and more frequent. Still, I refused to give in to fear. I willed myself to remain focused on my prayer, concentrating so intently on the words I was reciting that the cheers coming from the crowds outside were imperceptible.

The Lord is with me, the Lord will protect me, the Lord will provide. Lord, You do not give us a spirit of fear, but of victory. I declare victory, in Your name, Lord Jesus. I declare Your victory. I will not fear. I trust You Lord; I trust You Lord.

Behind me came the rumbling of servants and the voices of Juana's ladies, but I only prayed louder. I could hear Juana's voice shouting orders. I squeezed my eyes shut even harder and focused my mind on my words. A tingling sensation of anxiety spread from my stomach to my heart into even my shoulders, and I felt like I was going to burst into tears at any given moment. I grit my teeth, and even though I refused to cry, warm tears rolled down my cheeks.

There was a knocking on the door.

It is Enrique. He is here, it is over.

The knock grew louder but I didn't move, and instead remained kneeled and in prayer, refusing to open my eyes. The metal handle creaked loudly as it unlocked from the outside, and then I heard his voice.

"My lady."

It was Gonzálo.

"Princess Isabel, I present to you, your king." He bowed, sweeping his arm behind him towards my brother.

Rushing to Alfonso, I hugged him as tightly as I could.

"I promised you I would come back, Isabel. I will always keep my promises to you," my brother said with a strength and confidence that was never there before. Hugging my little brother to me, I realized that the child I remembered now returned as the declared king over all Castilla y León.

"I knew you would come back," I said, smiling through the tears in my eyes. "I knew you would be safe."

Holding Alfonso to me, I reached my arm forward and took Gonzálo by the hand. He had kept his word to me. My Alfonso had been protected, and I knew it was because of Gonzálo.

"Thank you," I whispered to him. And his warm, full lips delicately kissed the tips of my fingers.

"Your Grace is kind to wait for me," I said, exiting the little cathedral next to the Alcázar. He took my hand and placed it in the crook of his elbow, and Gonzálo, protector to the king, took his place a few paces behind us.

"I wouldn't have it any other way, sister," Alfonso replied, handing me a ripe orange. "It is good that you have a heart that seeks the Lord. I have plans for the future of Castilla, and a woman of devote religious observance is an example I want for my kingdom."

The three of us made our way into the city center and meandered through its bustling streets. The hour was still early, and even during the hot summer month of August, the air was fresh and cool.

"I don't remember it being so beautiful here," I said, breathing in the crisp morning air. After so much time spent inside the palace or secluded inside my own chambers, I felt like I was seeing the outside world for the first time. "Segovia truly is Castilla's most enchanting city."

The city was rich with vibrance and energy, as if it had its own heartbeat. My eyes took in the flowers ornamented in vivid color and trees reaching up to the heavens. I breathed in the city, aromas of freshly baked bread from the *panadería* mixed with the scent of leather, horses, and metal from the various workshops.

Segovia was a jewel to behold. Home to one of the kingdom's largest populated cities, it was a center of power and commerce, particularly from its production of wool, and I watched as the merchants moved about, preparing for their busy day ahead.

Gonzálo plucked a few small daisies and presented them to me.

"For a princess as lovely as you," he said gallantly, handing them to me.

My brother stopped walking and stood, staring at the butcher shop. His eyes were fixed on the hog, its foot pieced by a large metallic hook hanging from the ceiling. Alfonso's lower lip tightened, as if he were forcing himself from showing any emotion. I placed my hand on his shoulder, but he shrugged it off.

"I'm fine," he said, his voice firm and defensive. "I must behave like a king. Don Pacheco tells me I need to stop acting like a little boy. I must be a man now."

As much as I didn't trust the marqués de Villena, I knew that what he said was true. No longer could my little brother, who had only just entered his thirteenth year, enjoy his childhood. And the truth of the matter was, neither could I.

But something had changed in my brother. There was a sadness, even a darkness that had never been a part of his nature.

"Alfonso," I called out. "Alfonso, I heard about what you did to the exotic animals Enrique kept housed in Segovia," I said gently, tearing his attention away from the carcass. "Why did you slaughter them?"

He stood there in silence and refused to meet my eye.

"What came over you?"

Finally, he looked at me, and when his eyes looked into mine, I could see the hurt and fear and anger behind them that had sparked such violence against innocent creatures.

"I... I don't know. I don't know why I killed them. But something inside of me snapped. I was so angry at him, at Enrique. And I wanted to do something to hurt him. It was the only way I could do something that I knew would hurt him."

His voice cracked, as if he were fighting back tears. Something had happened to my brother. He wasn't the sweet boy that I knew before he left. And I knew that the marqués de Villena was responsible. My brother was under Pacheco's direct protection, under his tutelage, but whatever education Pacheco had exposed him to had left damaging scars. Though he may be king, I feared he was also a victim.

I grabbed my little brother by the shoulders and turned him to face me.

"Listen to me. From this moment on, I will not leave your side. No one has your best interest in mind like me. Do you hear me, Alfonso? I will be your support, your wisdom and foresight. You cannot trust Pacheco, and I fear that you already depend on him too much."

"No, Isabel. You don't understand. You weren't there. Juan Pacheco has done everything in his power to put me on the throne. He never left my side once, not even during the battle."

"But he isn't doing it for selfless reasons. The marqués is the most ruthless and ambitious courtier since Álvaro de Luna. While we were separated, he made a truce with Enrique, promising to return to his side if Enrique agreed to marry me to his brother. Do you know what that means, Alfonso? It means Pacheco was willing to deliver you into your enemies' hands so that he could garner more power."

"That's not true!" His voice cracked with frustration.

"Hush," I said in a stern, low tone of voice. "Or you will bring attention to yourself. Take a deep breath and gather yourself. You are king now. You must always act like it. I beg you to heed my warning, but you must also listen to your own counsel. I am here only to serve and suggest."

I knew there was little more I could say. My brother was clearly under Pacheco's spell, just as Enrique was under his spell before, and even my father was under the spell of Pacheco's predecessor, Álvaro de Luna.

"These men fought next to me. Pacheco served me well. Everyday I receive more support from the nobles because of his efforts. Even Don Pacheco's uncle, the archbishop of Toledo, donned armor. Imagine that, a leader of the Church riding undaunted into battle! And do you know why he was willing to set aside his ecclesiastical duties and wield a sword? Because Carrillo, just like Pacheco, is looking to me to overcome the chaos in which Castilla now lives. They believe in me. They fought just as hard as any man on that field, and that battle would not have been won without them."

"That's very good, Alfonso. That's very good indeed. You do well in acknowledging the dedication and loyalty of your men. My only suggestion is to learn from our past. Refuse to take a favorite. Do not let the marqués de Villena expect you to declare him as your favorite, or else he will soon be the one making the decisions and leading the kingdom."

My eyes stared into his, waiting for him to process the lesson I hoped he would come to understand. "Enrique was made too vulnerable because he didn't harness his royal power. During his reign, the nobles were able to exercise far too much control over him, and no one more than Juan Pacheco. The same was true with our father. Many say that Don Álvaro de Luna made all the decisions for the kingdom. But it doesn't have to be like that for you. You are at the dawn of your rule, and God has chosen you to lead a nation of selfish and ambitious nobles that seek not the best for the kingdom, but instead the surest means to line their pockets with gold. Let there be no favorite. Do not allow yourself to be governed by anyone but God."

Alfonso released a heavy sign and I knew he was submitting to my logic.

"You are right. Enrique was a weak king, and for that, he not only lost his right to rule, but he leaves no honorable legacy."

"Yes. And make no mistake, *you* can create a legacy that will change the future of Castilla. You can restore the honor of the

Peninsula, and bring the land back into Christian hands. It was no coincidence that you were born the same year as the fall of Constantinople at the barbaric hands of the Muslims. Christians have suffered under the violence of Islam for seven hundred years. Let it end with you. Bring this country back to God."

Chapter IX

"Careful with your footing," Gonzálo Fernández de Córdoba instructed before lunging towards Alfonso with his sword. "That's it!" The cadence of his voice rang out. "Mind your balance. Yes! Just so!"

Alfonso hopped with the lightest of steps from one foot to the next, blocking the attempts Gonzálo made at him.

"You see, sister," Alfonso called out to me, moving as gracefully as a dancer, just as he had learned from Gonzálo. "You have nothing to fear. I'm untouchable!"

"Untouchable? Perhaps," Gonzálo challenged, then attacked harder. "But we won't stop until you are invincible."

Alfonso leaped forward, advancing in his offensive against Gonzálo with one strong blow of his sword after another. Finally, the edge of his sword reached Gonzálo's throat and he submitted and bowed, a smirk across his handsome face.

"Bravo!" I shouted, clapping my hands and smiling. "You improve every day!" I called out with pride, though I knew that Gonzálo was still unrivaled in his swordsmanship, and had merely let my little brother, King Alfonso, win that match.

But there would be more battles for my brother, and as grateful as I was for Gonzálo, I couldn't help but worry about how much he dutifully risked his young life for the good of my family. One day I would be sure that he received his reward. Loyalty deserved to be duly rewarded. Gonzálo would know my gratitude.

"You look as if you would like to join them," came a voice from behind. Without turning, I recognized it to be that of Alfonso Carrillo, the Archbishop of Toledo. "I can see the longing in your eyes."

"Alas," I answered lightheartedly. "If only I could. Though I am a woman, I would argue that I should prove to be a fierce warrior. I would wager that there is no man who can protect the king better than me."

My words were truer than I would like to admit. I was strong and quick, and could ride as well as anyone else. I would have loved to fight alongside my brother, to wield a sword in defense of his crown, just as Joan of Arc did in defense of her French king.

"Have no fear, young princess, your brother will be safe, as will you, just as I promised. I assure you, my lady, I never fail to keep my word."

The archbishop was a tall, wide-set man, with a burly chest and a heavy gaze. But even though he could seem over-powering, I saw something good in him, something that told me I could trust him.

"He is much more ready and agile than the last time I watched them practice. Gonzálo has done him much good through his training."

Carrillo clasped his hands together inside the luxurious purple velvet of his robe and studied the two boys.

"Our Gonzálo is younger than what I would have preferred for Alfonso, but he knows how to give instruction in a way his pupil can benefit from. And he will continue to, I am sure of it," he added, as if calculating Gonzálo's worth. "One must remember, Gonzálo de Córdoba is the second son of deceased parents. His older brother enjoys the strings to the family purse. I understand that the brother is generous with Gonzálo, but by no means can Gonzálo expect to become a wealthy man. His entire future depends on the career he can build in the service of King Alfonso. So, you see, he has no choice but to serve your brother well, and hope to garner his royal favor."

I continued watching the interaction of the two young men until it occurred to me that, for more than a few minutes, my eyes gazed at Gonzálo.

"Indeed," I answered, breaking away from my stare. "It is good to have a man like that in the service of his Majesty."

"Particularly when we have such challenging days ahead." The archbishop watched for my reaction out of the corner of his eye, then he went on.

"Have no fear, *Princesa*. There may be more battles ahead, but we *will* win the war, especially after Enrique's cowardice at the battlefield of Olmedo, taking flight from his little brother. I am afraid the poor man could not have made a more foolish blunder. But it is just as well. The nobles have abandoned his cause, and one city after another pledges their allegiance to your brother."

I raised my chin high, exhaling slowly. "The sovereign of Castilla must be courageous. A Castilian will never support a coward for a king."

"That was one of Enrique's great failings, he never behaved like the king of the Castilians," Carrillo replied in a stern, disapproving voice that revealed his own condemnation of my half-brother. "Enrique forgot who it was that he ruled over, who he was defending and who he was defending against. With his glorification of the Moor, dressing in their silks and robes, lounging on overstuffed pillows strews about the floor, insisting on employing Moorish bodyguards… a Spanish king fashioning himself as one of *them*. Castilian traditions and Castilian bodyguards weren't good enough for him. He rejected the traditions of his own people." He shook his head in disgust. "A king such as that deserves to be dethroned."

My eyes rested on my brother as I turned Carrillo's words over and over in my head. *He never behaved as king of the Castilians, he fashioned himself as one of them.* Such words could not be easily forgotten.

I realized that a king was not simply born, he must be fashioned. Enrique had a part to play, and he failed his subjects because he failed to be *their* king.

It was but a short time ago, a matter of decades past, that Islam, the great enemy of the Christians, savagely attacked our sacred land — Constantinople. It was our religious duty to retake what God intended to belong to us. No one could deny that during Enrique's reign, he had now and again waged war on the Moors. But Enrique's battles were nothing more than half-hearted skirmishes, like a game of cat and mouse. Enrique was never truly committed to retaking the Peninsula. It was all an amusement to him. In fact, even during his campaigns against the Moors, he continued to honor them by dressing in the Moorish fashion, imitating their ways, and even surrounding himself with a Moorish guard.

The archbishop was right and his words were well chosen. A king must be mindful of how he fashioned himself, he must consider how he was perceived by his countrymen. The behavior of Enrique was folly. I would not allow my brother to make such a grave mistake.

Perhaps I would never be allowed to take up a sword and stand next to King Alfonso in battle. But I could serve him with my insight and guidance in a way that no other courtier could. I would be his chief advisor. He could trust no one more than he could trust me. I would use Enrique's error to our benefit. I would fashion the king into the ruler that our land had long yearned for — a warrior, a nobleman, sired by Catholic kings, the purest of Castilian blood running through his veins. My brother, Alfonso XII of Castilla y León, would be the prince our land had long waited for.

Chapter X

"Surely you must be done by now," my brother complained to the valet who was fussing with one of the clasps on the cape.

"Let him take his time," I said calmly. "Tonight, you must look your best, particularly when it is *your* birthday we are celebrating! And you really do look especially dashing this evening."

He looked back at his reflection in the mirror, running his eyes over his wardrobe, then stared back at himself, deciding if he approved of what he saw looking back at him.

"Yes, well if I look better than any other day, it's your doing."

He was still not happy that his valet was taking so long. If it were up to him, he would have donned a simple leather vest and cotton shirt, and been done with it. "Anyway, I'm happy with the man you sent here from Flanders."

"As am I. He had an exceptional selection of fabrics, the best I've yet to see. And the seamstress' work is superb," I added, smiling with approval.

I had made it a point to arrange for Europe's finest seamstress to design my brother's wardrobe, and it flattered me that he had taken my advice as to how to dress for tonight's occasion. Though I made sure that it was only a gentle suggestion. There was no need for him to think that the idea was mine; better to merely plant the seed of an idea and let him think he came up with it on his own.

I took notice of the intricate embroidery on my brother's vest and his fur-lined cloak. Truly, he looked majestic, as he deserved to, our august ruler. Surely, we both should have always had access to the finest of wardrobes, but our half-brother Enrique chose to withhold the inheritance our father had willed to us, and my mother simply never had the resources to outfit her children as was befitting for the children of royalty.

That would all change now. Appearance, as I had learned, was paramount. And with that in mind, King Alfonso was prudently dressed in a polished outfit that harkened back to Castilian tradition.

"May I suggest this sword for tonight, my lord," Gonzálo Fernández de Córdoba said, and handed Alfonso a freshly polished sword ornamented with three jeweled crosses on the tip of the handle. "Perhaps this one is not as practical as your battle sword, but it is appropriate for the occasion."

Gonzálo noticed my preoccupation with the self-image I hoped for my brother to evoke, and I was grateful that he understood the symbolic importance of the sword, especially for a freshly recognized king.

Gonzálo led us down the corridor, and as we neared the great room, the sound of celebration grew louder and louder. Alfonso and I waited outside the two large doors, and I could hear the footsteps of the courtiers lining up.

I reached forward for Alfonso's hand and squeezed it.

"Happy birthday, your Grace. You are our honored king," I whispered.

It was as much a means to make him feel celebrated as it was a reminder that he must behave like a king, like a man much older than someone who was only thirteen years old the day before.

Suddenly, I felt the pangs of sadness for the little boy I once knew, the innocent, gentle child Alfonso was before Pacheco got his hands on him. There was no place for that child in the world he was now to live in. Now, that child had no choice but to be a man, to be the king that Castilla needed.

Tonight must be spectacular. Castilla's king was young; thus, his entertainments must be equally as fresh and lively. Not a detail of the evening was overlooked, I made sure of it. Though I, personally, abstained from alcohol, I worked closely with our sommelier to ensure that only the finest of wines and ales, brought in from France, Holland, Italy, and of course from different parts of Spain, were served to our many distinguished guests. The chef had prepared twenty courses, each brought out to the tables on serving dishes covered in golden gilt, delicacies including stag, chicken, veal, wild boar and hare, fruits of every nature, jellies and tarts. Musicians played their instruments and troubadours performed their ballads throughout the evening. The illustrious poet and knight Gómez Manrique had prepared the main event, a short theatrical comedy, then eight muses dressed in feathers, and a ninth dressed in an ethereal white gauze descended, dancing in celebration of his Grace. It was magnificent, exactly what I had wished for him.

The preparations to make this birthday, the first he would celebrate as king, required a great deal of effort, certainly. But it was not enough. This year, above all other years, he must have more.

Though I would have preferred for the spotlight to be cast firmly on Alfonso, I remembered my vow to myself, to portray the image of a ruler that Castilla needed, an image that included the royal family. *You are braver than you know*, I promised myself, then prepared for my moment.

I ignored the clammy feeling in the palm of my hands and clenched my fist to steady their shaking, then stood and made my way around the long rows of tables and past the honored guests, seated by rank. King Alfonso stopped conversing with Archbishop Carrillo and turned his head towards me. He raised two fingers and the entire room grew silent.

Lady Ana of the Buendía family stepped confidently before the crowd and performed a perfect curtsey. As she stood, the candlelight appeared to sparkle as it reflected off the jewels sewn into her velvet gown. A prominent member of House Buendía, Lady Ana was a relation to the archbishop, and as a seasoned courtier, Carrillo had encouraged me to observe and learn from her.

"A gift," she announced, using her clear, sonorous voice, "for our lord and king, Alfonso XII of Castilla y León." Then, gracefully sweeping back her arm towards where I stood, Lady Ana backed away.

Immediately I felt the weight of all eyes resting on me. There seemed to be no sounds at all, so silent was the audience awaiting their princess. Never had I endured the weight of so much attention, all falling at once onto my person. My knees bent forward, just for a moment, and I quickly stiffened them with resolve and forced myself to breath normally until my cheeks stopped flushing.

"Go on," Lady Ana whispered to me, her voice low and gentle so that no one but me could hear her. "As we practiced."

Composure, child, remember who you are. It was the voice of my grandmother, reminding me of the wisdom instilled in me all those years ago, words that were now only too indispensible.

Yes, grandmother, I remember my identity. I am the true-born daughter of one monarch and sister to another.

Things had changed. My brother was now king. A new king in a broken and vulnerable kingdom, he needed every bit of security I could foster for him. Cringe though I might at such attention as this, there was no doubt that this would be the first of many performances and first of many audiences with their eyes cast steadily, inquisitively on me. No longer could I find comfort in the refuge of shadows.

I took a step forward and stretched to my full height, doing my best to project confidence, reminding myself that I could do this. This was my own work, poetry written in my own hand, and I had been reciting the poem for weeks. There was no reason to cringe.

On this day, the Lord doth bring
A blessing to our home, Castilla
 To every city, every villa
To Juan II, his heir, our King

Pelayo and El Cid look down from above
Offering protection and saintly love
Castilla hails her King

Excelente rey doceno(Excellent King)
De los Alfonsos llamados (among the line of Alfonso's)
En este año catorceno (In your fourteenth year)
Dios te quiera hacer tan bueno (May God make you so good)
Que excedas a los pasados (That you exceed all those that came before you)
En los triunfos y victoria (In triumphs and victories)
Y en grandeza temporal (And in temporal grandeur)
Tu reinado sea tal (May your reign be such)
Que merezcas ambas glorias (That you deserve both)
La terrena y celestial. (Heaven and earthly glory.)

At first, my words were awkward, feeble. But with each stanza, I grew more comfortable, even confident, as the center of attention.

You've found your place, sister to the king of Castilla y León, first member of the royal family.

My voice rang out boldly, dramatically rising in grandeur then falling to a smooth whisper, and I knew that with such a performance, the minds of everyone in my audience could picture the image I meant to portray. With each new stanza, Alfonso emerged as our promised hero, the inheritance of the valiant Spanish Visigoth forefathers that came before him, the product of legendary Castilian history married to the sanctity of the Catholic faith. Here stood our young, gallant, honorable Castilian champion of old Christian blood.

Finally, I fell silent and bowed. King Alfonso was the first to stand, a smile as proud and strong as the dawn spread across his face. Then, lifting his hands, he broke out in applause, and after him, all the other courtiers did the same.

"Bravo, *princesa*," said Archbishop Carrillo in a loud, authoritative voice, spreading his arms out wide. "Bravo, indeed." Then, addressing the crowd, he continued. "Let us carry on with the celebration in honor of our beloved king with a jousting tournament and Corpus Christi tomorrow."

At that moment all eyes should have been on Carrillo, but I had the sensation of someone staring at me. Intuition told me who it was without any need to turn.

The eyes of Juan Pacheco, the Marqués de Villena pierced into me, but I refused to grant him the pleasure of acknowledging him. The outrage and jealousy from the energy of his stare was palpable. I hoped he wallowed in it, hateful creature that he was.

Certainly, the man had good reason to be jealous. Pacheco now tasted what he had always feared most, the loss of his power, a power that entitled him to his position as one of the most influential men in all Castilla. Now, his authority was quickly turning to ash before his eyes.

Pacheco, no doubt, had always fancied himself as the de-facto ruler of rulers, a sort of puppet-master of kings. Just like Álvaro de Luna, my father's favorite, Pacheco assumed he would secure his position as favorite to Alfonso, as he had with Enrique. He had no idea how determined I was to hinder his ambition.

Wealth and privilege he had already amassed through closeness to kings, and such dominance had allowed him to sway the politics of the country. But he had never used his influence to benefit the best interest of the kingdom — his greed wouldn't allow him loyalty to anyone but himself.

The man sickened me. Even more so now, when he still held such influence over my little brother.

His eyes still clung to me, digging into my flesh like a falcon's claws. I exhaled deeply and a serene smile spread across my face as I held one thought firmly in my mind. No longer would any nobleman wield such influence that he was able to manipulate the king of Castilla. From this moment on, the power would lie centrally in the hands of the sovereign ruler that God had ordained to lead the kingdom. Juan Pacheco, the Marqués de Villena, would be the last of the favorites.

Chapter XI
Medina del Campo, Summer, 1468

Just for a moment I let my eyes linger on the wide, reaching towers pocked with kill holes of the old Castilla de la Mota, then continued along with the others, headed towards the town center, where Medina del Campo's famed annual fair was taking place. Behind us walked King Alfonso's most loyal supporters, an entourage that only seemed to be growing larger as more and more nobles pledged their loyalty to Alfonso, recognizing him as the one true king of Castilla.

The day had fast begun, and everywhere I looked, Medina del Campo was bustling with energy. In every corner, down every row, banners flew in the wind and colorful tents filled with merchants and shopkeepers bartered and sold their goods to the crowds in the open market.

"Something has caught your eye, my lady?" the shopkeeper with the receding hairline and kindly face asked as he polished a silver looking glass.

"Perhaps, sir," I replied, smiling to the man. His mustache was so prominent that it was impossible to see him smiling back at me, except for the warmth in his eyes.

He took a step backwards, as if to appear less aggressive in wishing to sell his wares.

"Do take your time. There are many a fine object to be found, objects from all over the world. My collection is small, but well curated; each piece is unlike anything you've ever beheld. I invite you to look at your leisure, if you please."

After a few minutes, the shopkeeper put the looking glass down, walked before me, and without saying a word, presented me with an antique vase.

My eye fell upon the object, and I leaned forward to scrutinize it more closely.

"It doesn't quite look Castilian. Is it French, perhaps?"

"Very impressive. My lady knows her antiques. It is French - through adoption, shall we say. Look at the rock crystal here, and here, at the gold filigree. Notice the craftsmanship." The shopkeeper fitted the suede glove over his right hand and presented it for viewing, running his gloved hand gently over the gold woven around the bottom of the vase. "This is one of my most valued objects, dating back to the twelfth century. It belonged to William IX, Duke of Aquitaine," he informed, proud to have an object of such worth in his collection. "I call it 'the Eleanor vase,' for his granddaughter, Eleanor of Aquitaine, who brought it with her to Paris upon her first marriage with the king of France."

"I know that name. Grandmother taught us of him," I said, turning to Alfonso. "William IX, they say he was the first troubadour. I'll take it."

I didn't bother to ask the price. If the vase truly belonged to Eleanor of Aquitaine's grandfather, its worth was invaluable. Besides, with the growing loyalty pledged by his subjects, my brother was amassing a fortune from the taxes Chacón and Carrillo collected from the cities that now turned away from Enrique in support of Alfonso.

The shopkeeper shook his head. "It is a gift, for the sister of our good king. I only ask, fair maiden, that the noble king and his lady sister remember the loyalty of a humble servant."

Alfonso nodded his head in recognition. "You are kind, sir. I can promise you that every man loyal to Castilla will be rewarded. But the sale of your goods deserves payment," Alfonso said. Reaching into the small leather purse at his side, the king handed the shopkeeper a generous amount of gold coin.

I stared at the coin, and a thought occurred to me. The king of Castilla must hand out coins with his own face on them, so that he will be as ubiquitous as trade and currency. I would speak to the archbishop about this as soon as he returned from Toledo.

With each passing day, my brother impressed me more. His leadership and integrity were earning the loyalty and winning the hearts of his people. This was the king Castilla had long awaited.

Alfonso turned to me. "This vase is but a small thank you, for the great effort it must have taken you for my birthday celebrations." Then, handing me my vase, he said, "No one is more faithful of a servant to the Crown than you, dear sister. And for your loyalty, I reward you with Medina del Campo."

"Your Majesty," I gasped, searching for the words to show my gratitude. "You do me too great an honor."

"Medina del Campo was always your favorite place to visit when we were little," he said, leading me by the arm. "The town is one of my greatest supporters, one of the first to declare its loyalty to me. Its wealth is immense. That wealth now belongs to you." He stopped and looked me in the eyes. "Isabel, no one has been more devoted to me, or believed in me as much as you. It gives me great pleasure to reward you."

"You have always been a prince, your Grace. You should have always been celebrated as such..." I said, stopping myself short from finishing my thought.

When we were children, Alfonso and I hardly had the means to be able to celebrate our birthdays. Although our father, King Juan, had provided ample financial support for us in his will, Enrique blocked us from receiving the inherited funds, and we were forced to live off little to nothing in Arévalo. But I didn't want to complain about days gone by, not now. Let the bitterness of the past stay in the past. I wanted my brother to keep his eyes on the future.

"And you have always had the heart of a king, dear brother. Now you *are* king, and there is so much celebrating to be had," I said, making my voice cheerful and rosy, and rested my head on his shoulder.

"Coming to Medina del Campo brings back memories, doesn't it?" Alfonso said.

"The best of memories."

"I used to love coming here with Chacón," he continued, sounding like his old self. "Whenever he knew we needed a break from our studies, it was here that he would take us, and it always felt like an adventure."

"Do you remember how much Grandmother loved coming to the fair? It was one of her favorite events of the year."

"And she always had a good story to tell. Returning to the fairs must have reminded her of when she was a little girl," he said.

"Hmm," I reminisced. "The foreign fragrances and baskets of spices, and the skins of exotic animals being sold have a way of doing just that - making us remember. Especially for a little girl, watching the sailors return to the Portuguese Court, bearing all sorts of rarities they picked up along their journeys, it must have been enchanting."

"I loved listening to her stories. It made me feel like the world was so large, I could spend my whole life exploring and still discover more."

"But they weren't just stories Grandmother told," I said. "They were lessons. She was teaching us how much bigger the world was outside of our quiet little existence in Arévalo. Grandmother was teaching us that all these exotic things we were seeing at the fair were brought here because of the sailors who braved the seas. Remember how she would talk of their courage and willingness to explore unchartered lands, how they brought glory to their kingdom. Captains of ships would return with greater knowledge of the world, of how much bigger it is than we ever knew. Grandmother taught that seafaring was the future, and seafaring would bring wealth through its discovery, and wealth bred power."

"Now, power lies in my hands."

"Now, power lies in your hands," I repeated. "And with it you can make the world a better place."

A teenage boy came running towards us, and Gonzálo Fernández de Córdoba protectively stepped in front of my brother and me and placed his hand on the hilt of his sword.

"The child is a page to Chacón. Let him pass," King Alfonso ordered.

"Your Majesty," the boy's voice was raspy, and he panted hard, trying to regain his breath. "My lord, Don Chacón has just arrived and requests to speak with you at once."

As soon as we arrived back at the royal residence of Medina del Campo, we went to the study and found Chacón pacing back and forth.

"My lord," Chacón said with earnest, and bowed respectfully to my brother. "Forgive the interruption, but the news is of urgent importance. I just received word from the archbishop of Toledo. The city is in open defiance against you. Carrillo writes that they have returned their loyalty to Enrique."

"How can that be? Toledo was one of the first to declare its support to us," I said, my voice growing louder, but Chacón's voice, by contrast, remained calm and controlled, reminding me that a royal was not allowed to lose their sense of control, regardless of the circumstances.

"Carrillo writes that Alfonso made a poor decision in not supporting the Christian cause and refusing to forgive them their violence against the Jewish *conversos*. Now the Christians of Toledo have turned their back on him."

"But what they did was wrong. I refuse to tolerate such injustice." Alfonso pleaded as if begging for us to understand the decision that I myself had helped him make. "I couldn't simply grant them forgiveness and turn a blind eye to their crimes. That is not how I mean to rule."

Alfonso had the right of it, and I couldn't support him more in his decision, but standing up for what was right came at a cost, and I began to fear how great of a price that might be.

Religious tensions between Christians and Jews had led to repeated outbreaks of violence, property destroyed, and a death toll that only continued to rise. And now the Christians of Toledo willed for the king to absolve them of their violent crimes against the Jews, while allowing them to keep the property they took from the Jews. Even worse, they expected that King Alfonso would indulge them simply because they knew he needed their support.

I stepped forward and looked Alfonso directly in his eyes. "The nobles must be made to heel at the foot of the throne now, immediately, from the very beginning of your reign, or else they will threaten to topple you, the same way they toppled Enrique. You cannot pardon them for the crimes they committed. A king must rule with justice, your Grace. Peace is born from stability, and stability is born from an iron rule."

"Even if it means losing the support of the city?"

"You won't lose the support of Toledo. Carrillo is the archbishop to the city, and he swore us an oath of loyalty. He would never allow Toledo to abandon you. But we must ride south. I will come with you. Let Toledo see her king, look at him with their own eyes. Once you are before them, they will be sure to support you."

Chapter XII
July 1468

The first rays of sunlight stretched across the plain. Gonzálo Fernández de Córdoba helped me into the saddle and examined the leather straps, making sure they were sturdy before tightening them.

"We must be off soon," I said. "There is no time to be lost. How far along is Don Chacón?"

"He has just passed Ávila, to a small town called Cardeñosa," my brother answered, pulling back on the reigns of his horse.

"The town needs time to prepare for the arrival of the king and his entourage," Gonzálo explained. "Chacón left with a few of his men before dawn. Most likely he is nearly there already."

Alfonso cracked his knuckles, a habit he always did whenever he was worried.

"Chacón means for us to spend the night at Cardeñosa. But it's precious time lost. I am anxious to keep pressing forward at full speed until we reach Toledo."

"Chacón has the right of it, your Highness," Gonzálo maintained. "A king must not be in such haste to pass through the towns of the small folk. Remember, the arrival of a royal entourage is an exciting event for the town, maybe even the biggest thing they will ever see in an entire lifetime. The peasants and farmers, they keep close to the towns they were born and raised in, never traveling further than maybe a mile or so. They'll want to see you with their own eyes, so they can tell their children and grandchildren about you."

Gonzálo had a point.

"The streets will be lined with subjects. If you were in too great a haste to rush past, it would make you appear disrespectful and fearful. We will do as Chacón bids, remain and enjoy the entertainments. Better to earn their love than their scorn."

"I'm famished!" Gonzálo said and leaned back comfortably in his chair. The servant, dressed in a grey, rough spun wool and suede cap, discreetly topped off his glass of red wine. A second servant approached, light blue eyes peaking out from below locks of long, thin strands of hair, unsheathed a carving knife and began slicing the meats.

The quaint town of Cardeñosa was not large enough to provide for royal lodging. Instead, Chacón made arrangements for us to stay at the posada, a large estate home that hosted people of influence.

"I must admit, your Highness," Gonzálo continued, turning toward my brother. "I have never seen a woman ride with such endurance as the princess did today. We need more soldiers like you, my lady."

"Perhaps one day I, myself, will be a soldier and join you in the battlefields, fighting against the Moors. I expect I could fight as well as any man, save the king."

But my brother made no answer. Instead, his mind was elsewhere, far from where we were now, and his eyes stared off into I knew not what.

The servant with the golden locks placed a large serving of boar meat before the king, and I noticed a small golden ring on his finger. It was unusual for a servant to own gold. Perhaps he was a bastard son who had been sired by some wealthy lord. But as I looked closer, the ring was shiny. It must be newly forged. Something about him made me weary. As I watched, the blonde servant unsheathed a second blade, carefully cutting the trout pastry, and presented the dish to Alfonso. I pushed the concern aside and instead worried that my brother hadn't touched his dinner, an act that could be considered a slight to his host, and we were in too great of a need for loyalty to displease any of the king's lords.

"What is it that troubles you?" I asked in a soft voice, so as not to bring attention to us.

My words seemed to break the spell under which Alfonso was cast. He looked at me, as if I had startled him, then let out a sigh of sadness.

"It's Mother. I worry about her."

His words were simple, but were replete with meaning.

Before we went to the fair in Medina del Campo, we visited our mother. She was overjoyed to see her children, but even with her smiles and warm hugs, it was obvious that something was wrong. It was as if she was out of touch with reality, and we knew that her mental condition had worsened.

"I worry, too," I admitted.

"It's not right that she is cloistered all alone in Arévalo, with so few servants to care for her. There must be something we can do."

I knew that Alfonso felt the same way that I did. Helpless. Our mother, the woman that loved us with such dedication and goodness, was sick, and there was nothing we could do to help her.

In the best of worlds, we could all be together. Nothing would make her happier than to be with her children. Even if we could not cure the challenges she faced with her mental health, just having us near would make her life better. I wanted so badly to be able to give her that gift, to be able to fill her life with more joy simply by being near to her, to give her the peace of mind that had evaded her since Father died.

But that could not be. My brother was king now. He could not return home to Arévalo to care for his mother and also fulfill the duties of the Crown. Nor could my mother join the ranks of an itinerant Court.

My brother was no longer just a boy. No longer did he belong to himself, but instead, to his people. Gone were the days when he could indulge in the comfort of staying in one palace, surrounded by his family. His days would be spent traveling to different cities throughout the kingdom. Such a truth was only more certain now, so early in his reign. With a crown placed only just recently on

Alfonso's head, it was critical that he establish his claim to the throne.

In my heart, I yearned to go back to the home of my childhood, to return to my loving mother's arms and to care for her better than any nurse could. When we visited home, I allowed no one to feed her or bathe her. Instead, I saw to her needs myself. It was with a deep sense of satisfaction to my heart that I was able to care for her. Mother's nurse begged me to move home, insisting that my place was at my mother's side. She had no idea what she was asking. Often, people readily cast judgment based on assumptions and the scant information they have at hand, unable to consider the world from another perspective. If I were to return home now, it would mean that I was sacrificing the great need Alfonso had of me in order to make my mother's life more comfortable.

My brother, the newly crowned king, was but a child fighting headfirst in a civil war. He was surrounded by courtiers that would have loved nothing more than to be the one the young king relied most on. Meanwhile, they themselves truly only sought lands and coin.

I couldn't let that happen. I couldn't allow my brother to be left vulnerable. And despite how much my mother may want me to be there with her, I knew in my heart that, were she to consider what it would cost her son, she would tell me that my place was by Alfonso's side.

Alfonso yearned for the ability to do something for our mother as much as I did. How was I to explain that, though he was king, he lacked the power to truly help her in the way she needed most. Still, I needed to make him believe that he could do something to help.

"These same thoughts plague me, as well. Soon we will be able to help," I smiled, trying to reassure him. "The mother of a king must live the quality of life deserving of her title. I will see to it that her staff is increased, and I will have Chacón personally oversee all her expenses. Meanwhile, it is best for her to stay where she is, with people that have cared for her for years."

He placed his hand atop mine and squeezed.

"Thank you, Isabel. You always know how to make things right." I could tell he still felt the weight of the world on his young shoulders.

Before I had the chance to say anything, the performers stood before us, and the *juglar* began reciting the Spanish epic poem, *El Canto del mío Cid.* The poem originated centuries ago, and recounted the heroism, honor, and loyalty of the great warrior, the nobleman Rodrigo Díaz de Vivar.

Pensively, as if lost in thought, Alfonso slowly cut into the trout pastry and lifted it towards his mouth.

"Do you really think we will be able to take back Toledo?" he asked.

"With the support of Archbishop Carrillo, how could we not?" I replied as lightheartedly as I dared, hoping that my words would reassure him and that the mind of this young, impressionable king could enjoy a moment's peace. "I can promise you with absolute certainty that Toledo will be back in your camp as soon as you set foot in the city. Once the people of Toledo see their ruler with their own eyes, their doubts will vanish away and their morale will be lifted, as will their confidence in you. Toledo," I said with perfect assurance, "is as good as yours."

Chapter XIII
July 5, 1468

The town of Cardeñosa was small, but it did include a chapel. The days to come would, no doubt, be taxing. To prepare myself for all the challenges that surely lay ahead, the early hours of the morning found me there, in the security and familiarity of prayer.

After morning Mass, I walked directly to the dining hall to join Alfonso and Gonzálo Fernández de Córdoba to break the fast. But when I arrived, I found neither vassal nor king.

"His Highness 'as not yet come down, *senyora*," one of the servants informed me, her accent gruff.

"No one's fast is to be broken until the king is present," I ordered.

My brother was a creature of habit. Such an irregularity as this was cause for concern. I stood and made my way to his quarters. As I neared, I found Gonzálo, loyal as always, standing guard outside his rooms.

"The King has not risen?" It was more a statement than a question.

"Not yet, my lady."

"That's unusual. He typically wakes with the break of dawn." My voice did little to veil my mounting concern.

I moved towards the thick wooden doors of the king's rooms and Gonzálo followed in behind me. Darkness filled the space, making the air morbidly heavy. The air felt thick, my throat constricted, and I stifled a cough.

"Gonzálo, the windows." I gestured towards the heavy velvet curtains, and as he drew them back, the rays of crushing sunlight eagerly stretched across the room.

And then I saw him, my brother, his face pale, nearly grey with sickness, and his skin covered in little purple spots. His small chest, barely lifting and falling as he struggled for each breathe of air.

The sight of him made me gasp and I stepped back in horror.

"Alfonso!" I cried out, rushing to his side. Kneeling beside the bed, I took his cold, clammy hand in both of mine, and he turned his face slightly towards me.

"I feel…" each word was a struggle for him. "I feel so very weak."

"Call for the physician." I had hardly noticed that the marqués de Villena and Archbishop Carrillo had rushed in behind me.

The town's most distinguished doctor examined the king, an old man with grey hair and frown lines around his mouth. His frown deepened further still after leaching my brother and examining his blood.

Within hours, Alfonso started to lose his senses, coming in and out of consciousness. "Mother," he called out. "Mother, it's cold. May I have another blanket?" Gonzálo looked from Alfonso to me, as if I had an answer.

I tucked a heavy quilt over my brother.

"Alfonso, dear. Would you like us to light the fire?" I asked gently and lovingly in the same voice my mother often used. If it brought him comfort to think Mother was there, so be it. Whatever he needed, I was willing to give, so long as he healed.

The physician examined him again and again. Each time I prayed for a miracle. But when the doctor opened his mouth, my heart sank in my chest when I saw my brother's tongue. It had swelled and turned black, as black as death. An hour later, and the king could no longer close his mouth.

Hours passed. Everyone left the room. Everyone except Gonzálo. He stayed by my brother's bedside, never leaving me.

The others had given up hope, I knew. The gravity of the loss of this young man's life, the hope and future of the kingdom, was too great for them, and so they bid farewell and mourned in private, itching to avoid the burdensome lingering shadow of death. And so, those that had the privilege to enter the king's chambers came to say goodbye, so doubtful were they of his ability to survive. But I remained, clenching to my faith and hope that God would deliver my brother. And Gonzálo, my loyal friend, never once left my side.

I took Alfonso's hand in mine. His hand seemed so small at that moment. I squeezed it, rubbing it to bring warmth to his fingers. But he didn't move.

"It's cold," I whispered, and my body felt the dread of those words.

"Alfonso, it is time for you to wake up," I said reasonably, authoritatively, speaking to him in the same way I did when we were little children, when we played "Master of the Mote." My eyes were fixed on his face, waiting for some movement, some sort of reaction.

"Alfonso!" I shouted louder, my voice cracking. I squeezed his hand hard, hard enough to hurt him — anything to get a reaction from him. "Brother, wake up!"

But he made no reply. Finally, I knew that my greatest fear had now befallen me. My brother, my king, my best friend, was gone.

My jaw fell agape, a cry of hysteria escaped my body, and I looked towards the heavens and moaned with an indescribable depth of anguish.

My knees gave way beneath me and I felt my body go limp. Just before I hit the ground, Gonzálo caught me in his arms. His embrace tightened around me, holding me steady, his strength bearing my weight.

I gripped Gonzálo's cloak and squeezed the fabric between my fingers. "Alfonso, please don't go. You are all I have left!"

Chapter XIV

"A word, *Princesa*," Juan Pacheco, the Marqués de Villena, requested, pulling his horse alongside my own as our company rode towards Ávila.

My eyes, swollen and red from tears, stared blankly at the chestnut mane of the horse I road upon and I made no reaction. Since the morning my brother was taken from me, I felt like I was trapped in a daze, and when the marqués spoke, I hardly heard his voice.

Chacón was quick to reply in my stead. "Forgive me, my lord. But the princess requires to remain in silence."

"Another time, then," Pacheco lowered his head respectfully, then trotted his horse back up to the front of the riders and next to his uncle Carrillo, the Archbishop of Toledo.

We rode on for miles in silence. All along the ride, I felt lost, out of touch with reality.

Alfonso had lost touch with reality, as well, just before dying. Perhaps I will join him.

Without saying a word, Chacón reached out his hand and offered me an apple, but I turned my face away.

"You must eat, child. You'll need to keep up your strength, to not catch a fever, too," Chacón said, implying that my brother had simply died from a fever. He rode closer and took the reigns of my horse into his hand.

"You can't really believe it was a fever," I retorted.

"Hush! Let it be a fever, girl. Let it be. And don't let anyone hear you make accusations of anything else." He remained silent for a long minute with a look of sadness and desperation on his face.

"I had a responsibility, to protect you and your brother. I loved him like a father loves his only son. And now…." His voice cracked. He cut himself off and exhaled harshly, gathering his composure.

Lowering his voice so that only I could hear him, he continued. "Remember, Alfonso named you as his sole heir. If someone dared to poison him, it was to take his crown. If you declare that he was poisoned, the killer may look at you as a threat."

The church was my one comfort, the only comfort I could find, and once we arrived in Ávila, I immediately went to hear Mass.

"Muy buenos días, *mi dama*," came the voice of Juan Pacheco, finding me just as I stepped out of the chapel. Immediately I felt uneasy. The marqués de Villena had never paid me such respect when he addressed me, and now here he was, waiting for me, right where he knew I would be.

"Forgive the intrusion during this time of mourning. My sincerest condolences on the loss of your brother. You must know that I cared deeply for our king, and I mourn with you."

I nodded my head in acknowledgment, but kept my eyes lowered.

"It was the Lord's will that he be taken," he added, as if trying to relate with me by showing that he, too, held some sense of piety.

I squeezed my eyes shut, clenching in the tears. Just hearing a man as wicked as Pacheco speak of God felt like blasphemy.

"Poor child," he continued, his tone unbearably patronizing, shaking his head in pity. "No father, no brother, and no husband to look after you, to guide you and protect you. And now, with Alfonso gone, for cities to be declaring you as their queen, you must be so frightened," I felt the weight of his stare, as if he were trying to read my reaction.

"I had no idea you felt such concern for me," I replied, but he failed to notice my sarcasm.

"Of course, I do. Women are, by nature, feeble, vulnerable, illogical creatures that make their decisions based on their emotions.

But you have no need to fear, girl." He placed his hand under my chin, forcing me to look him in the eyes. "I have my eye on you," he said.

My heart beat faster in my chest.

"I am a servant of the Crown," he went on, his voice shifting to a friendlier note, "my loyalty lays squarely with the good of the kingdom. And you are the only daughter of King Juan II. It would be folly to leave your future to chance. Have no fear, your future has been secured. Arrangements have been made. You are to marry the King of Portugal. I understand your mother and grandmother both hail from Portugal, is that not so?" He continued without waiting for a reply. "Then it will be a most natural fit. Most importantly, this is what is safest for you, and for Castilla."

"But, my lord," I interjected, searching for an excuse to make an objection. "I cannot indulge in the celebration of marriage, for I still mourn my brother."

The marqués de Villena raised his finger to silence me.

"No need for you to concern yourself with a thing. I will see to everything for you. The nuptial agreement is already underway. Simply leave matters in my capable hands. After all, I have much more experience in matters of state that you ever could."

"Excuse me, my lord. I cannot think of such a matter as marriage at a time like this. I must spend my time in prayer and solitude." I pulled the hood of the black robe over my head and quickly walked away.

There were few noblemen as cunning as the marqués de Villena, but I could see right through him. Marriage negotiations with any man of noble stock would have taken months, but for him to have secured a marriage with the king of Portugal so quickly after Alfonso's death? His move must have been premeditated.

Pacheco was aware of my previous refusal to marry Afonso, King of Portugal. He must have been plotting for months behind Alfonso's back. And now that my brother was dead, there was no one left to intercede on my behalf.

Afonso of Portugal had made his desire to marry me very well known, and when Enrique failed to secure the match, the king most probably considered turning to a more capable man. There was little doubt that such a union would please all three men. By marrying me off, Enrique would have removed me from the line of succession and further secured the throne for Juana while simultaneously strengthening the kingdom's alliance with Portugal. And as the one to have orchestrated the marriage alliance, Pacheco would find his way back into Enrique's graces. Most certainly, Pacheco expected that the king of Portugal would generously line his pockets with riches as a token of his royal gratitude. And of course, King Afonso would finally attain what he had been craving for years - to marry the only daughter of King Juan II of Castilla, the teenage bride he had lusted for since we first met, and if destiny presented the opportunity, Afonso could even argue himself a claimant of the Castilian throne based on marriage to me. Afonso of Portugal, Enrique and Pacheco, all well satisfied with the arrangement that benefited them but horrified me. Another virgin swallowed up by the gods of the patriarch.

And now, with neither father nor brother, I was defenseless. Pacheco was right, there was no one to protect me. The king of Portugal would take me as his bride, there was little that stood in his way. And once wedded I would quickly be bedded. Bedded and bedded and bedded, over and over until the Portuguese nursery was littered with royal heirs. Bloodlines were shared, wealth and titles were exchanged, political relations were strengthened and noble houses secured – and whatever reservations or fears a princess may have were quickly dismissed in the name of "duty." The marriage agreement was little more than an arrangement in which one man granted another access to my body, a body that, to them, was nothing more than a political pawn.

My stomach turned. This was wrong, all of it. If this were best for my *patria*, I would do my duty and marry the king of Portugal, regardless of my personal feelings. But it wasn't what was best for

Castilla. Afonso of Portugal was a man that enjoyed conquest, dominance, and territorial expansion. And if he were able to secure a marriage with me, the daughter of Juan II and declared heir to my brother Alfonso – whom many were already hailing as queen, there was every reason to expect he would try to claim Castilla as his own, waging war in my name against my own homeland. And as my husband, he would claim that it was his right, and not my own, to govern my land.

I've had my eye on you. There is no one left to protect you.

Pacheco's words ran over and over in my mind. I had no one left to protect me. But the one I needed protection most from was him. To Pacheco, I was nothing more than an object to barter with. He thought he could control me, just as he had controlled my brothers. And as a woman with no one to defend myself, the marqués no doubt felt quite certain that I would be even easier to manipulate than Enrique or Alfonso.

Juan Pacheco was a dangerous man. I feared I had no choice but to obey him, just as all the others. My breathing grew panicked. I needed to get away.

And so, I fled.

My feet shuffled faster and faster, kicking the black cape over my gown from under my feet until I found myself running at full speed through the streets of Ávila. I pulled the black hood tighter over my head so no one could see me, fearing that some bystander might recognize me or see where I was headed and report to Pacheco in exchange for a gold coin or a place in his service. The man, I knew, had spies everywhere.

When I finally found myself before the small wooden doors of the Convent of Santa Ana, I couldn't remember anything I saw or heard during my flight towards refuge. It was all a blur. Everything was a blur, ever since the day Alfonso died.

A small hatch in the door opened from the inside and the wrinkled brown eyes of an old woman peered out at me from beneath her white wool habit.

"Sanctuary," I begged, still breathless.

Her eyes widened. I knew she recognized me. My heart stood still, waiting for her to take me in or hand me over to Pacheco.

"This way, quickly," she whispered. Before closing the door behind me, she looked both ways to make sure no one saw us.

The nun showed me to a small cell, then left me alone to pray.

Evening came and still, I was left undisturbed.

The next morning I heard a key enter the door lock and turn from the outside. The nun opened the door and standing behind her was Chacón. He entered my cell and the nun lowered her head, turned and left us.

"Isabel," he said, and hugged me close to his heart. "I was so scared I'd lost you, too."

"I'm sorry. I never meant to make your worry."

"What are you doing here?"

I exhaled slowly and looked down. "Seeking the will of God," I replied. It was the truest answer I could give.

"Are you to become a nun now?" he asked, half-joking, and leaned back to look me in the face and read my reaction.

I looked up at the crucifix above the door. The low-hanging ceiling seemed to look back at me, and in desperation I closed my eyes.

"What is to become of me?" I wondered aloud. Then, I lowered my gaze and looked Chacón in the eyes. "Here may be my only refuge, my lord. Perhaps the life of a nun suits me, a retreat from this world and its folly. Anyway, I can do more good for Castilla by interceding to God through prayer than by being taken advantage of by the marqués de Villena. At least here, I am safe from the machinations of Pacheco, and not forced into a marriage with King Afonso of Portugal."

"You no longer have need to fear Pacheco."

No longer a need to fear Pacheco? I almost laughed aloud, if my soul hadn't been so utterly exhausted. There would always be need to fear Pacheco.

"He has gone. Most likely, on his way back to Enrique's Court."

"He has betrayed us, then," I stated, as a matter-of-fact.

"I was going to say that Pacheco had defected, but your choice of verbiage is much more appropriate, considering who we are speaking of."

"And his uncle, the archbishop of Toledo? Has he gone, as well?"

"No, Archbishop Carrillo is loyal to Alfonso's cause… to your cause," he said, carefully choosing his words.

"To *my* cause?" I furrowed my eyebrows, not understanding what he meant. Ever since the passing of my brother, it felt like nothing made sense anymore.

He exhaled deeply, gathering his thoughts before continuing.

"Carrillo is decided that you must take your brother's place, you must be queen. 'We have the tiger by the tail, we must strike while the iron is hot,' he says. One city after another is declaring you as their queen, and the archbishop believes that you must do what Alfonso would have wanted, and serve your nation."

My jaw tightened at the mere mention of my little brother's name, and his face flashed before my eyes. My mind was filled with the last image I saw of him, his perfect, childlike face, turned pale and lifeless. A precious life taken, and in that moment, I knew that with his death came the end of my childhood, as well.

I knew it had to be poison. And if that were true, then whoever killed my brother did it to remove him from the throne. And as his successor, if I were to take his place and allow the nobles to declare me as their queen, my brother's murderer would come after me next.

"And do you agree?" I asked him.

Chacón shifted his weight, measuring his words before answering.

"I believe that the tide will again turn. The nobles that chose your little brother threw their support behind him because he is the *son* of King Juan II, not the daughter. Many of those men would consider it unnatural to declare their ruler to be a young princess of sixteen. *If* you take the place of Alfonso and proceed in this civil war, you will find even less support than your brother. As such, you will be required to make compromises and promises you may find hard, even dishonorable, to abide by. It is a hard game for any man to win, even more so for a woman."

"Then it is best that I stay here," I concluded with resolution. "I desire neither to be the pawn of the nobles in their war against Enrique, nor the pawn of Pacheco."

Chacón leaned forward, dropping his head, and gripped his hands together.

"I loved your brother like my own. With every breath I take, I wish I could have taken his place, and let my life be taken instead of his. And I love you like a daughter, Isabel. You know that. I could tell you to stay here, where I know you would be safe. But if I allowed you to stay at the convent, I know that you would one day regret it, and your regret would be my fault."

In my heart, I knew he was right. If I were to stay here, I could dedicate myself to worship and study. But this choice would require for me to forfeit my claim to the throne, and once Enrique died, so would the Trastámara dynasty. Castilla would be ruled by Queen Juana's illegitimate daughter, Juana la Beltraneja. And the corruption and chaos that my little brother, Alfonso, sacrificed his life to fight against would continue.

I knew what must be done.

"I, too, have a duty to my kingdom." I reached out my hands and rested them on top of Chacón's. "If the nobility truly declares me as their queen, then they will obey me when I submit my authority to Enrique as our true king. I must make peace with my brother."

Chacón shook his head. "The nobles will never agree to it. To submit to Enrique now would mean that all their efforts have been in vain. They are through with Enrique's capricious and unpredictable leadership. The nobles will not stop until the ruler of Castilla y León can promise them stability and justice."

"Precisely," I emphasized, sure of my decision. "This is exactly how I intend to rule."

Chacón furrowed his eyebrows. I stood up and walked to the small table where my rosary lay next to the open Bible, resting my fingers on its pages.

I thought of the patriarchs of the Bible, men like Jacob and King David. Neither were firstborn sons, and yet they were the ones chosen by God. Though they were least among many, it was from their line, the tribe of Judah, that Jesus Christ was born.

"God has rejected the firstborn son, he has rejected the tribe of Enrique, and he did not choose the tribe of Alfonso," I said, running my fingers along the text of the Bible. "It is God's will that the future Trastámarian heir comes from neither Enrique nor Alfonso, but from me." I turned towards Chacón and continued. "My proposition is this. Tell my brother to let us once and for all be united under his rule, that he is our crowned king and we honor him as such, but that he must declare me to be his sole legitimate heir. Those are my conditions."

Carrillo stared, unblinking, at the wall, as his mind calculated all that could become of my suggestion. A smile spread across his face.

"Very clever. You are wiser than your years give you credit for, young Isabel. Such a bargain brings peace to the country, shields you from suffering the same fate as Alfonso, and allows you time to prepare to govern."

"And most importantly, it protects the sacred right to rule, a right which now belongs to me alone."

Chapter XV
September 1468

Fall was approaching, my favorite time of year. The summer heat began to wane, and Beatriz de Bobadilla and I sat under the canopied umbrellas and enjoyed the caress of the soft September breeze.

"It is good to see you, Beatriz. You have no idea how much I have missed you."

"I only wish I could have come sooner," she said warmly, and squeezed my hand. I knew, just through her touch, that this was her way of comforting me for the loss of my brother, without forcing me to relive the pain by saying his name. She leaned back against the studded leather chair. "You have only grown more beautiful since I last saw you."

The servant placed an ornately carved silver platter of manchego and goat cheese, figs, grapes, almonds and chestnuts, ripe oranges and candied orange peels before us.

"It seems that no matter how much time has passed, our friendship is never touched by time," I said.

"Too true," she let out a lighthearted laugh. "But so much has changed, Princess," she said, emphasizing my title. "I commend you for your wisdom. You have somehow managed to outsmart them all."

"Have I?" I replied playfully, appreciative of the compliment.

"Why, of course you have. Don't you see, the nobles meant to rule you, just as they rule Enrique. In fact, they assumed you would be even easier to manipulate. After all, are we not but the docile beings of the weaker sex?"

"I only meant to protect myself and to make peace with my brother," I said, a touch defensively.

"Yes, very good. And by doing that, you have removed the power from the hands of the nobles." She tilted her head and smiled her relaxed smile before continuing. "You see, if you had obeyed their wishes and continued this war in Alfonso's place, you would have needed supplies, soldiers, food, and a great deal of money. And to get it, you'd have made many promises. In short order, my dear, you would've been beholden to many a great lord. Make no allusions, your good Castilian aristocracy expects compensation for whatever they would have given you to support your war effort."

I looked up at the stones cemented into the walls of Ávila dating back to the Romans and Visigoths. These walls were a part of Castilian history, of my own family's history.

"As the future ruler of Castilla y León, I refuse to allow myself to be put into a position of submission. Not now, not ever. All that matters now is making peace with my brother and bringing peace to our kingdom. And I am determined to achieve this."

Enrique had made grave mistakes. But I knew I couldn't hold him entirely accountable for the decisions he had made. For years, he had been under the control of one noble or another.

That cycle stops now.

Beatriz de Bobadilla smiled. "You must be looking forward to seeing your brother again," she said.

"I am. Though I won't deny that I am also nervous. I don't know if he is quite so eager to see me, considering all that has transpired."

"You have no need to be nervous, Isabel. It's time that both of you put your past behind you."

"I couldn't agree more. Despite all that has happened, everything, Enrique is my blood. It is time to move forward, as a family."

"And the king needs family now more than ever, considering what he is going through. When the news came out that the queen had given birth to a second child, and that the father was the nephew of Bishop Fonseca, Enrique well knew how foolish he looked to try and maintain that little Juana was of his seed."

"I wish I could have prevented my brother from enduring such shame, especially at the hands of that obscene wife of his."

"Hmm. Well, at least it explains why the king was so willing to sign the agreement that required him to divorce Queen Juana de Avís and declare their daughter a bastard," she said, referring to the agreement made between my advisors and those of Enrique that had been signed in August.

I exhaled deeply. "Hopefully, now he can understand why I insisted on choosing my own husband," I added, referring to one of the agreement's specifications, "though I did promise that I would not marry without Enrique's approval."

"Precisely what propriety calls for. After all, he is not only your king, but the only living male in your family."

Beatriz was a woman of great virtue and decency, principles that she had encouraged in me since I was a little girl. It was one of the reasons why I valued her opinion above most others.

"You must know, the matter of your marriage is the most popular topic at Court," Beatriz said, changing the conversation and lightening the mood. She leaned forward and plucked one of the grapes from its stem. "Is there any one man that has caught your eye? It seems you have grown quite close to your pet, Gonzálo."

"Gonzálo is not my pet. He is a most loyal friend. And I, a woman of noble blood. The man I choose to marry will be selected with discernment and tact. Noble in spirit though he is, Gonzálo Fernández de Córdoba could never serve the needs of Castilla that a prince or a king could."

Beatriz nodded in approval of my response, then turned her face towards the sun. She knew the sacrifice that existed in such a response — I would not have the liberty to choose a husband based on the purity and simplicity of love. My marriage would be a matter of duty and service to my *patria*.

"Have you heard who is on the list of contenders for your hand? It is rather impressive," she said, and I was grateful that we no longer had to speak of Gonzálo.

"I understand that the brother to the king of France, Charles of Valois, Duke de Berry is interested. As well as King Afonso of Portugal, of course."

"I have heard that Richard Plantagenet of England is also competing for your heart. And I am certain he is as handsome as his brother, King Edward."

"They are not competing for my heart, but my dowry." I sighed sadly. "But I refuse to marry anyone that will require me to leave Castilla. I am the sworn successor to the throne, and though I desire for Enrique to live a long life, there will come a day when I inherit the land. I cannot be married to a foreigner that will force me to leave, and I refuse to wed anyone but a prince or king."

Beatriz hugged me tightly, as if she wanted to shield me from what the future may hold. We both knew that there was nothing she could say that could save me from the responsibility that rested on my shoulders as a princess, and the sacrifices my heart would be required to make in service of my country.

"When God presents you with your true match, you will know it in your heart." It was the most comforting thing she could say.

Chapter XVI
September 17, 1468
Toros de Guisando

"I need not remind you how important this first encounter with the king is. All eyes will be watching you," Archbishop Carrillo said, reminding me of how little experience I had in such matters. Carrillo was protective of me, for certain, but whether because I was a woman or because of my youth, he underestimated me. "The goal is in sight, but we must now redouble our efforts," he continued, clenching his fist.

But there was no need for him to warn me thus. I understood my position had changed in the blink of an eye, and that there was much work to be done. Still, it displeased me that the archbishop was bringing a spirit of reluctance and aversion into this pivotal meeting with the king, especially after all had been accomplished by my advisors and the papal legate in the days prior.

"Are you not pleased with the results of the agreement, the progress we have already achieved? His Grace has granted me the rights to several lands, among many other things."

"As always," he exhaled, his voice revealing a sense of superiority, "it is one thing to receive a promise from Enrique, it is quite another to see those promises realized."

Carrillo was a man that unabashedly stared reality in the face, and his disillusioned perspective cast a shadow over my hopefulness, making me doubt my brother's sincerity.

"Even now, must we still have such little faith in our own lord and sovereign?"

"Even now."

At this hour, as the mid-morning heat grew stronger, the sun lurked so brightly overhead that I had to shield my eyes from its rays. We left Cebreros hours ago, and were to meet my brother halfway, at Toros de Guisando, a location wrought with historical significance.

"Now, we move slowly," Carrillo ordered, the sun reflecting off his smooth, freshly-shaven face. His long silk robes hung just a breath above the dirt road, and the dust began to gather along the tip of his hem, but the luxurious depth of the grey hew of the fabric's dye hid the dirt. He must have dressed with this in mind. Even in his wardrobe, the man acted with foresight.

The archbishop dismounted, leaving his horse with one of the men behind us, and took the reigns of the mule I rode atop. I had suggested that, instead of entering the arena proudly seated on a horse worthy of royalty, I take a humbler approach, riding in on the back of a mere donkey, just as Christ rode into Jerusalem. I knew King Enrique would appreciate that such a gesture intimated modesty and recognition of his superiority.

"There is no need to appear as if we are in a rush," Carrillo added. Tugging firmly on the reigns, the beast understood that the archbishop was now his master, and must proceed in obedience to his will.

My eyes scanned the meadows, then finally rested upon the ancient sculptures of the stone bulls carved by the Celts during the 2nd century BC, even before the Roman arrival on the Peninsula. Something inside of me intuitively told me that today would change the course of Spanish history forever.

Behind these ruins stood Enrique, with Juan Pacheco, the Marqués de Villena, standing half a step behind him.

Pacheco. He runs to and fro, from one king to the other, with such agility, they should call him "Pacheco the pendulum."

With the death of my brother, Pacheco must have realized that his position of power was waning. After having rebelled against Enrique, he now found himself in a rather precarious situation. Perhaps he felt he would wield more influence if he were to return to Enrique's side, and that's why he turned his back on me so quickly. And, of course, he knew as well as the rest of us that the king was always too lenient, forgiveness was in his nature.

Now, after such disloyalty to Enrique, here he stood, pardoned, and at his side.

"If you sense any irregularity or feel uncomfortable in the slightest, I am here," the archbishop reminded, though it was less of a promise than an instruction. Carrillo was an experienced courtier and knew that the machinations of politics were like a web that one could easily find themselves ensnared in.

My stomach tightened. I was not sure how my brother would react to seeing me. We both wanted peace, in this, we were united. But I did not forget that it was but a short time ago that we were on opposite sides of a civil war.

For weeks, our envoys had shuffled back and forth, negotiating the terms to our agreement in which I acknowledged him as king. He, in return, declared me as his sole legitimate heir:

Princess and legitimate inheritor of said king and of said kingdom, and after the death of the king, she is queen and lady of said kingdom and lands.

I was, of course, named as princess of Asturias, a title that was now rightfully mine according to my position as heir apparent. I was titled with the lands and rents of Ávila, Huerte, Ubeda, Alcaraz and the towns of Molina, Medina del Campo, and Escalona. Additionally, all the nobles that had formerly declared loyalty to Alfonso or to myself would be forgiven by Enrique, and would, in turn, pledge their loyalty to him, acknowledging him as king, and me as the *infanta* and future ruler of Castilla.

I was well pleased with all that my nobles had accomplished, and only hoped that my brother felt equally as satisfied.

Carrillo halted the donkey and helped me to dismount. I stood to my full height, stretching my neck and holding my chin high, slowly pacing forward until I reached Enrique. Then, with the greatest of reverence, I lowered myself, bowing before him. In silence, I lingered, my head held low, waiting for him to address me or to reach out his hand and allow me to kiss his ring in demonstration of my loyalty.

Instead, I felt the warmth of his embrace. Reaching out to me, he placed his hands on my shoulders and gripped.

"Sister," he said, helping me to rise. His voice, like his embrace was firm and loving. Then, to my great surprise, he wrapped his arms affectionately around me, hugging me to him.

Turning to the crowd, Enrique stretched out his hands and exclaimed for all to hear, "I present to you, Isabel, Princesa de Castilla y León, my one and true heir."

He spoke with pride and authority, and in his voice, there was a peace-of-mind I hadn't heard before.

Then he chivalrously held out his arm for me and we proceeded to walk together. My hand rested on his elbow, and he affectionately placed his hand on top of mine.

"Dear sister, I cannot begin to express my great distress at the passing of our brother, Alfonso," he said with sincerity.

I kept my eyes lowered and wondered if he had any idea if Juan Pacheco was involved in the death of our brother. After all, with Alfonso's death, an obstacle that had been in Enrique's way was now removed. If Pacheco had sensed that Alfonso was losing support, he would have been quick to shift allegiances and to align himself with the ruler that would preserve his power. Nothing was more important to the marqués that protecting his own power.

No, I decided, Enrique couldn't have known. He didn't have the stomach for something so heinous as killing his own brother. Enrique was a pacifist; he would never take the life of an innocent. He couldn't bear to endure the blood on his hands.

"I know how close you were to him, and I can't take away the pain of your loss, but I want you to know, I will always look out for you. Even more now that I'm all you have," he said warmly, the creases of his eyes curling with his smile and the lines along his large, lion-like nose wrinkling. "I only wish I could have taken better care of everyone I care about."

There was a deep sense of remorse in his voice. I knew he was referring to young Juana, the daughter of the queen. My heart broke for Enrique. I couldn't imagine how he must have felt to endure the humiliation of having to publicly proclaim his daughter as a bastard, or the shame he must feel as a king whose queen had just given birth to another man's child.

"I imagine being a sovereign is a great challenge, requiring many sacrifices, especially personal sacrifices, in order to do what is best for Castilla." I tried my best to be both politically astute and empathetic.

"I'm glad you understand. And that's why we must act as one, because there will come a day when you will rule."

I nodded in acknowledgment.

"Indeed, your Highness, though, I hope with all my heart that such a day is far from now."

The entire town of Ocaña was a lavish array of the colorful and bizarre, a mix of chivalry and carnival. In celebration of our unity, my brother had made a point of honoring me with one spectacular event after another, all of which I presided over.

The trumpets blasted, signaling the beginning of the next event, and my ladies-in-waiting watched with wide eyes as the peacocks and monkeys and other foreign animals passed by. King Enrique wisely deemed that, as heir, I must now have my own litter of ladies-in-waiting, and my mother was more than happy to curate a group of women of known virtue to serve under me. And I was grateful to Enrique for honoring my mother by allowing her involvement in such a selection.

I made sure that, as my ladies were now in the service of the heiress to the throne of Castilla, they must be dressed appropriately. Each one had several gowns prepared for them, all made of the finest of fabrics, as well as elegant jewelry. His Grace had sent his own tailors to oversee the dresses of my ladies, as well as to design an entire new wardrobe for me.

I ran my fingers over the little sapphires sowed into the soft velvet gown. Even though I knew that my confessor would claim that my enjoyment of these luxurious gowns was materialistic, I couldn't help but smile to myself as I touched these beautiful stones and soft fabrics. No, indeed my confessor would not approve of such extravagance, but he would have to be reasonable; these jewels and gowns were a luxury that I really had no choice but to indulge in. After all, the way I presented myself to the world must evoke the regality and authority of my title. I was heir apparent; it was essential that I present a majestic image.

The ladies that now formed my entourage showed an impressive amount of composure for women who had never ventured far past the confines of Arévalo, and certainly had never seen anything as extraordinary as what their eyes took in today. Just in the past few hours, they had watched the performance of bullfighters, singers and musicians, and exotic creatures from lands they had only heard tales of. There was even a half-naked man from Africa riding atop a fake lion, and monkeys bound to their masters with gold chain leashes. All of this would be vastly different to the quiet, sheltered life they lived in Arévalo, but they, as well as I, would adapt to our new lifestyle.

Sitting proudly atop a great white horse, the king looked chivalrous and brave as he rode up to the colorful tent under which my ladies and I sat.

"Virtuous princess," he declared, and stretched out his lance before me so that I might receive his silk handkerchief, colored red and white for Castilla y León.

"Most noble king," I replied and received the handkerchief. It was not only a gallant gesture in accordance with his *mentalité* of courtly love, it was also an act to be observed by the public, to further acknowledge our unity and my position. By such acts as this, all could see that their king had finally united the realm and secured the future of the Crown.

Never, in all our years together at his Court had he treated me with such sincerity and affection. But he was a different man. Now that the queen was removed from his life, Enrique was no longer under the influence of a woman that scorned me at every turn.

Yes, Enrique was different… we both were. Life, it would seem, had a funny way of doing that.

A sense of tranquility now reigned over his kingdom in a way it never had, and the king was aware that such harmony was the result of my willingness to submit to him, and my declaration for my men to lay down their weapons and bend the knee. And for this, he was grateful, even taking measures to ensure my utmost comfort. His Grace, himself, oversaw to the arrangements of my stay at the home of Chacón's nephew, Gutierre de Cárdenas, where he knew I would be most comfortable. Even more importantly, promises were made to ensure access to my wealth — of which I now had great need of, as I must manage the expenses of my ladies and household.

Soon others began treating me with deference. After all, I was now heiress to the powerful kingdom of Castilla y León. Yet, as much as I appreciated the recognition, respect, and privileges bestowed upon me, what meant the most to me was the healing of the relationship with Enrique. I could only hope that the redemption of our family would lead to the redemption of Spain.

The king and his opponent both rode out, each outfitted in their finest armor, prepared to show off their military prowess as they faced off against one another. The herald cried out, and I felt my nerves mount for my brother; a joust may be chivalrous in nature, but it could be lethal. With lifted lance, both men bravely charged one another. But the rider's lance, predictably, lowered just in time and the king smashed his opponent to the dirt floor.

"Bravo, Sire," I stood, applauding my brother. But I couldn't help but wonder if the king's courtiers always let him win.

"Lady Isabel," came a voice I didn't recognize.

A man approached. His height exaggerated the elegance and pride of his gate, while his thin lips and pale skin made him appear serious. His manner and dress were modest yet clean, a simple black wool robe belted with a rope. The only piece of value he wore being a long chain with a gold cross hanging from it.

"Forgive me, I do not mean to interrupt your enjoyment of the entertainment."

"Not at all, father. Please," I said, and gestured for him to sit with me.

"I am Friar Martín de Córdoba," he said, folding his hands across his lap. "I am the professor of theology at the University of Salamanca."

"It is with the greatest of pleasure that I finally meet you. Stories of your teachings have reached me since my earliest days. And I am a great fan of your work, *Compendium of Fortune*."

He looked down and smiled, pleased that his reputation proceeded him. "My lady, I come here in order to convey the deepest respect to you, and to hope to serve you in any capacity that I may."

"Thank you, Father Córdoba. Your philosophies and religious insights are much appreciated."

"Your words do me honor. If that is how you truly feel, then might I be so bold as to present you with a gift… something I have prepared especially for you."

He unlaced the leather strap of the sack he carried, and removed a small collection of papers beautifully bound in leather.

I opened the front cover and read the title aloud.

"*El Jardín de las donzellas,*" I said with curiosity. "Is it similar to what you wrote for Álvaro de Luna?"

"Quite different, as a matter of fact. This work is a treatise specifically written for you, the lady and future queen of the august kingdom of Castilla y León."

He leaned forward and proudly ran his fingers over the finely etched design on the leather binding.

"Years and years ago, when you were just an infant, I had the great pleasure of meeting your father. Your mother was with him. Very few times in my life have I encountered a woman with such profound virtue. And from what I have heard of you, I have little doubt that she raised you to be a woman of honor."

"And is that the subject you write on?"

"Lady Isabel, you have little need for advice on propriety and virtuous behavior. Indeed, you already exemplify such integrity in your conduct. However, you are called to become much more than a woman of noble character — in the years to come, much more will be expected of you than to merely behave in a dignified manner. But to answer your question, yes. My writing does provide instruction for proper behavior, though not that of a common noblewoman, but instead of a queen."

Friar Córdoba placed the text in my hands with great solemnity.

"My service lies in my counsel and guidance to you as heir to the crown of Castilla. This work is but a means of preparation for how one must behave as sovereign of a nation, how a female monarch is to composer herself, her values and conduct."

"I couldn't agree more. A woman's behavior must be above reproach, but a queen must also be irreproachable."

"Precisely," he answered, pleased that we were of the same opinion.

"May I?" I asked, and he nodded his consent. Carefully, I opened the cover and quickly scanned the first page.

"As you study the text," he instructed, lifting his thin grey eyebrows, "you will also find an additional intention of mine with this work."

I stopped reading and looked up, and his eyes, filled with gravity, met my own.

"You have been chosen by both God and king to reign over this land. It was predestined that you would rule Castilla, the noblest of kingdoms." I sensed his words were buffering me for what he was to say next. "But ours is a kingdom that has never had a queen that ruled without the guidance of a king. Therefore, the land must be prepared for a female ruler, while still honoring both tradition and your role as a wife."

"Hmm," I sighed, a shade annoyed. My marriage was a subject that everyone seemed to have an opinion on, but few allowed me to voice my own. Still, this was a man of vision. I set aside any assumptions I was making and chose instead to acknowledge the wisdom that surely lay in his suggestion.

Friar Córdoba leaned back in his chair.

"I imagine, my lady, that now is a most pivotal moment in your life. You are soon to choose a husband — a king for Castilla."

"Indeed. In fact, as we speak, the subject of marriage is one of the foremost matters in my life. However, whomever I marry, I alone will govern my people."

He nodded his head and absorbed the resistance in my words.

"And rule you shall. Though, some might not be supportive of the notion of a woman acting as king."

"There is no law that prohibits this. And when we consider that God has removed the possibility of a legitimate male heir, it only further confirms to the Castilians that, male or female, there is but one being alone that has been accorded the sovereign rights."

"Precisely. My writing merely provides a logical rationalization to encourage the same thought in those that might, in their ignorance, disagree with your right to rule, simply because you are a woman. However, such concerns will dissolve once you marry and produce the desired heir."

"Naturally. Such is the duty of all women, to marry and bear children."

"And yet so much more is required of you. Consider, just as a sword is united with its sheath, a husband is united to a wife. The king, like a sword, delivers justice, while the queen, the sheath, protects her subjects with mercy and clemency. Likewise, just as you, fair princess, look to the Virgin Mary as an example, like Mary, a queen must be like a mother to her people, as well as serve as an impeccable model of chastity and obedience, an example that women of noble lineage will strive to replicate."

The friar paused before continuing, letting the worth of his words sink in.

"Do you see, my child? Providence has placed a great responsibility on your shoulders. As queen, you have the unique ability to purify Castilla, to redeem the land from chaos and corruption, and to foster a national spirit of religious devotion."

I began to see how complex my role as both sovereign and wife would be.

"Your gift is of unrivaled value and purpose, father."

Friar Córdoba lowered his head respectfully. Understanding that his message was received and the conversation ended, the professor stood and walked away.

Of course, I had no allusions to the fact that I must marry. The choice of whom I would commit my life to was of utmost importance. So much rested on this one decision, and I knew that the choice would not be mine alone to make. But neither would I be a victim without any agency of my own in a matter that would forever affect the future of my kingdom.

Yet once I was married, it would be expected that I step down into a position of wifely obedience and submission, and allow my husband to act as the true leader of the country. Being the *infanta* and heir apparent did not exclude me from my duties as a wife, instead, they bound me to them even more.

I tapped my finger on the wood of the chair's armrest and stared into the distance, thinking. The friar's concerns were well-founded. The kingdom must be prepared to accept a female ruler.

Friar Córdoba had been involved in the trappings of Court for decades. I knew I had every reason to study and learn his instruction. However, I also knew that once informed with his insight, the power of his wisdom lay in my own hands, and I could apply his lessons in the manner that was of most use to my own objectives.

The crescent moon shone down on us, and the streets were filled with both nobles and commoners alike, all celebrating the continued festivities. The king had ordered a masked ball to take place after the day's events, and everyone was there, out in the streets, in the fresh open air, ready to indulge in the celebrations.

My ladies-in-waiting all stood in a circle and danced to the sounds of flutes and violins and drums and guitars. I threw back my head and laughed, savoring the freedom of dancing in the crisp naked air. Just behind me sat King Enrique, unmasked and nearly reclined on rugs and velvet cushions, focusing on his fingers strumming the guitar.

"Your Grace," I said, "will you not dance with me?"

"Later, perhaps," he answered, smiling gently up at me. "Your ladies dance beautifully, Doña Isabel," he added, turning his eyes away from me and back to the guitar as his fingers lightly ran across the chords. "But none dance with such grace and elegance as you, sister."

"You flatter me, Sire," I replied cheerfully. Lifting my mask off my eyes and resting it atop my head, I decided to stay and spend a moment with Enrique. "Your song is lovely. Did you write this piece yourself?"

He shook his head briskly, his eyes still downcast. "No. If only your king were that talented." He tilted his head back and gazed up at the stars, and I once again saw the haunted look in his eyes. "No, child. I merely imitate the troubadour. These are but the notes to one of their ballads."

I sensed that something was troubling my brother. Instead of enjoying himself and his company, he sat here and kept to himself.

"Perhaps I will join the troubadours and run off from town to town, singing my songs to the people," he said, and dropping his head, the king gazed at the mask that rested on the cushion by his feet.

He was surrounded by life's pleasures, the happy cries of a city of his people, and yet he seemed so distant, as if he had been abandoned, or had perhaps instead abandoned the world.

I patted down my skirt and sat on a step just below him.

Enrique had a habit of entering a dark place in his mind, and once he entered that place, it was difficult to save him from himself. I couldn't restore his peace of mind, but I could keep him company.

"Good king, the celebrations you arranged this week were exceptional. And how wonderful it is to share in the festivities here, in the fresh air, alongside our people," I said to distract him. But he wouldn't be put off.

"Do you know the origin of the troubadour?" he asked, tilting his head a bit and looking at me out of the corner of his eye.

"They are French."

He looked down and let out a short, almost mocking laugh.

"No, no, my love. They did not come, in fact, from France. That is a common error. Truly, it's an error of prejudice. Most believe that the first troubadour was William IX, grandfather to the beguiling Eleanor of Aquitaine. And it is a pretty idea to have of the troubadour. After all, Queen Eleanor was a great patron of the art of courtly love, as well as the troubadours that flocked to her Court. But, alas, her grandfather cannot take credit for what he did not originate himself. The troubadour is a Moorish tradition."

He stopped to look me in the face and see my reaction. Then, wagging his finger at me, he let out a little laugh.

"Ah, you stare at me with disbelief, it exposes your own prejudice. But I speak truth. Everyone assumes that courtly love and the performance of the troubadour originated in France, but it's false. William IX wasn't the first troubadour. In fact, everything he learned was simply the result of the short period of time he spent at the Moorish Court and from the hundreds of Moorish slave girls that were brought back to beautiful Aquitaine when he was just a boy. Ironic, isn't it? That the entertainment performed before royals originates with lowly slaves.

He clenched his jaw and his lips grew thin.

"These Castilians, they are so ready to reject and despise the Muslims, but denunciation of the Moors is a denial of themselves. The Arabs and Moors are part of us — of every man and woman that call themselves Spanish. Muslims ruled these lands for seven hundred years, they produced some of the finest art, literature, and science we know, and yet…" his voice trailed off. "And yet, despite all my efforts to integrate them into my Court, these Castilians only seem to want to villainize them… and me."

"Forgive me, your Highness, but I do not share your respect for the Muslims. They attack and destroy one Christian city after another, enslaving our young men into their legions of soldiers and forcing our Christian girls into their harems. Their king has outright declared that he means to destroy our faith."

He narrowed his eyes at me, his thinning blonde waves of hair and large, flat nose making him look again like a lion trapped in a cage. "You don't understand. But so few do understand me."

He was right, I didn't understand him. Enrique was an enigma, but this was only so because he had made himself so impossible to understand. And even while my heart broke for the unhappiness that ruled over my brother's heart, it didn't excuse his weakness as a father to a country that needed strength from its leader.

These carnivals and tourneys and feasts that I now presided over, they were a means of reminding the people of the king's regal authority, of his capacity to guide and direct his kingdom's future, and of manifesting the power of the sovereign. And power must be used to bring order. My brother wished for harmony, but harmony was an impossible endeavor without first fostering order. I wondered if, even during this period of peace, could Enrique prove to be the king Castilla needed.

Our lands were only recently relieved from threats of civil war, of one Christian fighting against another. The kingdom needed the restoration of justice now more than ever before. And yet, as long as Enrique insisted on giving such honor to the Moors, the nobles of

Castilla would scorn him. No *cristiano viejo* would respect a king that placed such value on those they considered their enemy. Our loyalty must be first to the Faith, then to king and crown. The nobles would view his behavior as anti-Castilian, even if that was never the king's intention. I had to warn him.

"Sire, I understand the worth of these festivities and celebrations, their purpose. They are meant to exude our royal supremacy, but they also are a display of monarchical beliefs. Perhaps it is not wise to attempt to interweave two conflicting beliefs at a time such as this."

Pacheco stood up, towering over me with glaring eyes.

"Hold your tongue, girl! How dare you question your master," he said through clenched teeth. "You are nothing but a child, and the king is not to be questioned."

My eyes widened at the sudden harshness of the marqués de Villena's words. I waited for my brother to defend me, to say that I was not merely a child, that the marqués was addressing the future of Castilla, that I was his one true heir, and that my opinion was valued.

Instead, he stared at me with his cold, hardened eyes.

Chapter XVII

"The king will see you now," the servant announced, then turned to escort me into the royal chambers.

Enrique's elbows rested on his knees and he stared with furrowed brow at the chessboard before him.

"Your move, Sire," challenged Juan Pacheco, the Marqués de Villena. His voice showed no reverence for his master, but instead was slightly taunting, as though they were but two old friends playing a match against one another. I cringed at how familiar the king allowed his vassal to treat him.

Upon entering Enrique's presence, I performed a respectful curtsey. From under his furrowed eyebrows the eyes of the king raised from the board game to find me standing before him.

"Ah yes, that's right," he said, finally taking notice of me. "I almost forgot I had requested you join us. Do sit." He flicked his fingers slightly towards an oversized velvet chaise. "We are nearly finished here," he added, then turned his attention back to his game with the marqués.

Pacheco waited for the king to decide on his next move.

"Do you play, Isabel?" he asked without daring to lift his eyes from the chessboard.

"Yes, your Highness, but I am still a novice."

"Oh, but you must play more often, then," Enrique said, his voice carrying more animation than I'd heard from him in weeks. "I assure you, Pacheco, my sister is a quick study. The girl is more of a challenge than you think."

"Indeed, your Majesty. I have no doubt," Pacheco mumbled, a response replete with significance.

"Do you remember the *Libro de los juegos*, the Book of Games that Father kept in his library, the one that belonged to Alfonso X?"

I asked the king. "I loved leafing through the parchment paper. Each page was so beautifully painted, especially the ones that spoke of the game of chess."

"I'm familiar with it," interjected the marqués. "A true family relic," he added with a shade of sarcasm.

"The text dates from the 13th century, but the game dates from far before that. Can you guess when?" the king inquired, clearly enjoying himself. "Chess is another gift, given to Spain by the Moors in the sixth century."

The king seemed to find any opportunity to defend the reason behind his affinity for the Muslims. But, despite his efforts to encourage others to share in his enthusiasm, it was only a subject of contention. Knowing that we shared different opinions, I decided it was a matter I did not wish to discuss.

"It is a game of cunning and intellect," I said. "Personally, I enjoy the game for the value of its martial strategy. Your Highness, if I might have a word," I began, attempting to address the matter for which I had waited for an opportunity to speak with the king about. "It seems that there may be a slight oversight in the matter of the funds from the lands I received, as in accordance with the Treaty of Guisando." My brother had agreed to place several territories under my jurisdiction; however, I had hardly received any of the revenue I was promised.

"There is nothing for you to concern yourself with, Doña Isabel," said Pacheco, responding on behalf of the king, who continued studying the chessboard. It was almost as if my brother preferred to ignore me, and instead allow his favorite to handle the matter.

Pacheco had now fully returned to the good graces of the king, as if none of his duplicity had ever happened. Once again, he was the favorite, even speaking as if he were the "mouth" of the king, as if he himself were the one wearing the crown.

"There *are* more pressing matters that must be addressed... your marriage." The marqués de Villena maneuvered the rook and placed it on a black square. "Most women of noble birth are wed by fourteen. The time has come for you to marry as well. An *infanta* must do the king's bidding. And at your age," he said, his voice growing surly, "you are more than ripe for the plucking."

His words were vulgar and offensive, but what else could be expected from the brother of Pedro Girón.

"May I remind you, my lord, that according to the treaty, just so long as I receive the king's blessing, it is my right to choose the man with whom I will wed in holy matrimony."

"Documents are always subject to an amendment or two." Pacheco flicked his hand back and forth, as if brushing my reservations aside. "You will learn these sorts of intricacies of the Court soon enough."

Only a man with no honor could say such a thing, essentially admitting that the king's word held little worth. But I must remember, Pacheco was the same man that, within the span of a few hours, publicly swore allegiance to little Juana as heir after her baptism, and then privately signed a document declaring that he did not believe she was the legitimate child of the king, thus he could not be held to his public statement of loyalty.

"The king must do the choosing. After all, you are merely a child. It is dangerous to leave any woman with the weighty responsibility of choosing her own husband, let alone a princess. It's for your own good that you leave matters to those that know how to properly manage them."

"There!" Enrique shouted gleefully and picked up Pacheco's queen. "Give me but a moment, and this game will be quickly won." I realized he had no interest in interjecting himself into the conversation between Pacheco and me. He would simply rely on Pacheco to settle the matter.

"It's a shame that a queen can be so easily defeated," Pacheco noted with significance, then handed me the little queen figure.

"Look at her closely. Knights, bishops, rooks, pawns... she is the only female chess piece on the board. The queen is surrounded by men. It is little wonder that this piece finds herself so limited in her movements, reduced to one feeble step at a time. Our little queen is nearly helpless. Take it as a lesson, my lady. Just like the chess piece, a princess has so very little power that she truly wields, and is dangerously vulnerable. Just look, Enrique was able to take my queen because she was poorly protected."

"But you, my dear girl, I would never let that happen to you," my brother said, only now deciding to enter the conversation.

"Allow me to explain," Pacheco continued, speaking to me as if he were speaking to a small child. "You no longer live within the cloistered walls of Arévalo. The world is a dangerous place, and a woman needs a man, a father or a husband to protect her," he emphasized with a patronizing tone. "Furthermore, remember that *you* are an example to other women, and as such, you must behave in the proper fashion and marry. We have already received a great deal of interest in your hand from an impressive list of suitors, even the brother of the king of England."

"A brother to the king of England? The same king that had previously jilted me after agreeing to our engagement?"

"Yes, the youngest of the Plantagenet brothers," Enrique answered, ignoring my tone. "Though, *I* favor a union with the king of Portugal. He still desires your hand, and how could he not. You are the most beautiful princess he has ever beheld, and your pious and virtuous reputation reaches all corners of Europe. And an accord made through marriage between Portugal and Castilla would be in the best interest of the kingdom. But there is also Charles de Valois, the Duke de Berry, if you prefer. He is the brother of Louis XI, King of France," Enrique added. "You can expect to meet with the French envoys in short order and decide then."

"I understood that my marriage would be my choice." My jaw clenched, holding back my desire to argue with my brother. I felt my chest heated with growing frustration, but I forced myself to gain self-control. This was not the moment to react. I needed time to consider the best response.

"Sister," the king said in a soft tone of voice. "Choosing the best partner for marriage is terribly complicated, and as your brother and king, it's best that you leave such matters to me," he said, not even realizing that he was merely regurgitating the same notion that Pacheco had pushed forward moments before.

"Checkmate," Pacheco said, pulling my brother's attention back to the chessboard. Then he turned towards me. "Your brother and I will advise you on who is the best match," he concluded.

"Isabel, come. Play with me. I challenge you to a game," came the relaxed voice of the king, as if he were entirely ignorant of the overwhelming tension in the room, as if all my trust in him and his promises hadn't just turned to ash.

"Another time, your Highness," I answered, then curtsied and exited.

I tried to maintain a calm pace but my feet moved as quickly as they could to the chambers of Beatriz de Bobadilla. The handmaiden opened the double doors and curtsied to me.

"Where is Doña Bobadilla," I asked, doing what I could to veil my anxiety.

"My lady is out, but she will be back shortly," her handmaiden informed me.

"I will wait here then, until she arrives."

Once I was alone inside her rooms, I restlessly paced back and forth, stewing on Pacheco's words and the implications of the king's broken promise. Everything had changed. Everything.

But rehearsing the conversation only made me grow more frustrated. Instead, I stood and looked out the window. That's when I noticed something in my hand. It was the queen, the little chess piece that Pacheco had handed me to look closely at, so that I might compare my own lack of freedom and agency to this little wooden piece.

"Isabel, my dear," Beatriz said upon finding me there, then turned, her crimson gown swaying, as she gently shut the door behind her.

I remained standing by the window and waited for her to come to me. Inside the palace, there were ears in every corner, even inside the privacy of one's one bedchamber.

"What is the matter?" she asked and took my hands in her own.

"Oh Beatriz," I said, shaking my head. "He lied. The king has broken his promise. He made a solemn vow, and he has broken it. He means to marry me off, like a prized ox to the highest bidder."

My head dropped, and I squeezed my eyes shut, but tears filled my lashes and threatened to spill down my cheeks.

Enrique and I had spent the past nine months together. Nearly every day I found myself by his side, entertaining his guests, riding alongside him on horseback, dining in the place of honor beside him, presiding over elaborate events he arranged in my honor. We had grown closer than we ever had, and now all of that trust was shattered.

"How could I have ever believed him? How could I have been so foolish as to believe the most indecisive, wavering man in all of Europe?"

Beatriz exhaled deeply.

"I was afraid this would happen. Especially after all the criticism the king received."

"Criticism?"

"Of course, and in abundance. His public decree that declared little Juana as illegitimate has circulated throughout the entirety of his kingdom and has been the cause of discontent for more than one noble house who still supports the girl, and no one more than her mother, Queen Juana. The queen is not a woman to be underestimated, and if need be, she will move Heaven and Earth to protect her daughter's birthright. Despite her fall from grace, the child's mother has the support of the Mendoza family, and from what Andrés tells me, House Mendoza has gone so far as to reach out to the Pope about the matter," Beatriz explained. Few were more informed of the workings of ambitious nobles than Beatriz, particularly since she was married to Andrés de Cabrera, treasurer of Segovia and trusted advisor to the king.

"Because the king couldn't endure the criticism, he has reneged on his sworn oath?" I asked a question I needed no answer for.

"And what's worse, all this time he has Pacheco, the Marqués de Villena, in his ear, whispering that *you* are the cause of his people's dissent against him, and that if it weren't for you and Alfonso, his entire country would have never been divided."

My jaw dropped in shock at how conniving Pacheco proved himself to be.

"It was not Pacheco, but *me* that presented the king with an olive branch of peace. I alone had the power to restore unity within our family and our kingdom, or to carry on with civil war. *I* chose peace. *I* instructed all the nobles, men who so staunchly stood against him, to bend their knee to the king. I surrendered that power in order to unite our country under the rule of King Enrique, on the single condition that I be declared as his sole legitimate heir. And just as soon as Pacheco saw that I no longer had the support of the nobles who pledged their loyalty to me as queen, he took advantage of my trust in my brother. And now that Pacheco finds me defenseless he means to use me as a piece of collateral to be manipulated and used for his bidding."

I squeezed the wooden chess piece in my hand, and looked up at my friend.

"If Enrique has his way, he means to marry me to the king of Portugal." My voice cracked, revealing my desperation. "Just like this little wooden queen, I am surrounded by men that plan to use me for their own will. Pacheco was even so bold as to lecture me on the propriety that a woman, and above all, a princess, must exemplify. He handed me this little queen, and reminded me that a woman's place is obedience and submission, and that a husband must protect her from her own vulnerability. He explained that this was why the little queen chess piece is so easily restrained from freedom of movement."

I placed the chess piece on the windowsill.

"If you marry King Afonso of Portugal, you will be required to leave Castilla. Your children will not inherit the kingdom, for he already has a son and heir," Beatriz stated.

"Precisely... a son whom Enrique intends to marry Juana to. In his eyes, that would solve everything. I would become queen for a time, but it would be Juana's children that would inherit the throne, not my own. And with a bastard child impersonating a true *infanta*, thus would end the Trastámara dynasty."

"As much as I hoped that his intentions were pure, something told me that we couldn't trust the agreement His Highness made at Toros de Guisando. His hand was, in many ways, forced. There was too much pressure placed on him from the nobles. And even amidst all the drama of his wife giving birth to another man's child, the king is still convinced that Juana is his own. My husband even overheard the king say that God chooses who is to rule the country, and that he simply feels he doesn't have the right to disinherit her."

My stomach filled with rage. I had been taken advantage of.

"The Pope, himself, had even sent his envoy to help settle the matter of the Treaty of Guisando. Enrique and I had made a solemn oath before God, and now he uses the holy name of God to legitimize his lies." My fists clenched. "I don't know how to free myself from the chains Enrique means to cast upon me, but I refuse to break with the agreement I made," I said with determination.

Beatriz stared into my eyes with her thoughtful gaze, then sighed deeply before continuing.

"So then, what will you do? Be controlled, doomed to the fate Pacheco assigns for you?" Her eyebrows lifted and she smiled. "No, dear. That is not for you, not for my Isabel. My love, you have more control than you think. You will simply have to change the rule of the game." Beatriz picked up the chess piece from the windowsill. "Life is very much like a game of chess, and Pacheco thinks he is making all the rules. But, just as Enrique says, queens and kings are appointed by God, and not restrained by nobles. The queen chess piece should have the freedom to move in any direction she chooses, as far as she wants to go. So then, it is up to you to change the game."

"Shall I trade in my knitting needle for a sword, shall I be like Joan of Arc, and amass an army to fight beside me, to save Castilla from the tyranny of Pacheco and the instability of Enrique?" I joked.

"You have a lion's heart, as ferociously dedicated to your country as Joan of Arc was to hers. But no, you won't win this war or gain your freedom through an army. This chess match requires more subtle means."

She walked over to the windowsill where the little queen chess piece waited patiently and sat at the drawing table, picking up the cards.

"Did you notice how they forgot about the queen chess piece? Both Enrique and Pacheco were so negligent with it that they forgot to ask for it back."

"I suppose so."

"Then let them forget about you as well. Allow yourself to be overlooked."

"What do you mean?"

"You must learn how to use their own oversight against them. They underestimate you, do they not? After all, you are no male heir; you pose no threat to them. In their eyes, you are nothing more than a teenage girl, a trifle, a chess piece that can be shuffled about at their will. Your role is to obey, to do as you are bid. So then," she said, drawing to her point, "let them think just that, let them think you are merely acting as an obliging servant to every one of their whims. And above all, raise no suspicions."

Beatriz, I realized, had learned much and more from her exposure to the cunning schemes of the courtier. She had grown wise at the lessons of court intrigues, and yet she somehow retained the goodness and purity of spirit that was ingrained in the essence of her being.

"And what if I am told to marry the king of Portugal?"

She picked up the queen chess piece from the windowsill and casually inspected it, a nonchalant look on her face.

"Never declare an outright refusal to the Portuguese marriage," she answered, her voice remaining calm, almost aloof. "Instead, simply don't commit yourself with a promise. There is power that lies within the liminal; it is a wise woman who can learn to harness it." She smiled, and I began to understand. "Subtly make your own arrangements, and when the time is right, you'll have changed the game, and it will be too late for them to react," she concluded, and placed the little queen chess piece back in my hand.

Once again, I retreated into my one safety, to prayer. Since childhood, the church was the one stable foundation that I could rely on. Prayer was my sole source of peace.

And I was desperate for peace.

As the days passed into weeks, my brother grew more and more paranoid and distrustful of me. I sensed it in his behavior towards me, and in how others began to treat me. Soon, it even became evident that my entourage was not my own, but his — people he had placed in my midst in order to surround and spy on me, to ensure that I did not stray from the king's wishes.

But as much as I wanted to loathe him, I couldn't. I knew that this chasm that was growing between us was Pacheco's doing. Enrique's fault was not that he was hateful, but that he was capricious, impulsive, unreliable, and so easily influenced. The true enemy, the source of conflict and instability both in our family and in Spain was, and always would be Pacheco. Despite how disappointed, hurt and frustrated I was at Enrique, I knew that he was being manipulated.

Beatriz was right. A queen would always be at the mercy of the other players of the game until someone succeeded in changing the rules. But how much could these rules, rules that created a paradigm that governed our daily existence, actually be changed?

Next to my bed rested *Jardín de las donzellas*, the treatise gifted to me by Friar Córdoba to help prepare me to rule Castilla y León. As carefully as the first time I beheld the text, I lifted the front cover of the treatise and reread the preface once more.

The friar was so careful to begin his work with a logical argument for a woman's right to act as sovereign, even citing legal and spiritual justifications. And yet, the more I read, the more clear it became that friar Córdoba intended that my right to govern as queen regent only be recognized up until I was married, at which point I must submit to my husband, not only as a wife, but also submit my own authority to govern my lands into the hands of my mate.

Of course, there was much in the writing that I was entirely in agreement with. A woman, particularly a princess and heir to the Crown, must be pious and chaste, and spend a great deal of time in prayer. But there was an undeniable expectation that I would not, in fact, be the one leading. My place, according to Friar Córdoba, was as queen consort, and instead of acting as the true sovereign, I must find a suitable mate to do the ruling for me.

I was aware of the great possibility that, although the nobles of Castilla might rally behind me, it would not be in support of me as queen regent. In their minds, it made no difference that I was not the first woman to rule. There had been predecessors, female sovereigns such as Urraca or Berenguela, but even with them, pressure was applied for them to relinquish their authority of governing to their young, impressionable sons — sons who inevitably were ruled over by great lords, just like Pacheco with Enrique.

Marriage was the one thing both Enrique and the nobles required of me, a rule I knew I had no choice but to obey. But if these men assumed that I would surrender my sovereign right to govern over my own lands to my husband, and be contented with fulfilling the maternal role of producing bonny princes for the kingdom, they had forgotten one very important fact. After Enrique, I alone was the only legitimate heir of King Juan II. There was no other living soul with the right to rule the kingdom but me.

Yes, I would marry, just as he wanted me to do, just as was appropriate for a woman of my age. But I wouldn't enter into a marriage that would separate me from my kingdom, or force my allegiance to a foreign land with foreign interests. I could not marry a man that would force me from my realm.

Yes, I would marry. Such was inevitable. But I would choose whom, just as I stated in my agreement with King Enrique.

More and more, especially since the death of Alfonso, men had taken notice of me. As was Court custom, I began receiving love poetry praising my delicate beauty, the bluish green hew of my eyes, my calm, pleasing countenance. My brother, as well as Pacheco, was aware of the reputation I had gained as a beautiful young heiress, a worthy match for any man. But along with the overtures of courtly love paid to me came equal pressure from my brother, the king, to marry me to Afonso of Portugal. Meanwhile, Pacheco had his own plans for me. The marqués of Villena was doing everything in his power to formalize a marriage contract with France.

As much as I tried to remain coy and out of reach, as Beatriz had suggested, there was only so long that I could remain elusive before I was going to have to make a commitment to one of the contenders for my hand. And just as Beatriz suggested, I would take advantage of Enrique and Pacheco's underestimation of me. Despite what they thought, I was not so new to the games of the Court, and it had been from my observations of them – the king, the marqués, and particularly the queen – whom I had learned most from. Ready or not, I was to play my own match.

The king and the marqués de Villena were not the only ones moving the chess pieces anymore. While they were preoccupied with debating over suitors for me, I had my own short list of potential marital partners in consideration, each one garnering the support of one or another of my close advisors. And amongst these few, there was one name that had stood out to me above the rest, the very man who had gained the support of Chacón, in whom I had more confidence than any other advisor.

Indeed, my mind was set on this someone. Curiously, we had been betrothed to one another years ago, when I was just a little girl. At that time, neither he nor I were expected to inherit the throne. At that time, such a union meant little more than a marital contract of two powerful houses. But life had changed our course, and now we were both the future heirs to the Crown.

Even still, a marriage to the heiress of Castilla y León was too lofty a hope for the young prince. Originally, Pierres de Peralta, our neighboring kingdom of Aragón's most honored diplomat, was sent to Castilla to detail a marriage alliance between Fernando of Aragón and Pacheco's daughter, a marriage that would have elevated Pacheco to become the patriarch of Spanish royalty. But after spending time in Castilla, the astute Peralta quickly concluded that the best match for Fernando, heir apparent of Aragón and King of Sicily, to aspire to was not merely the daughter of a wealthy nobleman, but to the *infanta*, heiress to the throne of Castilla y León.

Much hung in the balance, thus making the choice of a husband of utmost importance, but the more I learned about Fernando, the more I felt secure that this was the man that would be my true match. Strong, handsome and cultured, Fernando was also a warrior and natural leader to his soldiers. Thus, a partnership with him would serve to bridle Castilla's unruly nobles under our yoke.

It was true, Prince Fernando already had a handful of illegitimate children and was known for his liaisons, but even that unsavory fact didn't hinder my interest in him. Instead it made him an even greater asset. It all but guaranteed that we would be able to have children, and that meant I would never have to endure the humiliation that my brother Enrique had faced ever since the failure to consummate his first marriage.

But there were other factors that made him the most logical choice. Fernando had already been named king of Sicily, thus marrying him would immediately make me a queen. It would be to my benefit for Castilians to recognize me as such. We spoke the same language and shared the same customs and traditions. His kingdom of Aragón was neighbor to Castilla; therefore, marriage would not only be a holy union, but a union of our lands, a union of two of Spain's most illustrious kingdoms under Christian rule.

It's decided, then. Fernando would be my choice.

And I knew exactly the man to help me make the arrangements.

Chapter XVIII
Spring 1469

"That book looks familiar. It belonged to your father, did it not?" Beatriz asked. "My goodness, it has been years since I've seen it."

I looked up at her and smiled.

"El Libro de buen amor," I answered, naming the 13th century book's title. "He left it to me," I let out a deep sigh, and smiled with nostalgia. "The pages even have little notes in them written by my father," I said, running my finger along his handwriting. "In a way, it makes me feel like he is still with me."

"I can still remember him reading it. It must have been one of his favorites. He loved that book, especially the poetry and prayer in the beginning."

"It is a beautiful way for a love story to begin, with poetry and prayer."

I knew my own story might not ever include love. I was a princess, and princesses often do not enjoy the delights of romance inside the bonds of marriage. It was a fact I had no choice but to accept.

The door opened and a servant entered.

"Señor Gutierre de Cárdenas," the servant announced, then bowed and exited.

Back so soon?

My eyes widened in surprise. Chacón had arranged for his nephew, Gutierre de Cárdenas, to be sent, along with Alonso Fernández de Palencia, to Aragón to begin the marriage negotiations with King Juan and his son Fernando, a visit that Enrique had no notion of, and I meant to keep it that way. But I couldn't believe he was here already, at Enrique's Court, and had been allowed to visit me. The king had been increasingly paranoid, and it seemed that, with each passing day, he grew more restrictive with my freedom, privileges and access to my finances.

"My lady," Cárdenas said and bowed respectfully.

Beatriz gave me a knowing look, then moved to sit with the other ladies-in-waiting. Immediately she began chatting with animation about recent baptisms, upcoming social events, and the latest visit from the French. I spoke with Cárdenas about mundane unimportant topics until I knew that the ladies were paying me no mind.

"Sir, you've returned from Aragón quicker than I expected," I said, my voice almost a whisper. "I am eager to hear your progress regarding the matter." I dared not name the prince directly. I wouldn't risk this secret being found out. My ladies-in-waiting were decent and moral women, but I still could not trust that they were loyal to me. Loyalty could be bought if the price was right, and I had little doubt that one or two of my ladies might be reporting my movements to Pacheco.

"It is handled. My lady will be pleased." His tone of voice was grave and serious, and I felt confident in Chacón's suggestion to entrust Cárdenas with the substantial task of acting as envoy.

The details of the marital agreement were of such a sensitive nature that we could discuss the matter no further while inside my chambers. Instead, I requested that the envoy join me and my ladies-in-waiting for a walk through the garden paths. Once on the grounds, Beatriz led the women several feet behind me, giving me space to carry on my conversation with Cárdenas privately.

"King Juan was very eager to finalize the marriage proceedings. He believes that the future of Aragón rests on the unity of you and his son."

Of course, he does. The king of Aragón had had his eye on Castilla for ages. Nothing would make him happier than to think that his grandchildren would be the wealthy inheritors of both Castilla and Aragón, and as Aragón was riddled with rebellions and struggling with France and Barcelona, he, no doubt, expected that a union with Castilla meant that he would find himself in a stronger position against enemies and unruly subjects.

"As of March, all have come to agree with the terms set out for your union. I am certain that you will be married before the end of 1469," he continued.

I nodded my head in approval, but gave no other reaction. There was little doubt in my mind that the king of Aragón would agree to a marriage between his son and me. The true success of my envoy's work lay in the details of the marital agreement. Herein lay the merit of Cárdenas capacity to negotiate.

"What was their reaction to the stipulations I require?"

"King Juan and his son are pleased that a union with the Trastámara family will signify a more united Spain, and understands that Aragón would benefit exponentially from the union," he began, then shifted slightly in his chair. "However, the king of Aragón was concerned with the specification that his son is not to reside in his kingdom, but will instead be required to live in Castilla. He was additionally concerned with your refusal to allow yourself or your future children to be removed from Castilla. In the end, though, he came to agree that this was most suitable in order to secure the Crown." Cárdenas folded his hands together and leaned back against the leather seat. "I must add, both the king and his son found certain requirements… not to their liking," he added as diplomatically as he could, speaking slowly and carefully choosing his words.

"Oh? Which?" I asked, though I already knew without being told.

"They were surprised that Fernando is not permitted the right to dispense justice as he sees fit, or to give titles and honors. And he was most shocked that the purse strings of Castilla y León are to be controlled entirely by a queen."

"Such a stipulation is necessary, for the good of the realm. They will grow accustomed to it, I'm sure. Fernando would be foolish to refuse becoming king of my lands because of a few limitations. What of the matter of the coin and coat of arms?"

He raised his eyebrows and tilted his head slightly. "That subject required much and more negotiation. Traditionally it is the king that is represented on such objects and devices."

I had well expected resistance from the Aragonese advisors regarding the restrictions I placed on Fernando's access to the treasury and his ability to exercise justice and administer rewards, while using the coin and crest to promote a public image of marital unity. However, it was our only option. The Castilians must not view Fernando as a foreigner from a separate kingdom that now ruled over Castilla, with access and ability to exploit her wealth.

"However," he carried on, "after much consideration, they came to agree that, in order to foster an image of marital harmony, it is essential that both parties enjoy equal representation on both currency and the royal crest. Fernando suggested that the depiction on the coin be the facial profile of the royal couple facing one another."

"Very well, you have my approval."

"King Juan also had further concerns," Cárdenas said.

"In what way?"

"My lady, up until this juncture, the king has been in open negotiations with Pacheco regarding the marriage of their two children, as I am sure you are aware. You must understand, by breaking that contract and marrying his son to you, King Juan will make himself an enemy to one of the most powerful and ruthless men in Christendom, as will you. The marqués de Villena has given his daughter his word that she will be wed to Fernando; he will hold you responsible for thwarting his plans and discrediting the worth of his promise. More importantly, there are many whisperings that Enrique intends for his daughter Juana to inherit the throne. Should such a development occur, a marriage to you would reap no benefit."

I nodded, pensive. "Juan of Aragón is justified in this concern. But he must trust Providence. God is on *our* side. If his son hopes for my hand, then there will be risks he must be willing to take," I said, unshaken by the obstacle. "What more?"

"There was inquiry regarding your traits."

I had expected as much, but was still amused.

"I see. And what did you tell him?"

"The truth, madam. That your years betray the depths of your wisdom. That there is no other that could compare to your devotion and piety."

I knew that such a suggestion was made in order that they would understand me to be a good and obedient wife.

"That is kind, sir. I can only assume they inquired as to what I look like. Pray tell, what did you say."

A faint smile spread below Cárdenas mustache. "They did, as is only natural of any young man that is to marry a woman he has never beheld with his own eyes. Again, I told them the truth. I spoke of your illustrious beauty and youth, of your golden hair, kissed by a hint of strawberry, your eyes that shame the colors of the sea, that you have eyes a man can trust, and a gaze that is as steady and calm as it is captivating."

Coming from a man as austere and reserved as Cárdenas, such words took me by surprise. "My lord, I had no idea you were such a poet. Your words do me great kindness."

He bowed his head in acknowledgment.

"The prince inquired of you as well," Cárdenas continued.

"Oh?"

"He wanted to know if you... his exact words were, 'does she have passion.'"

An intriguing question. It made him only more attractive to me.

"And you replied, how...?"

"I said that there are few women that are as passionate as you — that your passions are specific — your faith, your country, your family."

"That was kindly said. Thank you, sir."

Cárdenas leaned forward in his chair.

"It must be noted, my lady, that your prince is a true *caballero*. Palencia told them of your bravery, that you are bold enough to defy the danger and tyranny of Pacheco and Enrique, who essentially are holding you as a captive. Palencia explained in great eloquence how Enrique has gone back on his promise. The prince was notably moved by this, and requested to speak privately with Palencia. He expressed great angst to come rescue you, and intended to come immediately."

"He wasn't concerned about the risk?" I asked, unable to suppress my surprise. Such an act was chivalrous, certainly, but not without peril.

Cárdenas shook his head once.

"For Fernando? No. They say he is fearless. Certainly, he must be if he intends to attempt this plan. The danger he faces is not merely of opposing King Enrique and provoking the enmity of Pacheco. The prince must find a way to get to you first. But your betrothed is determined, my lady. He swore that his bride would not endure these challenges alone. Fernando knows that you are taking a risk in defying your brother. He plans to take that risk with you."

Meanwhile, King Enrique's distrust of me only increased. The restrictions he placed on me grew more burdensome, and soon I found myself unable to even afford the expenses of a household. One by one, my ladies-in-waiting fell away from me, and soon I was left with but two loyal women, Beatriz de Bobadilla and Mencía de la Torre. Mencía, a few years younger, was my junior, and her mentality revealed her youth. Nevertheless, what she lacked in wit and maturity, she made up for with her good-nature and devotion.

No doubt, such an act on their behalf was intentional. Enrique and Pacheco thought that I would be more easily maneuverable if I found myself stifled by financial limitations and few friends. Instead, his actions revealed to me the ones in whom I could truly place my trust.

Not to be outdone by Pacheco, I created a web of my own.

With each passing day came a new letter from Prince Fernando, each one peppered with words of love. Though we had not yet met, we were promised, and with that, both of us considered ourselves eternally bound to one another. Still, despite the romantic sentiment of his letters, which I of course matched with words equally as tender in my responses, I knew that this was merely the proceedings of courtly love and must not be confused with real love that blossoms naturally between two souls.

"The marqués de Villena requests your presence," the servant said.

Quickly, I placed my letter to Fernando under a stack of papers so that the servant wouldn't catch sight of it and report me to Pacheco.

The servant led me down the corridor into the privy council. Pacheco stood at the head of the table, waiting for me.

I straightened my back to my full height and held my chin high, refusing to allow him to think he had any ability to frighten me. Breathing slowly and steadying my gaze, my countenance remained serene and calm. Perhaps I couldn't control a small part of myself always feeling anxious when I entered his presence, but neither would I allow him to think he had the power to provoke fear in me.

"Señor Pacheco," I said, and curtsied.

The marqués gave a slight bow, and as he stood, his purple velvet cape swayed, showing off the richness of its fabric.

"Please, sit," he ordered, gesturing to the finely carved wooden chairs covered with crimson satin and gold detailing.

"Lady Isabel, I come bearing the happiest of news for you. His Grace has come to an agreement with Afonso, King of Portugal. You are to be married in a matter of days. Congratulations, *mi dama*, you are soon to become the queen of Portugal."

The muscles of my neck tightened and my jaw clenched, but my face remained unchanged. This was a move I had waited for with bitter expectation.

"Has good King Enrique forgotten the terms of our agreement? The meeting at Toro de Guisando was not so long ago," I stated, my voice flat and controlled. "You will recall, sir, that *I* am to choose my husband, and I have the right to marry whom I desire, just so long as his Highness approves of my decision."

A sinister smile spread across Pacheco's face.

"Ah, yes. That." Pacheco's voice was cool and unaffected. "However, might I remind you, madam, your lord brother is head of your household." He gave a firm wave of his hand, as if swatting a fly away, a habit I imagined Enrique had learned from him, and it was clear he had all but dismissed the terms of our agreement. "Besides, as we have previously discussed, it would be inappropriate for any young woman of seventeen years to choose her own husband, much less a princess."

"You are mistaken. I am not merely a princess, but the *infanta*. I am heir to the throne."

He lowered his eyes and glared, annoyed to have to argue with one he considered a petulant child that knew nothing of political negotiations or matters of State. "You are to marry the king of Portugal, and your niece Juana, the king's daughter, will marry his son." His voice grew stern. He picked up the quill and began overlooking the documents before him, as if to imply that this was the end of the conversation.

I looked down at my folded hands, then up at him, waiting for him to meet my eyes.

"Our agreement was the means to end a civil war. We came to peace based on Enrique's promise that I would be named heir apparent, and his daughter would be declared illegitimate."

He sighed deeply, then tilted his head to the side.

"Perhaps such an agreement would be honored if the king hadn't discovered that his sister was a traitor." He paused, letting his words hang in the air. "It has come to his Majesty's attention that you have entertained ideas of procuring your own choice of husband outside of the options that the king offered you. This alone is shameful. But for you to have chosen to pursue a marriage with the one man the king told you that he disapproves of — such deceit and subversion from his own blood. How could such an act be forgiven? His Majesty was not pleased to discover his half-sister was a woman of such great insolence."

"So instead, the king plans to marry me against my will. Did he forget that he must first legally receive my consent?"

Pacheco made no attempt to answer my question.

"The marriage will take place. You would be wise to acquiesce to all that Enrique desires, as well as to all that the king of Portugal desires. Should you take it into your pretty little head to act in defiance, you will be considered an outlaw, and anyone that helps you will be faced with the unified armies of Enrique and Afonso. It would be a shame for you to be the cause of the punishment and imprisonment of those dearest to you."

Months passed and still I heard not a word from my brother. None of the restrictions he placed on me were lifted, none of the promises to allow me access to finances accumulated from my landholdings were granted. Instead, I found myself treated less like a princess and more like a hostage held captive in the palace of Ocaña.

The sounds of men mounting their horses and the rumbling of the animal's feet as they prepared to leave broke the silence.

The door creaked open, and Andrés de Cabrera entered.

"Husband," Beatriz said, walking towards him.

"There has been an uprising in Andalucía, some sort of dissatisfaction from the administrators of the region. The king plans to head south to restore peace."

"But surely *you* don't need to go," she said, taking his hands in her own.

"I expected King Enrique would have preferred me to return to Segovia. There is much to be handled there, and no one to oversee it but me. But the king has instead requested that I accompany him, along with the others."

Beatriz's eyes grew moist with tears. "Perhaps if you just told his Highness that…"

"Once a royal command is given, there is little that can be done," Andrés interrupted.

"But the danger. Should you encounter criminals along the road…"

Her husband gently stroked her cheek, calming his wife without words.

Beatriz was among the fortunate few. She had married a man that held a powerful and important position under the king, which therefore made her marriage to be considered a success. But unlike so many, she married a man with whom she found love and mutual respect.

"No danger at all, my dear," he promised, though I knew he was only trying to calm his wife's fears. Andrés was a man whose strengths lay in thinking more than fighting. "Unfortunately, the king has discovered that he has left far too much power in the hands of the magistrates, and now his subjects have grown more loyal to them than to their true master. Pacheco will handle the matter, have no doubt. I am there strictly to offer my counsel. I will return to Segovia in a few days time. But I must ready myself for the journey. The king wishes to depart immediately."

"And am I to not ride alongside my brother?" I asked.

Cabrera turned to face me, surprised at the suggestion. Still, I insisted with logic.

"If the king wishes to reinstate his control over unruly subjects, he must make a display of his power. Having me, his declared heir, ride alongside him surely presents an image of authority through unity."

"Your brother, the king, wishes for you to stay put" he emphasized. "Isabel, listen very closely, Enrique desires for you to be obedient, and to stay where you are. You must understand, the king is tormented by the accusations Pacheco makes about you. The wisest thing is to do as he bids, or else you are putting yourself and others at risk."

"What do you mean, 'at risk?'" Beatriz asked.

"Enrique wills that none of you are to leave, and should you ignore this request," he said, turning once again to look me in the eyes, "it will be the marqués who decides your punishment."

"Here," I said, handing Mencía de la Torre a long black cloak. "Put this on, and pull the hood over you. Let no one see who you are."

"It's too late for us to wander the gardens," Mencía said, not understanding.

"Indeed," I answered vaguely, then continued searching for another cloak for Beatriz.

Mencía stood there with lifted eyebrows, staring down at the cloak resting in her hand. Beatriz de Bobadilla walked over and picked it up out of her hands.

"Isabel, what are you up to?" She sounded more like a big sister than a lady-in-waiting.

"Making sure we are prepared."

"What do you mean, 'prepared?'"

"For escape."

"Isabel, didn't you hear what my husband said. The king made it very clear that we all are to stay here."

I took the cloak from her and draped it over Mencía's shoulders.

"Do what you will, then. But it has been a year since my little brother died. I have every right to visit his grave, and no one, not even the king, can prevent me from paying my respects. Besides, Enrique is away, Pacheco is away. They have been gone for days, and won't even know that we left before I have done what duty requires of me. This might be my only chance. I've been held here like a prisoner for far too long and I refuse to allow myself to remain here instead of honoring Alfonso. As for yourself, stay here or join me, but if you come, come now, and dress warmly. Once I leave, I will not turn back."

"My gown," Mencía de la Torre complained, inspecting the fabric of her dress. "The hem is covered in filth. And it's so dark out. I can hardly see a thing. How do you know we are even headed in the right direction?"

"Trust me, I know this road. I was born in Madrigal de las Altas Torres, just down the way. This road is like home to me."

"Still, this midnight excursion… it is too dangerous. We could come across thieves or gypsies. And we have no one to defend us."

Beatriz let out a laugh. "I dare any man to try and stand up against Isabel when she puts her mind to something."

"You laugh, but all sorts of criminals are out here. I've heard stories of the soldiers, deserters who rape and steal everywhere they land. And we haven't a man or a sword to protect us."

"Such villains as these deserve more compassion than you know," Beatriz replied.

"Compassion? To rapists and murderers?"

"Most of those deserters are nothing more than small folk and farmers who were told by their lord to join the ranks and fight the good fight for the king — whatever king that may be. So they go, brothers and friends, fathers with their sons, fighting one bloody battle after another. They've watched their kin die at the stroke of their lord's enemy, one by one, until all their relations have been left to the crows at one battlefield or another. If fighting doesn't kill them, disease will. It doesn't take long for these men, simple farmers who, years before, were tending their fields and flocks, to discover that the gold and adventure that was promised was a lie. But by then, most everyone they knew before the war is gone. There isn't a home for them to return to. No friends, no family, no home — it is little wonder that these "criminals" soon take to stealing, and killing if the situation requires. What more of a choice does survival grant?"

All three of us remained silent for a long moment.

"You see, Isabel. This is folly," Mencía carried on. "We should really just go back before we are found out."

"You didn't have to come," Beatriz replied, clearly exasperated with Mencía's endless grumbling. "No one forced you to come. But here you are. If you head back, you will be going alone."

"It's too late, Mencía. We can't go back now. And it's too dangerous for us to separate. The night sky hides us well and we are nearly there. Just be brave a little longer. We need to just keep pushing forward." I tried to sound reassuring.

We had been traveling under the cover of darkness, but the gentle light of the sun's rays was beginning to breach the surface of the land.

I exhaled with relief upon seeing the gentle light of the early morning hours crawling up along the edges of the earth. We had nearly arrived. I was finally home, in Arévalo. Ahead, I could almost make out the high walls of the town of my childhood home, a sign that brings the nostalgic heart comfort in a way few things can.

Finally, the horses paced towards the thick wooden gates, then Beatriz stopped her horse a few feet in front of me.

"Open the gates," she shouted. "Isabel, Princess of Castilla y León, has arrived."

The guards stared blankly down from the top of the wall above the gates.

"Forgive me, my lady, but we cannot grant you entry. We have not the permission."

I stood there, dumbfounded that I was being refused entry to my own hometown. My hands were nearly numb from the cold morning air, and I felt the muscles ache as I clenched them in frustration. My horse trotted in front of Beatriz' and I faced the guards with as much authority as I could muster.

"I've come to visit the grave of my brother Alfonso. I demand that you open the gate!"

"We cannot, my lady. We are under strict orders from our master, the count, to now allow you entry."

"Ah," I said bitterly to Beatriz. "Of course he does, the coward. The count denies me entry out of fear that I have come to reclaim Arévalo for myself, a territory that by right should have been under my jurisdiction."

My frustration quickly turned to sadness. This was the place I grew up feeling so safe in, and instead of being a home to me now, Enrique had placed it under the protection of the count of Plasencia. He had taken so much from me already, I dared not think what else there was to lose.

Mencía stared at us with eyes that looked like she was on the brink of tears.

"Never mind them," I said, hoping to stiffen her resolve. "Let them deny our entry. They will not refrain me from honoring Alfonso. I *will* still pay my respects to my brother. We are going to the convent, and then I will find a way to visit my mother."

"I'm going back," Mencía de la Torre retorted.

Beatriz turned to her with eyes as cold as ice. "You will do no such thing. We are here to serve the princess. Your place is here, with her."

"Don't you see, we will all be punished for this — not just Isabel, all of us," she cried. "At this very moment, your husband is in Andalucía, with the king. Do you not realize that you and your husband will both be made to face Pacheco's wrath?"

Beatriz inhaled deeply and held her breath, weighing the seriousness of the situation that I had brought them into.

"The princess is wise beyond her years; I am sure she will act sagaciously."

But nothing worked out how it was supposed to. After being refused entry from the town that should have been under my control, I made my way to the monastery where my brother was buried, Cartuja de Miraflores, to bow and pray at the foot of my brother's tomb, the young man that held such promise for the future of Castilla y León. And all the while, as I poured my heart out in prayer, all I could think was that this was not how it was meant to be.

Things only grew worse from there. Visiting my mother, I was confronted with the reality of the severe deterioration of her mental state. As much as her attendants tried to help, there was nothing to be done. More and more, they found her carrying on conversations with herself, and when they asked who she was talking to, she calmly answered that it was Álvaro de Luna.

Never in my life had I felt so utterly alone.

Going home only reminded me of those I had lost. I missed my brother, and I missed my grandmother. I needed comfort and protection, but even coming back to my home and to my mother, I discovered that here I found neither the comforts of home nor of a mother, and I wondered if peace-of-mind would ever return to me.

The cool water ran over my fingers as I refilled the clay water pitcher I took from my mother's chambers. The sound of gentle footsteps came from behind me, and I knew it was Beatriz.

"I have something I need to tell you," she said in a weak voice.

Despite feeling as though I had been drained of all my strength, I turned towards her, giving her my full attention.

My tired eyes looked into hers, but then she looked down at the palms of her hands, as if helpless.

"Enrique knows you are here…. He knows because my husband told him… at my bidding."

"Why would you do that?" my voice came out like a hiss.

"Before you say anything, I have to tell you, I did this for your own good." Her words spilled out rapidly. "Isabel, you are getting in over your head. You are taking big risks without any protection for yourself." Beatriz stared at me, biting her lip, and I knew she had more to tell. She took a deep breath in, as if mustering the courage to continue. "Pacheco wrote to me. He promised that the king understands that you needed to pay your respects to Alfonso, but that you must go no further. Return now to Ocaña."

"You've been in communications with Pacheco? Of all people, I would have never believed *you* would be the one to betray me."

Her jaw dropped at my accusation.

"Betray you? How can you dare say that? I am not betraying you. I've risked my life and my husband's good name to stay by your side. But we've come to a point now that is too dangerous."

Her voice began to rise, then she stopped speaking, and didn't continue until she gained control over herself. "There is still time to return, it's the safest thing to do…. There's more. Isabel, if we press forward and refuse to come back now, Enrique will punish anyone in Madrigal who helps you."

"It's too late to go back now, Beatriz!" I cried out, frustrated and hurt at discovering that I had no one, not even Beatriz, to confide in. "Don't you see? Enrique will never allow me to marry the man of my choosing, especially the prince of Aragón. If I go back now, I will be forced into a marriage against my will, or else Pacheco will see to it that I am locked up as a prisoner. No." My heart thumped in my chest like a hammer pounding stone. "No! I am not going back. If my brother knows where I am, let him know. I made an agreement with him at Toros de Guisando. I am to choose the man I am to marry, and that man has been chosen. I am going to marry Fernando, there is no better match for me than him. There is no better match for Castilla than him."

"Isabel, I am so sorry. Pacheco threatened both Mencía de la Torre and me. He told us we needed to keep an eye on you. And I was afraid. I've never met a woman as determined to have her way, and I was afraid that such dogged determination would blind you and put you in danger."

Beatriz dropped her head and covered her face with her hands. I could see tears running down her cheeks. "You are my dearest friend, the closest things I have to a sister. Please know that I was only trying to protect you. And I don't know how to." She sobbed openly and bitterly, and I could see the sincerity in her eyes.

"I know you did. I understand." I reached out my hand and rubbed her back. "But I'm not going back. Beatriz, when I decided to flee Ocaña, I was determined that I would never go back. And I won't. I know Prince Fernando is coming for me…. And if I go back to Ocaña, to the clutches of my brother and his puppet-master, Pacheco, I will lose all control over my destiny."

There was no time to lose. I stood and walked to the door. "Make ready Mencía de la Torre while I bid my mother farewell. We will be leaving after nightfall. My destiny is to reign as queen of my realm, but first I must get to my prince."

Placing my hand on the door, I turned once more to Beatriz and quoted my favorite verse from the book of Revelations. "We cast the dice, but the Lord determines how they fall."

Chapter XIX
August, 1469

But the journey only grew more daunting. No matter where we went, we found the doors of the town bolted shut. No one was willing to give us entry. We had no choice but to press forward, and that meant more time on the roads. Mencía stopped complaining of her fears of highway robbers, but there was no need for her to voice what we were all thinking. The roads were dangerous, especially for three young women traveling alone. The longer we found ourselves on them, the more likely it was that we'd find ourselves victims.

Our legs ached from riding on horseback from one town to the next, exhausted from the August heat. Our backs were sore from sleeping on the hard-wooden beds in convents and eating whatever the nuns were kind enough to share with us. No matter how far we went, no one welcomed us in. Pacheco's messengers had reached them before we did, declaring their warning against anyone who gave aid to the disobedient king's sister.

Beatriz and Mencía rode next to one another, just a few steps behind me. After days of being shooed away by one town official after another, even my own resilience began to waver. It didn't take long before silence took the place of chatter, and as the horses pushed forward, the three of us barely spoke a word.

Anyway, what more was there to say? Mencía probably wanted to slap me for turning her into a traitor, at least in the eyes of Pacheco, and for bringing her with us on a journey that proved more dangerous than expected. And I had nothing to say to Beatriz de Bobadilla. Ever since she admitted that she had been communicating with Pacheco behind me back, I couldn't look at her the same. I had forgiven her, yes. That was God's will, for us to forgive, just as He has forgiven us. But I couldn't stop worrying about the fact that Enrique knew where I was, and even though I had escaped Ocaña, Pacheco had managed to find a way to infiltrate even my closest allies and instill distrust. Things were falling apart at the seams, but I had no choice but to continue onward.

It took all day before we reached the safety of Valladolid. The day was miserably hot, and the first layer of my underclothes was sticky with sweat from the summer heat. Still, I kept the thick black hood over my head. The paleness of my skin and blonde locks of my hair would surely give me away as being of noble birth, making me a target for anyone looking to earn an easy ransom for a princess. Mencía grimaced at having to keep her hood over her head as well, but at least she stopped complaining.

"We are all exhausted," I said. "But we can't risk letting ourselves be caught. Be strong just a little longer, we are almost to the city."

As we traveled through the Castilian countryside, I observed the land I would one day rule and the people that cared for it. The country was in disarray. I knew it, just as well as any of the other nobles, whose duty it was to oversee to the wellbeing of the citizens of their lands. But walking along the same roads as the common people, I could feel the unrest of the land, an unrest that disturbed my bones.

The city of Ávila had turned us away with a grave warning, claiming they were suffering from the plague. Entering the same area where even one man alone suffered from plague, or touching the garment of one who had died from the disease, was deadly. At first I had argued, thinking it was just another excuse. But once I realized that most of the city's citizens had already fled, and smelled the smoke in the air of the houses they had burned where the infected had been found, we moved on without further complaint.

The poverty was overwhelming. My lands were failing. I couldn't erase the image of a small child I had seen outside the city walls. Her mother sat in a chair, breastfeeding a baby she'd wrapped in a coarse wool swaddling blanket. Strands of hair fell from her mother's sloppy bun, and the heat of the scorching sun caused her hair to stick to her forehead. She looked worn, her eyes hallowed, as if the burdens of life had added years to her age, taking from her and giving nothing back. Poking out from behind her, I saw a little girl's face as she clung to her mother's skirts and watched our horses trot by. The little girl stood barefoot, her feet covered in dry earth, her hair just as unkempt as her mother's. But what troubled me most was how gaunt the child looked, her clothes hanging off her little body, her little tummy protruding from under her dress. The nobility had a responsibility to these peasants, and yet these people who had so little, were suffering from the lack of protection of the landholders who were neither concerned for the peasant's health nor their safety.

Both the mother and the girl looked so thin, and I knew there was little food in the land. Even if their lords were generous, there was little to be offered. My heart broke to see this, such suffering at such a young age. I felt desperate to help them and rode over, handing the little girl a small leather pouch containing the last of my gold coin. She stretched out both of her hands to take the gold and looked up at me with a big smile on her face. Despite the biting harshness of her reality, her eyes still had the brightness of childhood in them.

The land was desperate for healing, but Enrique never had the stomach to make the tough decision and necessary sacrifices. He never secured enough authority to administer the justice that cultivates prosperity.

Scanning my eyes over the sad acres of country that would one day kneel under my rule, a story our nursemaid often told came to mind. It was the legend of Alexander the Great and his challenge to untie the Gordian Knot. No one had succeeding in its untying. So, taking out his sword, the warrior cut the knot it two, claiming that it mattered not how the knot was untied, but only that the solution was found.

I had every intention of adopting the same philosophy, and decided that the image of the Gordian Knot would be included in the royal coat of arms. I would do whatever was needed to give this country back what was taken from it, regardless of the methods needed to secure safety. One day, when I ruled, I would do everything in my power to protect my people's innocence and to provide for my Castilians, like a mother willing to care for her children by any means necessary.

The sun had already disappeared, and the last of the light remained on the land before us, making the rocky fields look somber and funereal.

The night sky will soon be bright with stars. That will be light enough.

I stopped at the sound of horse hooves beating against the dry land, growing louder as they drew near. I couldn't see far enough ahead to make out what was coming, until the faint light of dusk revealed a group of men on horseback riding towards us. My heartbeat quickened, and my hand went to the small knife I kept hidden inside my sleeve. Beatriz hurried her horse to ride alongside me. Since confessing her communications with Pacheco, this was the first time she dared to ride by my side, and I knew it was her way of protecting me.

"Ride behind me, my lady," she said, and I could hear the concern in her voice.

"Don't worry, Beatriz, they won't hurt us." But she dared not trust a soul.

Moments later, the men were before us. The wind beat their banners violently back, as violently as my beating heart, and I wondered if we were to be once again turned away, or worse yet, taken captive. My mare trotted cautiously forward, and I removed the hood of my robe to reveal my identity.

"Doña Isabel, we have long awaited your arrival. On behalf of Señor Juan de Vivero, we welcome you to Valladolid. This way, please." They turned and led us into the heart of the city.

We dismounted from our horses and entered the palace. A servant dressed in fine livery of House Vivero led us past the great corridor, through rooms covered in elegant tapestries and large paintings, then to a large wooden door hinged under a pale stone archway.

"Her royal Highness, the Princess of Castilla y León," announced the servant.

Quietly, I walked into the chamber. Before me stood a man dressed in a black velvet doublet with gold buttons, and his wife wore an azure blue silk gown that draped richly to the floor. Both bowed deeply before me, a show of respect.

"Princess Isabel, I am so relieved you are here. I am María, and this is my husband, Don Juan de Vivero," she said with great warmth and simplicity. "Please know you are very welcome in our home."

"You honor me with your hospitality."

The servant approached, pouring a glass of wine into fine crystal glasses.

"I hope your Highness will enjoy this. It is among my finest reserves," Juan de Vivero said, gesturing to the wine.

"My husband is somewhat of a connoisseur," María added, her smile soft, yet proud. "We have some of the finest wines in all the kingdom. This particular wine is from Ribera del Duero. It is a—

"A tempranillo," I said.

"Yes, my lady. You are exactly right," she smiled graciously.

"Our land is richly blessed with fertility, and produces some of the greatest wines in all of Europe. Though I do not drink, I know what my land cultivates. It's only right that a ruler knows their kingdom well enough to distinguish which region her wine comes from." I inhaled deeply, enjoying the aroma of the wine, and felt my body relax for the first time in as long as I could remember.

"It is wise for those who wield great responsibility to protect their mind from the lack of clarity caused by alcohol," María de Vivero replied.

"Señor and Señora Vivero, forgive me, but I fear my energy is escaping me. Would you be so kind as to excuse me for the evening?"

"Of course, Princesa. This way, please. Let me show you to your quarters."

She led me once more through the great hall.

"Your chambers, my lady." Maria opened the wide-set wooden door, the room already lit with a fire and thick wax candles, as if it had been awaiting my arrival.

My eyes took in the artistry of the rooms, gilded ceilings and painted silk walls adorning the wide-open spaciousness of the area. The palace was magnificent, but the rooms they had chosen for me were truly remarkable.

"I hope you will find these quarters to your liking. I took the liberty to personally furnish the room myself," María said, walking in just behind me. She reached out her hand in front of her, guiding me to a wall near the far corner of the room. "If you pull the tapestry to the side, like this," she said, showing me where to place my hand, "you will find a hidden door. It leads to a small private study. There, you will find ink and paper. There is already a letter waiting for you from my uncle, the archbishop of Toledo. He requests that you write to him immediately. But your Highness must be tired. Surely the letter can wait until morning. I will let you retire for the evening. I bid you goodnight. Please, rest assured that you are safe here."

"Señora Vivero," I said, meeting her at the door. "I am indebted to you and your husband, as well as to your uncle, Archbishop Carrillo. Your home is a sanctuary to me."

She nodded her head in acknowledgment.

"We are here to serve you in any way we can. Without a doubt, the honor of welcoming the one who will one day reign over the kingdom of Castilla is ours." She placed her hand over my own. "My uncle is determined that you will come to rule. He is doing everything in his power to place you on the throne, and he is a man that is sure to achieve whatever he puts his mind to. I have always trusted in his council, and you are wise to do the same."

During the weeks I spent at the palace in Valladolid, I was treated, for the first time in my life, as the heir apparent. Archbishop Carrillo had every certainty that I would be queen, and made sure that his family was the first to treat me like a princess and heir. He stressed how essential it was that I was perceived as the future ruler of the kingdom, and promised that once others saw how I was being treated by a family as distinguished as House Vivero, more noble families were sure to follow.

Juan and María de Vivero were the most generous of hosts, and every evening prepared fresh entertainment or a private dinner, but I had very little time to spend enjoying such delights. Royalty or not, there was little leisure time, not when I had so much at stake, and so much to be accomplished in so little time. My hours were consumed inside the walls of the study. Every morning, new letters were received and responses were sent.

Carrillo, too, was busy at work, casting his web and drawing in every one of his contacts to my side. He worked tirelessly, determined to place the crown upon my head. Every one of his letters sent to the Castilian nobles, as well as their responses, was presented to me, as the archbishop agreed that I must be kept apprised of all matters. Each one of my lords had their own agenda, concerns, fears and ambitions. Some were bold and cunning, while others were easily managed. I needed to know each of them, and they needed to know me. Such exposure was an imperative step in learning how to rule.

"Sign here," Archbishop Carrillo said, handing me a document. I looked it over carefully while he used a small knife to sharpen the end of the quill. Then, opening the sterling silver handle of the inkwell, he dipped the quill and handed it to me to sign.

"What progress are we making in Rome?" I asked. It was the one question we all were waiting on, and the one task I needed Carrillo most for.

He exhaled deeply, a bad sign.

"The Pope is obstinate. He still refuses to provide the papal bull."

"The blessing of the Holy Father is the one thing that is essential for my marriage. Without it, all our efforts are in vain."

To marry a second cousin was a regular practice, for both noble and royal houses, but a papal dispensation was requisite, and without it, all his work, all his connections, were utterly useless.

Carrillo held his breath before speaking, and I knew he was worried.

"Not all things are so simple to acquire. Enrique's envoys in Rome have tremendous sway with the Pope, who has already provided Enrique with one dispensation for you to marry the king of Portugal. A second dispensation for the same princess is not easily attained," he said defensively.

It felt like we had hit a brick wall, and I couldn't help but worry. Great risk had been taken to escape Enrique's palace in Ocaña and flee to Valladolid. I couldn't turn back now. But without papal support, I could not marry Fernando. My whole future rested on this one document.

"Then your envoys must press further," I replied, steadying my gaze. "Surely they can find a means. Enrique's dispensation is only valid if it is to be used."

"Do not let this discourage you, my dear. The matter is being handled." Carrillo was obviously displeased at such forthrightness coming out of the mouth of an eighteen-year-old girl. "You can have no doubt that I will find a way. Even now, Fernando's father, King Juan of Aragón, has put his men to work in Rome to handle this matter. You can trust me when I say, you will have your dispensation."

The archbishop poured the wax over the envelope and used his ring to press down on the seal.

"In the meantime," he continued, "you must be content to stay put. Here is the safest place for you, at least until you are wed and bed."

"I've already escaped one prison. I do not mean to be held within another."

With his chin bent low over the letter, he lifted his eyes and stared at me.

"I advise you to consider the danger that lingers, waiting for you, outside these walls. Remember, the nobles who once supported you and young Alfonso…they now have sworn their allegiance to Enrique, at least at present. Meanwhile, the land is wrought with crime and poverty. Should you leave and get yourself caught, your captors would be paid a pretty reward for delivering you to the king and Pacheco."

"And Fernando? What of him? If it is too dangerous for me, a princess, to leave, surely it is too dangerous for him to come here!"

"Better he come here than you attempt for Aragón. You would do well to remain within the confines of this palace, if only to further establish yourself as the future queen of Castilla. It will be poorly seen if you flee from the kingdom you mean to reign. Fernando must come to you, there is no other way."

"But the road between us is dangerous. Is there not somewhere I could meet him that would make his journey safer?"

"Have no fear for your prince — the boy has the undaunted spirit of youth and love. Look at the letters he sends you. Fernando is enamored with you, young princess. More importantly, he has the same ambition you do, unity. The prince will find his way to his bride, I have no doubt. I've known him since he was just a child. He is braver than you think, as you soon will find out."

Chapter XX
September, 1469

I sat on the edge of the fountain in the center of the courtyard and listened to the gentle sounds of the water. Droplets splashed from the spout and fell, creating little wet circles on my gown.

"There you are," María de Vivero said, coming up from behind me. I turned towards her, startled. "Forgive me. I did not mean to frighten you." She came and sat next to me, tucking the delicate yellow fabric of her gown beneath her. "It's beautiful here, isn't it? May I join you?"

"Please." A soft breeze caressed our skin and gently blew María's thick golden-brown curls from underneath her pearl headpiece. "Of all the rooms in the palace, this space is my favorite," I said.

"I'm glad you were able to leave the study today. You do spend so much time there. I've hardly seen you allow yourself a moment's reprieve. My uncle requires much of you, but you must take care of yourself, as well."

I dipped my fingers in the water, enjoying its coolness against my skin.

"It is peaceful here. I came here to clear my mind, I suppose. Being inside for so many long hours makes it impossible for one to think clearly."

"Hmm," she agreed, taking a closer look at me. "Is there anything I can do to help?"

I looked up from the water. "You are too kind. If only there were. But I thank you anyway."

"I'm a good listener. Sometimes, when my mind is troubled, just talking to a friend helps me to feel like the weight of the world no longer bears down so heavily on my shoulders."

"Where to begin?" I replied, turning away the invitation. There were so many things that troubled me. How could I begin to explain it all?

Instead of accepting my refusal, she waited patiently for me to continue. My first instinct was to remain secretive. Years at King Enrique's Court taught me to protect my innermost thoughts and to never reveal my true fears and desires. But something inside of me told me I could trust María, and I knew that right now, more than anything, I needed to unburden myself from the weight of my thoughts.

"I suppose, at the root of it all is my brother, the king. I can have no peace while our family is so deeply fragmented. And as things stand, we will only grow more distant."

"In families as powerful as yours, unrest can easily evolve into bitterness, until soon enough, you've discovered your brother is your enemy."

I looked off in the distance, and let her words sink in. "Never would I wish to make myself an enemy to my brother. But I fear I have no other choice but defiance. He refuses to honor our agreement and accept my wishes to marry Fernando. But my betrothed already has my word — I will not go back on my decision."

"If the king fails to honor your agreement and refuses to give his blessing to the one you have chosen as your mate, as he promised in the Treaty of Guisando, then don't you agree that the treaty is summarily void, thus freeing you from the promises you made in the contract?"

"That's true," I said, though I hadn't viewed it from that angle. "But 'a house divided cannot stand.' I fear if I break with my brother, it will be the end — for all of us."

"You speak with a wisdom well beyond your years. It was indeed Christ who first said these words, though I'm sure you already knew that."

It comforted me to know I was sharing the deepest concerns of my heart to a woman who revered God as much as I did.

"The chasm growing between the king and I only widens, especially with the web Pacheco weaves. It's as if he knows my every step. He has even gone so far as to intimidate those closest to me, Mencía de Luna and Beatriz de Bobadilla. That's why they told him of our escape from Ocaña to visit my brother Alfonso's grave. Visiting my brother's grave could be considered understandable, even excusable. But if Pacheco learns where I am now… I can only guess at the pleasure he will take in my punishment."

María turned towards me. "My uncle Carrillo would never allow that to happen. You are safe here, Isabel. Pacheco thinks he is powerful, but he will need a great deal of courage if he plans to attack *this* city, with its fortified walls, towers and moats. Why, we are nearly impregnable. And the king? It takes a bold man to try to pursue the heir to the throne while she is under the protection of Valladolid."

"You have no idea how persuasive Pacheco can be. He has some sort of sick power over my brother. Whatever he says, my brother will do. And if he sets his mind to getting me into his custody…"

"Please don't worry. Even though many nobles support Enrique, there are many who stand by you and would send their army for you at a moment's notice."

"Perhaps. But not as many as before."

She pursed her lips. "I understand. The issue is complex. But complicated as things might be, in the end, you and Enrique are family. Often, miscommunication leads to hurt feelings, and hurt feelings lead to hurtful actions. It is my opinion, *Princesa*, that the only remedy to fix hurt caused by miscommunication is to communicate. As simple as it sounds, creating room for both of you to share your thoughts will bring a great deal of resolution. So then," she said, her voice lifting cheerfully, "I propose for you to write to him. Tell him how you feel and what you plan to do."

"But that would put my fiancé in even more danger. Fernando must travel through territory controlled by Enrique's loyal supporters. If Enrique knows that Fernando is coming, he will do everything in his power to stop him."

"But by telling Enrique of these events even before they happen, by not going behind his back, you will make him realize that you honor him as your king, and truly want to be a loyal and obedient servant."

"A loyal and obedient servant, yes, but a pawn to be manipulated at will, no. I refuse to give him all that he wishes of me. I am not willing to surrender my sacred rights to the throne and relinquish my inheritance to Juana la Beltraneja. I don't want to defy the king, but I also refuse to renounce my future."

"I'm not suggesting that writing to him will solve everything. But consider this: even if you can't count on you brother's approval of your marriage, at least he will see that you are honest and forthright with him, two traits that are rare in this debauched, self-serving world we live in. Writing to him may not fix the problem, but it could be the first steps in the right direction. And at the least, by being transparent with him, you are doing what you can to restore your relationship with your brother and acting with royal dignity. And that, most certainly, will bring you peace of mind."

And so, I wrote.

Dipping my quill in the ink, I paused, staring out the window. Summer had come and gone. Autumn was fast approaching, and I couldn't help but wonder what this season would bring, resolution… or civil war. It all lay in the balance.

There was so much I wanted to say to my brother, but where things stood, I couldn't just pour my heart out. This letter required tact. Each of my words carried weight, and even though I wished with all my heart that he would read my letter with an empathetic mindset, willing to find resolution, it was impossible to tell how he would interpret my words.

And so, I cast the dice.

The ink pressed a deep black scar onto the paper, and just as the black liquid left a mark that couldn't be erased, I knew that once my words were before my brother, their mark was permanent.

The letter began by addressing my purpose for writing, my decision to wed Prince Fernando of Aragón. I begged his Grace to recall the peace forged and agreement made in Guisando, and explained to him the care and consideration my advisors and I took in selecting our choice among the four marriage candidates: Fernando of Aragón, Afonso V of Portugal, the duke de Berry of France, and Richard, brother to the king of England. As was agreed, it was my right to decide whom I would marry, and my choice was made. Fernando was a non-negotiable.

I wrote that, even though I knew a marriage to Fernando was not Enrique's preference, I asked for him to accept my decision and to acknowledge that, despite what might be perceived as disobedience, I wished to honor him as my true sovereign king. For above all else, my actions reflected our singular shared desire for peace.

This first portion of the letter was performed with diplomacy. After that, the words began to pour out of me. I pointed out that my prerogative for peace was evident since the day I refused to take our brother, Alfonso's place as queen. Even though I was Alfonso's legitimate heir and had overwhelming support from the nobles, I rejected the opportunity laid at my feet to be named queen and refused to dishonor my lord and king. After all, are we not siblings? And do we not share the same desire for harmony and prosperity for the kingdom? In these two regards, at least, we must surely be of the same mind.

Lastly, I addressed the issue that had caused the greatest injury to my brother's pride: my decision to marry Fernando. Enrique was indignant that I, a woman, chose my own husband, but I explained that this was not, in fact, the case. Again, I explained that, among the suitors, Fernando was the one that rallied the most support from my noble advisors. Enrique knew just as well as I did that unity with the neighboring kingdom of Aragón was the final wish of our grandfather, King Enrique III of Castilla. If the king acknowledged this, then he must also recognize that my marriage to the heir would thus realize our forefather's longed for aspiration, and unite two of Spain's most powerful kingdoms. This act would be for the betterment of our realm, and we had no greater duty than to Castilla.

But the letter did not end there. It couldn't. If it did, then King Enrique would look at this letter and see himself as innocent and I as the villain, an obstinate child arguing her way to forgiveness and acceptance after wantonly disobeying her lord and master. Enrique must be made to recognize his own sins.

And so, I took up the quill again, this time airing the great injustice he had allowed Alfonso and I to endure at the bidding of his wife. And yet, despite the bitterness of the past, I wished to move forward, and expressed my deep hope to be accepted as his obedient servant, a desire that was equally shared by my husband-to-be, Fernando.

Days passed, each one making me more anxious for a reply. Instead, Enrique chose isolation, abiding by his usual course of inaction.

Was he playing some sort of game, waiting to see if I would truly follow through in my defiance? Did he doubt my resolve to wed the man I willed to marry? Did he doubt the resolve of my fiancé?

Days turned into weeks, and my brother made no attempt to communicate with me. Carrillo was not surprised.

"Enrique was never known to be a man of action," he retorted, disparagingly. "Besides, consider how this is being portrayed to him? The marqués de Villena is your declared enemy. It's in his interest to see you destroyed, and no one has the king's ear more than Pacheco. I can guarantee you that the nullification of the agreement made at Toros de Guisando was his doing."

"El marqués," I fumed under my breath. "I wish I could just as easily blame Pacheco with my brother's disloyalty towards me. But the truth can't be so easily ignored. My brother, somehow, has an affection for that child, even if it isn't his," I said, my thoughts turning to la Beltraneja. "I admit, I feel sorry for the girl. But not so sorry that I am willing to sacrifice the future of my family's dynasty and my own children's inheritance to the illegitimate offspring of a wonton mother."

"Isabel," Carrillo's voice was controlled and masculine, "trust me when I tell you, it is you who will rule over Castilla. But the situation we now find ourselves in is much more precarious than before, when your brother Alfonso was declared as king. If you had only listened to me then, we might not find ourselves where we are today. We had support from powerful lords across the kingdom. Now that's gone, all that support that your younger brother had mustered. Those same nobles now shrink from you, fearing that rallying behind you will eventually lead to another war between siblings. The nobles may believe in your rightful claim to the throne, but their willingness to lend you their support has limits."

"But my prerogative is peace."

"Also true of your brother, no doubt. But you are only willing to allow peace on your conditions. You want to reign. And Enrique wills to impede that."

"Tsk. When a threat goes unpunished too many times, the fear vanishes. Enrique's threats have lost their sting."

"Exactly, and in a way, his lack of credibility in the eyes of his vassals levels the field. In the minds of the nobility, it is just as probable for you to end up as the future queen of this land as Juana. But what leaves so many of these nobles unsettled is the fact that, invariably, the keys to the kingdom lay in the hands of a woman. You must gain the upper hand. The solution is simple: marriage. Fernando must come, at once."

"Now? But it's still too dangerous. We still haven't attained Enrique's consent, and the land is overrun by my brother's supporters. If Fernando comes now, he could easily be captured."

"Haven't you heard? Fernando is a gambling man. He'll take his chances, whatever the risk, to get to his princess."

Chapter XXI

The archbishop's voice bellowed through the hallways. I frowned and felt my chest grow agitated; Carrillo should not have begun the discussions with my advisers without my presence. I was just as anxious to hear what the envoys had to say as he. Especially now, when everything lay in the balance, but it disturbed me that he would act so precipitously, so presumptuously, as to begin without me being there, as if he were leading instead of me.

All grew silent and stood when I entered the room.

"Welcome home, gentlemen," I said to Gutierre de Cárdenas and Alonso de Palencia. Turning to Cárdenas, I continued, "I am sure your uncle Chacón is pleased to see you again. Please, let us begin. I am eager to hear your report."

The men remained standing until I took my seat. Gutierre de Cárdenas and Chacón sat, followed by my second envoy, the courtier Palencia and the lawyer. But Archbishop Carrillo remained on his feet. His clenched knuckles turned white as he leaned forward, pressing them violently into the table.

"I regret to inform you, *Princesa*, that things did not go according to how I had arranged. These two men," he said through clenched teeth, "were to meet Fernando at the Franciscan monastery. I had made specific arrangements to ensure the delivery of Fernando to Valladolid."

"That is correct," said Palencia, sitting up straight in his chair to interrupt the archbishop. "And we arrived at the arranged meeting place, as you required."

"And was Fernando not there?" I asked, growing nervous.

If he were, Carrillo had every right to be furious. The envoys were to safely bring my fiancé to me, and they had returned empty-handed.

"Upon our arrival, one of the monks, I do not know whom, led us to his private cell. It was there that Fernando awaited us."

"A private cell? Was such a precaution necessary?"

"I have no doubt that it was. Apparently, while Fernando's men were in town, there was a rumor circulating that Isabel's envoys where soon to arrive. The prince's safety could very well have been compromised if such precautions were not taken."

Carrillo scoffed. "The prince decided to meet you in the monk's cell because he didn't trust the friars of the monastery? Or was it that he didn't trust that I had provided a secure location?" Condescension dripped from Carrillo's lips, annoyed at Fernando's disobedience.

"Yes, my lord. And he refused to return with us. Fernando assured us that he would find his way to the princess, but it would not be by coming with us."

"Oh, is that right? And how, pray tell, does the prince of Aragón plan to exit the city unrecognized and travel unprotected through two hundred and twenty-five miles of treacherous terrain?" Carrillo bellowed.

Images of Castilla's geography entered my mind, its dangerous slopped cliffs and icy mountains, that all must be crossed in order to arrive here, to Valladolid.

"Do you have any idea how important your mission was? The princess must be married, the alliance must be cemented. How dare you return here without fulfilling your duty to your princess."

Palencia ignored the archbishop and turned directly to me.

"I have never seen a man so eager to get to the side of his betrothed," Palencia said. "Have no doubt, Doña Isabel, that your prince will make it to you. He is as clever as he is daring."

Carrillo cut him off. "And yet, here you are, both of you, without completing your mission. You had one objective, to bring the prince to Valladolid."

"Nephew," Chacón interjected calmly, addressing Cárdenas. "Tell us more of what happened? What does Fernando plan to do?"

"He decided it would be too great of a risk for us to escort him back here. Instead, he ordered us to dress in our finest clothes and present ourselves publicly as diplomats of the princess, to behave in a way that garnered attention. We arrived and did as he bid, declaring that we had come to escort the prince to the princess Isabel, and then grumbled that Fernando had failed to come. We spoke loud and clear so that everyone could hear that the prince was not there, but instead had joined his father, King Juan II, in the north, in Cataluña. We left, making sure our complaints were heard."

"He had you put on a spectacle? I thought we'd sent noblemen, not actors," Carrillo shook his head. "I arranged for him to be escorted here under the protection of a hundred lances, and now he has put himself, and this entire enterprise, at risk."

Carrillo expected to be able to take control of the situation, but it was too late for frustration and regret, the matter was done. I could not change the fact that my fiancé was not here, and may have very well put himself in danger. Instead, I had to trust that my future husband acted with prudence and would come, just as he had promised.

"Where is the prince now?" I turned to face the envoys, ignoring the archbishop and returning to how to best resolve the matter at hand.

"Your betrothed is traveling with a few of his closest companions. They are disguised as traders, and he is acting as their servant," Cárdenas explained. "He will be traveling day and night to get to you, I can swear it," he promised.

Cárdenas walked to the center of the desk and pointed down on the large map, tracing his finger along a path.

"The prince showed me the route he plans to take to get here, so that we can send help should anything arise. He will first make his way through an old road along the Montalvo Mountains, then through Berdejo and the Puerto de Bigornia, then to Gómara. His plan is to get to Burgo de Osma. If he can make it there, he will find the support of the count of Treviño and his men."

"How can we help?" I said, turning to Archbishop Carrillo.

The archbishop tapped his fingers loudly on the marble table and pursed his lips as he thought.

"I will write to my brother, el conde de Buendía," he answered, resting his two fingers over his mouth as he thought aloud. "If the prince can avoid Enrique's spies and make his way to Osma, then he will be able to travel with armed guard to my brother's land, Dueñas. My brother will be able to provide refuge and a good night's sleep for him, and secure his safety the rest of the way to Valladolid."

"Thank you, my lord," I said, acknowledging the archbishop's help. "The prince faces a harrowing journey through high altitudes and dangerous roads, with cold days and colder October nights. I know Fernando will be grateful for the safety you are able to provide."

And still, no word from my brother. The thought of my promise to not marry without his consent plagued me day and night, but I knew that if I didn't take this step and marry Fernando, I would be forced to marry the man of his choosing, or worse.

Days turned into weeks, and yet he made no attempt to react to the letter I had sent in September informing him of my coming nuptials. I wanted a response from him, some type of reaction. I wanted him to communicate how he was feeling, even if he were angry, at least it would be our first step towards resolution. But time was passing too quickly, I had too little of it to spare, and I couldn't afford to wait and hope that a letter from him would soon arrive.

I decided to write to him again.

October 12, 1469

To his Majesty, King of Castilla y León, Enrique IV,

To my honored king and dear brother,

I write to you again this cold day in October to remind you of my coming nuptials. My betrothed, the prince of Aragón and king of Sicily, is already in Castilla.

I begged you to accept that this is the man I have chosen to marry, and though you have not given me your approval, I remind you again that Fernando was the choice of the great advisers and highest noblemen of the kingdom. Marriage to Fernando would mean the unity of two of Spain's most powerful crowns, an endeavor I know is dear to your heart, as it is to mine. Marriage to the prince of Aragón will pave the way towards the unity of Spain under the leadership of one religion, the Catholic Church, and nothing can be more essential than this.

I must remind you of my choice to acquiesce my own right to rule Castilla y León at present as a show of my allegiance to you. My beloved younger brother, King Alfonso, declared me as his legitimate heir to the throne. And despite the opportunity to take the title of queen, I obediently chose peace. I chose to prevent my countrymen from entering into a civil war between a brother and a sister. I chose to declare you as my king, and avidly encouraged my supporters to accept you as their king. And instead, we agreed that upon the end of your reign, I would be your sole legitimate heir.

And yet, instead of treating me with the love of a brother and good master, you oppressed me. You did everything in your power to take away my freedom, to control me and cage me within the walls of your castle. You threatened me with imprisonment should I leave. And you now threaten to take away my sacred inheritance.

Your Majesty, I write to inform you that my fiancé, the prince of Aragón and king of Sicily, is already in the villa de Dueñas. Our wedding ceremony will be celebrated shortly. I write to assure you that we mean to cause no scandal. My husband and I, we are your servants, and our greatest desire is the same as yours, peace. Please be assured of my most profound sincerity.

Your humble servant and sister, Isabel.

Chapter XXII

My betrothed was on his way to me, just as he promised. Carrillo was occupied preparing for the wedding, just as he promised. And yet we still lacked the most essential element: the dispensation from the Pope.

The door to the counsel chamber gently closed, and I recognized the loud, firm sound of boots hitting against the floor to be the footsteps of Chacón.

"Doña Isabel, we have no other option. Fernando will have to wait. You cannot dare to wed without the dispensation."

It almost sounded as if he were giving me a command, as if he had forgotten to whom he was speaking. Chacón, it was true, was confusing me with the child I once was. The man had been in the service of my father, then my mother, since my earliest memories. That would make it difficult for him to adapt his treatment of me as future queen and sovereign, instead of the little girl he had dedicated himself to guiding and instructing.

I was a different woman now — for better or for worse. Much of the innocence of the child he had once known in Arévalo was gone. My childhood had ended the day my brother Alfonso died. But my time at the king's Court had been put to good use. Instead of becoming a victim to the machinations of the courtier and queen, I had become a student — and I meant to make use of Juana, and even Pacheco's piteous lessons. Now, life had spit me out the other side, and with this marriage to Fernando, I would be a queen in my own right.

I looked up from the letters I was busily penning in my own hand to various nobles in an effort to fortify relationships and prepare the way for the road that lay ahead.

"Do I dare to wait? There is too much at risk, time I cannot afford to lose. Every moment of inaction is like a gift to Enrique and all those who support him….. I have no choice but to trust that Carrillo can accomplish this task."

"You are willing to place such great trust in that man?" I knew the thought of Carrillo's growing power and my dependence on him disturbed Chacón.

I put down the quill and looked up at him, giving him my undivided attention.

"Carrillo assured me that he can and will have the dispensation. The archbishop has never once failed in his promises, now is not the time to begin questioning his capabilities. He *will* find a means to procure the necessary document."

"And what about the fact that the Pope has already provided a dispensation for you to marry the king of Portugal? He will not provide a second dispensation for the same woman; you cannot ignore that. And Enrique has ties with Pope Paulo II. I don't see how you expect…"

Chacón had a way of repeating himself, and I had heard his reasonings on the matter too many times already. Once he had an idea of what he considered best into his head, the man could never just mention it once, but instead would bring the same concerns and recommendations up until he had his way. My mother and little brother Alfonso were docile, passive creatures, easily accepting any idea pushed on them. I was not of the same temperament.

"The dispensation is for Carrillo to be concerned with," I calmly, yet firmly interrupted. "I trust that when the moment comes, he will have what we need. Anyway, once the public witnesses the ceremony with their own eyes, and sees me presented with a legal document approving my marriage, what more is there to want? An archbishop of the Catholic Church is unlikely to be questioned, the matter will be indisputable."

"But should we not receive the dispensation in time…" he carried on, then stopped, fell silent, his jaw agape. "You couldn't mean... for the archbishop to create a papal bull?" he said, aghast. "Do you have any idea the danger you will put yourself in? To marry a man against the will of both the king of Castilla and the Pope. It's sacrilege! Your marriage will not be considered valid. Your children will be illegitimate."

"Please, my lord, hear me. First, you are assuming that the Pope will not come around, when we have every indication that he, in fact, will support my marriage. Still, should the document be... delayed, we must proceed with our plans."

He writhed his hands, still worried.

"Come, Chacón. Please don't fret. Things will all work out as they should, I am sure of it. Why, just think, even now we have the Pope's own envoy, Señor Venier, speaking with His Holiness on our behalf regarding the matter. Rest assured, he is rather eager to be of assistance."

During the Treaty of Toros de Guisando, Rome sent Venier to act as Pontifical legate to see to the success of the treaty. The Pope was eager to establish peace in the Christian kingdom of Castilla, and had placed his confidence in Venier, and the legate had assured the Pope that he would bring resolution to the conflict between us. But when Enrique broke the agreement made at Toro de Guisando, Venier took it personally, as if it reflected his capabilities. He would not allow Enrique's duplicity to tarnish his credibility, and swore to lend his support in the matter of my marriage to Fernando.

"The legate," I continued, "wields a great deal of power; the Pope has placed little restraint on his faculties. He has given me his word that I am to have my dispensation. Why should we not have the utmost confidence that our objective will be reached? And in the meantime... In the meantime, there is but one thing to do, move forward. This is a risk I have no choice but to take. It's wiser for me to proceed as planned, to take action now with matters that I can make a difference with, and, if need be, ask for forgiveness later."

Chacón frowned. "And Carrillo is willing to take this risk for you? To defy the will of the Church? Should this not go according to plan, the archbishop will be putting his career and his future at stake."

I sighed. "Carrillo has made it clear that he has every intention to ensure this marriage takes place. He understands he has 'tied his horse to my carriage,' so to speak, and with my rise comes his own. There will always be risk involved, but we have taken preventative measures. Besides, if the Vatican's spiritual representative has assured us that the dispensation is ours, then we must trust him at his word."

"Hmm. And for all Carrillo's efforts, what does he ask in return? I assume he has made his desired reward clear."

"You know the archbishop too well," I laughed, then sighed at the nature of ambition that drove many of those I relied on most. "Alas, he has, as always. Carrillo wishes for his son, Troilo Carrillo, to receive the Villa de Atienza. I would rather not reward the illegitimate son of a man of the cloth, but so be it."

"That can't be all he demands. I know the archbishop too well, he's too shrewd a man to not ask for more, especially when he knows you have found yourself in a desperate situation and that you cannot achieve your wishes without his help. Carrillo is putting his neck on the line by promising this dispensation, and he knows you need him."

"Very well. I admit, we do depend on him. If it were not for the archbishop of Toledo…" I paused. "Fernando and I are indebted to him. And he has made his wishes clear. He desires for us three, Fernando, Carrillo and myself, to be of one mind and act as one body as we govern the country, that no decision be made without his approval."

Chacón sat before me and stared, his eyes fixed on me. I knew he was thinking, calculating the repercussions of such an agreement.

"Isabel," he said firmly, then paused, softening his tone. "Isabel, I am the closest thing you have to a father. I cannot express how protective I am of you. But I am not your father. No, your father was a king, and you are to be a queen. You have the vision and foresight of a great ruler. The archbishop is a man with an appetite for power. Not necessarily a man of greed, but certainly opportunistic. To grant him such a favor is like putting handcuffs on your wrist and giving him the key."

I smiled, and placed my hand on his. "You *are* the closest thing I have known to a father, it's true. And I am no fool, I see what Carrillo plans to do. He recognizes vulnerability, that we are unable to realize what I mean to achieve without his help. He means to take every advantage of this, and to rule through me. But Castilla will not be a puppet in the hands of a puppet master, just as Castilla will not be ruled by an illegitimate daughter of that licentious queen. But I have no other option but to acquiesce in this matter, at least for the time being."

"All I advise is to keep your eyes wide open, especially to those closest to you."

Chapter XXIII

The fire crackled under the high-reaching hearth, its warmth heating my back through my gown. The hour had nearly reached midnight, and I sat alone, waiting for my prince to arrive. My only company: an adolescent girl staring back at me in the reflection of the mirror.

The girl looking back at me from inside the looking glass was pretty. Her pale white skin still savored the freshness that birthed with the dawn of youth. She sat, elegantly dressed in her finest gown of an exquisite sapphire blue silk tightly bodiced against her chest, with her delicate hands resting patiently on the flowing skirt of the gown. Her lips appeared almost crimson from the cold autumn air, and behind her wavy blonde hair, her blue eyes stared back at me imploringly, asking a question I did not know the answer to. And all I could do was stare back at the face in the mirror and smile, reassuring myself that I was exactly where I was meant to be.

The prince would arrive any moment, and soon I would be wed to a man I had only known through a small portrait sent by one of his envoys, and through his colorful reputation. Fernando, they say, was just as much a warrior as he was a paramour. Yes, he was known as an admirer of women, women who apparently loved him back. Women that must have been beautiful, clever, desirable, or else the prince of Aragón wouldn't bother himself with them.

Indeed, the man I, a virgin, was to wed, already came to the altar with a handful of children from various lovers. Though I wouldn't considered this to be a fault. At least, not in my present situation. In fact, his virility was one of the reasons my advisors chose him to be my counterpart. At least it proved that Fernando would not present the same fertility issues that Enrique had. With Fernando, Castilla could expect an heir.

And as soon as I was made a bride, I would be expected to produce this heir — the future of Castilla y León. To bear a child was my duty to my husband, as well as to my kingdom. Still, a little voice inside of me made me shrink with worry. Fernando had proven his ability to sire sons, but I was still a maid. There was no guarantee that I could have children.

Nonsense, I told myself. *There is no room to doubt yourself.* I need only to have faith. I must remember, God Almighty placed me here to rule this kingdom, to repair and redeem the land. It was the words I heard in my head time and again: just as God chose Mary to bring Christ into the world for redemption, I was to bring a son into Spain to heal this fragmented home. All of this rested on the man I was to meet tonight.

He would be the man I was to spend the rest of my life with. Looking once more into the mirror, I exhaled deeply and gathered my strength, resolute in my decision, ready to perform my duty.

But the girl in the looking glass stared back at me, begging the one question it was forbidden for a princess to ask. Would my prince love me? Would I be desired? Or is he here for no more noble of a reason than that a royal father desired for his son to become king of the largest Christian kingdom of Spain?

The door gently creaked open. Gutierre de Cárdenas stood before me, and I knew his presence meant that Fernando had arrived. I smoothed down my gown and rose, silently walking through the doorway and the halls, the only sound coming from the toll of the church bells, signaling midnight. Now began a new day, and with it a new life.

Within the high reaching ceilings of the Great Room, my advisors and Fernando's entourage stood awaiting my arrival, all dressed to perfection.

"*Este es*, that's the one!" Cárdenas whispered with excitement. But there was no need for him to indicate which man was my prince. Just as quickly as I entered the room, my eyes were drawn to one man alone. The side of his mouth turned up into a roguish smile, and I instinctively knew that this was my bridegroom.

My heart beat faster, and I felt a tingling sensation in my chest. Never had I been so drawn to a man. It was as if something inside me, some energy I had never knew existed, recognized something inside of him, and demanded to be one with him. My flushed cheeks felt hot and I lowered my eyes modestly, hoping to veil the palpable desire I felt for him. I remained like this for but a moment, regaining my composure. And then, inhaling deeply, I stood straight, and looked at my betrothed square in the face.

Yes, I was a virgin. Yes, I was a woman of piety and modesty. But he must realize now, from the very inception of our life together, that I was his equal, and would not be made to submit.

His eyes looked back at me with curiosity and confidence, analyzing the woman that was to be his bride and queen. His eyes, eyes that smiled with a mixture of playfulness and the sinister, that seemed almost ready to laugh, eyes that undressed me, and just as a swaggering smile spread across his freshly shaven face, he performed a low, respectful bow.

Yes, Este, es, este es. This is undoubtedly the one.

Three months had passed since the day we were united before God and man in holy matrimony. And just like that, I was in love. Entirely. All consuming love.

For so many years I was strong, confident, cold and untouchable, but there was always an emptiness inside of me. And now? Now, I realized that I felt whole. For the first time in my life, I felt complete. The yearnings of my heart were, in a word, satisfied.

Three blissful months before, we had said our vows and made our promise to God and to one another to share the rest of our lives together. That day, I felt all the fretful flushes of nervousness as I walked down the aisle, and even more nervous as the entire Court stood in our bedchamber to witness the consummation of the royal marriage.

It was a tradition no bride enjoyed, but one that must be endured, to see the royal couple to their marital bed, and then to display the bloodstained sheets. But Carrillo demanded more, and I could very well not refuse, no matter how ashamed I felt.

The archbishop insisted for prudence sake that the Court remain in the room in order to witness the act of consummation. That way, there could be no question as to the legitimacy of our children. More importantly, should a problem arise, Fernando would not be able to nullify the marriage or claim that the marriage was not consummated, like my brother Enrique had done with his first wife. The lesson I learned from Enrique's failure to sire a son with his first wife, Fernando's half-sister, had earned him the scorn of the kingdom, as well as the monicker of *el Impotente*, "the impotent one." After years of marriage, Enrique finally returned his wife to her father, claiming that she was as much a virgin as when he had married her. Carrillo would not allow such a fate to befall me.

As a girl, I only dared imagining such a moment when I was alone in my room. I had seen horses mate, and had even accidently walked in on Queen Juana's ladies with one of the king's grooms. When I had been promised to the king of England, I imagined what our first kiss would be like, what his mouth might taste like. Such romantic illusions were not to be my lot. The moment was not private, and without privacy, intimacy could not exist.

Since leaving my mother's house, no longer did I belong to myself. No longer was I a private citizen, my identity was as princess of Castilla y León, and now queen of Sicily. I must accept that my life belonged to the public.

Mortifying as the moment was, it had earned me the support of the people, and there was little doubt how greatly in need I was of their support. The efforts failed, neither Venier nor the archbishop of Toledo was able to garner the backing of the Pope. The papal dispensation never came. Chacón's fears were better founded than what I was willing to believe. But *el pueblo*, the people, I could depend on. The good people of Valladolid shouted our names at the wedding, witnessed our vows before a priest, and the holy consummation of our marriage. With promises of loyalty, *el pueblo* hailed us as their own.

"It is nothing to concern yourself with," Carrillo said, after having to inform me of the Pope's refusal. "It would have been ideal for his Holiness to provide a more recent dispensation, but not all is at a loss. Years and years ago, when you were a child and no one thought you to be of any political import, you were given a dispensation to wed Fernando. It will suffice. Your marriage is valid enough."

He stood before the crowd alongside the envoy from Aragón, Mosén Pierres de Peralta, with the document he declared as the papal dispensation in hand, and read aloud for all to hear.

"As long as we have the people's support, we need little else," Carrillo promised me. "Popes come to wear the crown with grey hair already atop their head. They come as quickly as they go. But your people… it is the love of the *pueblo* that we need most."

I left it at that. There was little more that could be done… Besides, my heart was so entirely in love with my groom, my Fernando, that I didn't want to spend my energy on problems that couldn't be fixed, at least not yet. Life was so beautiful, it was almost as if it were a dream, with no one else in the world other than just us two.

Married, and savoring all the throws of passion. But wealthy? Wealthy, we were not. I could almost laugh to myself at how little we, the children of kings, actually had. For a couple that was destined to one day reign over the kingdoms of Castilla y León, Aragón and Sicily, we were surprisingly poor. But wealth matters little to those so rich in love.

The more time passed, the more I grew to respect a man that was truly my soul mate — as if he were made from the very fabric of my being. We were so similar in so many ways. Just like me, Fernando was born from his father's second marriage. He had an older brother, the first-born son, who was meant to be heir to the throne. Just like me, Fernando grew up in a country ravaged by war and hostility. He, too, knew what it felt like to grow up feeling exposed, vulnerable.

From the moment I first laid eyes on him, I felt deeply connected to him. And as time passed, I found him to be a man who was truly a counterpart — a man of integrity and grit, a patriot who lived to defend his faith and protect his Church.

And just like me, he was a man of great scholarship. His mind was astute and dynamic. We could spend hours debating, challenging each other's opinions. His education was well-rounded, his father had seen to that. And his mother, God rest her soul, had made every effort to ensure her son was given an education that prepared him to one day rule his land, despite not being the first-born son.

Our conversations were rich, engaging. He could talk for hours about the growing popularity of humanistic debates currently being discussed in Rome, Florence, Naples, and other Italian kingdoms. He often quoted Petrarch, one of his favorites, and hoped to one day instill Petrarch's philosophies into the united kingdom we were creating together. And when he wasn't discussing philosophy, he regaled me with tales of adventure and battles.

I found myself enchanted. And I wasn't the only one. Fernando had the gift of charisma. He was a natural leader, invoking loyalty and devotion from his men.

The words of Cárdenas reverberated in my mind again and again. *Este es, this is the one.* Indeed, he was. For, my kingdom needed a leader that was both scholar and warrior, and I needed a partner that could inspire support for our cause. We would need him to muster all his charisma, for soon, I knew, there would be battles to confront, and men who needed leading.

And yet, though this man was loved by so many, there was one man that he could not get along with, Alfonso Carrillo, the Archbishop of Toledo.

The archbishop had, at one time, been Fernando's greatest supporter. Few had used their influence with such overwhelming effect to sway the Castilian nobles into casting their vote for Fernando, as Carrillo had. But things had soured between these two, and I didn't know how I could fix it. Carrillo demanded more and more control. Fernando disdained the power that Carrillo already wielded over us and the promises I had already made to Carrillo, for us all three to rule as one body.

With each passing day, Fernando pressured me to put Carrillo in his place, but he had no idea what he was asking. Carrillo had risked his life and the future of his ecclesiastical career for us. Time and again, the archbishop used all his resources to protect me and secure my future. And we still had so much need of him. The nobles of Castilla were still as untamed as ever, and I knew those who had supported my brother Alfonso were now securely in the camp of Enrique. Without Carrillo's financial assistance, we had nothing. Enrique had done everything in his power to cut me off from receiving any form of income. Most of the territories that should have been under my control were now under Enrique's, and the few towns that did declare loyalty to me were only held in place because of the tireless efforts of Gonzálo de Córdoba, Chacón, and his family. Even Valladolid wasn't safe for us. The city had been a refuge for long enough, but we knew we needed to leave.

Again, we would have to depend on Carrillo's connections. Again, it would be Carrillo who would ensure our protection.

Chapter XXIV
Dueñas, Spring 1470

Just as the first flowers bloom overnight with the coming of spring, a Court soon formed around us, a development that couldn't have been more natural. We were *the* royal couple, the future of Castilla. Young and beautiful, everyone wanted to be a part of the world we were creating. Courtiers were quick to flock to our Court in Dueñas, and just as soon as they swore their undying loyalty to us, they were busy finding ways to curry favor.

Such pleased my husband, reasoning that the growing size of our Court not only validated our position of power, it fed it. All eyes were on us, and as more and more came to us with promises of loyalty, others were galvanized to follow suit.

This growing popularity of our Court pleased me as well, though for me, I viewed this opportunity differently than Fernando. By keeping my nobles close at hand, I was afforded the unparalleled benefit of centralized power. It was a lesson King Enrique never learned. His mistakes would not be my own.

My husband took great care in the curation of our Court. We were creating a center, one that was young, cultured and elite. The prince of Aragón was a true man of the Renaissance, and as such, he wished to establish an environment that fostered the arts, painting, architecture, and philosophy that had spread from Italy into the rest of Europe, that we wished to now bring into Spain.

I shared the same desire — not only for the sake of the reputation of our royal identity, but also for the future generations we were to produce. I wanted my children to grow up surrounded by wisdom and culture, to be exposed to ideas and worlds unknown to our forefathers, to experience the magic of exploration like my grandmother did when she was a little girl, and for their minds to have the freedom to discover new possibilities.

"King Edward IV has won one victory after another. He is a warrior, and his soldiers are loyal to the death. Have no doubt that he will keep that crown atop his pretty head."

My husband stood surrounded by courtiers, listening as the others discussed one of the most polemic topics of conversation: the civil war taking place in England, the War of the Roses. Across the sea, England was in the thick of it, and in early March, the Plantagenet king of House York had won a resounding victory against young Henry Tudor of House Lancaster.

"Very well. We all know his prowess on the battlefield. But the question is," one of the courtiers countered, "will Edward be able to keep the throne? A chasm exists between warring and ruling."

"I, for one, doubt he will last," answered yet another voice. "After all, he is nothing but a pretender and has no right to the Crown. Besides, now that the earl of Warwick and Edward's own brother, Richard, have turned on him, I don't see how he has a leg to stand on. Edward is but the creation of Warwick, the 'King Maker' they call him. Without the support of the earl, Edward has no chance of keeping his rear seated on the English throne."

"I beg to differ. Edward IV is England's only hope. He rescued the kingdom from that Lancaster king, who was nothing short of an old madman. Surely you can't expect *him* to rule."

Fernando listened to the opinions of all the men, but added nothing himself. With my hands folded, I quietly stood next to my husband, listening. It was his opinion alone that I desired to hear.

"What say you, my lord husband?" I asked, stretching my neck to gaze up at him. He gave me a wink, then kissed me on the lips before answering.

"I believe King Edward is wise to rid himself of Warwick. The earl of Warwick is merely another Pacheco. He is greedy for power, and willing to have it by any means necessary."

"But King Edward means to forgive the earl of Warwick and bring him back into his camp. After all, the earl is a powerful man. Would you not think it good for the king to have his support?" I questioned, eager to hear my husband's perspective on a situation that was not dissimilar to that of our own domain.

"Warwick, Pacheco, Álvaro de Luna… the ambitions of such men know no bounds. They are favorites, the lot of them. They mean to rule over those whom God has appointed. I would fall on my sword before I let that happen to us."

"The Yorkist king is a fool to forgive," I agreed. "A man that is willing to betray you once must never be trusted again."

My husband smiled, as if approving of such an emboldened, unapologetic statement coming out of the mouth of his wife. He gave me his arm and led me from the crowd to a chair to sit and rest.

"Any word from your brother?" Fernando asked, sitting himself next to me.

"Nothing of yet, or else I would have told you, my lord," I answered, resting my hands on my swollen belly where my baby slept inside of me. "I've written him twice, and still, he does not respond." An anxious sigh escaped my lips. "I don't understand it. He is getting everything he wants. I promised him peace and power. All I ask in return is for him to honor his word, and to not rob me of what is rightfully mine."

"And what rightfully belongs to our son," Fernando added, placing his hand on my stomach. Then he leaned back against his chair, as if he wanted me to relax and do the same. "Peace, my love. Don't let these matters upset you. The baby needs you to remain calm." He reached up to stroke my cheek and rested his hand beneath my chin. "Perhaps you will have more success if someone intercedes on your behalf. Write to the conde de Plasencia. Ask the count to speak to King Enrique, to help him see reason."

I wanted so badly to make peace with my brother. And I knew that in his heart, it was what he wanted most too. But Pacheco was by his side, pouring poison into Enrique's ear, and the king's favorite was determined to make me his enemy.

"A game of cards?" Fernando asked me, gesturing to a small table where several friends from his inner circle played their hand.

"Another time, my darling. But you go, play for me."

He plucked a red rose from the bouquet and lifted it for me to smell.

My back was beginning to ache, but I maintained my posture as I sat in the chair. A royal was never permitted to appear tired or weak, even when pregnant. All eyes, I knew, were on me. And my eyes were on them.

As I scanned the room, my fingers toyed with the petals of the rose my husband gave me. The petals felt like velvet to the touch, and the stem was smooth and pleasant. A violinist paced through the room while playing. A woman's laughter mixed with the murmur of courtier's conversing. Rows and rows of thick, tall candles dripping wax and standing candelabras lined the halls, casting a romantic, ethereal glow.

With our marriage we built a Court, with this babe we built a family. Soon, we would build an empire. Distracted with all these thoughts, I hadn't noticed the sharpness of the rose's thorns until a warm sensation ran across my hand and down the length of my arm, forming warm drops of blood. The blood gathered into a small pool on the lap of my gown.

This is a promise, and a warming — the first drops of blood that will be poured out in the name of the Crown.

These words passed through my mind, but I didn't know where they came from. Was this some sort of foretelling? I didn't believe in gypsy's prophesies, those diabolical dealings of magic. But still, these words were not my own.

My mind raced, searching for their meaning. Could this mean war? Was Enrique remaining silent because he was planning an attack, when he found me vulnerable from pregnancy?

That last word, pregnancy, brought me back to my senses. The tightness in my chest relaxed. I could have laughed at myself. I was like an old woman, worrying about nothing and everything. The blood was not an omen of war on the battlefield, but instead for the war of the birthing chamber — a woman's war.

"Mi hijo," I whispered to the growing child inside of me, placing my hands atop my belly. "Everyone says you are sure to be a boy. They say they can tell by how great my belly has grown."

Our son's name had been chosen. He would be Juan, an easy decision. The name honored our fathers, both named Juan, both men being kings of their realm, but it was also the name of my patron saint, John the Baptist. In a name there was power, and in this one name, my child would embody the unity of God and country, of one united kingdom, Castilla y Aragón, protected under the wings of the Almighty.

"Again! I would play you once more," shouted Fernando's cousin peevishly, throwing his cards to the table.

"And I would win again," replied Fernando lightheartedly, unaffected by his cousin's antagonistic tone.

"Only because you cheat..." he retorted, his voice growing increasingly terse.

My jaw clenched. I stood, and the Court stopped and turned towards me, watching as I walked directly to my husband and placed my hand on his shoulder.

"You forget yourself, sir. It is the crowned king of Sicily and prince of Aragón you speak to," I said, my eyes piercing into my husband's relative.

"Forgive him, your Grace," the cousin's brother said, hoping to assuage the upset. "My brother meant no disrespect. His words were only meant in jest. Fernando, my brother and me, we have always gotten along thus. We are, after all, the king's blood."

My stare bore into him. "Blood," I repeated, unappeased. *That word finds me yet again.* "His Majesty, the king has no family, only vassals."

My voice was icy and fierce. The Court, nobles, princes of the blood, even the common folk — all would come to realize the weight and power of our title. Fernando and I were set apart. We had no equal but one another.

Soon enough, the others would dare not assume that familial ties meant familiarity. Every one of them would come to find that my husband was above reproach, by all but myself. Fernando would one day be king, I would permit no one to speak to him the way his cousin just had, and hope to keep his tongue.

Despite the growth of our Court, I understood that we lacked the support we needed to maintain a position of power. Such vulnerability made it even more imperative to protect an image of authority. Even slights made in jest would not be tolerated. The courtiers, I knew, would soon learn their place.

Even my pregnancy, though the source of our greatest joy, put us in danger. Every passing day that I was pregnant from a marriage that was not sanctioned by the Church meant that I was that much closer to giving birth to an illegitimate child. Pacheco would use this to hurt me, he was too sinister to make waste of a chance to tear away my support and strengthen Juana la Betraneja's claim to the throne.

I looked down at my stomach. "My prince. We will soon have our boy, and with him, all will be well," I whispered, and my fears began to subside.

As soon as my son was born, once the people saw that I had given birth to *el infante*, no longer would there be a question of loyalty. The throne would belong to our child, the sole legitimate heir.

I inhaled deeply, and raised my chin, feeling my body fill with confidence. Just as our Holy Mother Mary was chosen to give birth to Jesus, I had been chosen to bring this child to Castilla. And with his birth, the birth of the heir to the Trastámara dynasty, there would no longer by any question as to who has been appointed by God to rule this kingdom. With the birth of our son, our entire family would be secure, safe, indisputable.

Chapter XXV
October 1470

The rosy little hand wrapped around my finger, gently squeezing me tightly. And within the hand of my child, my first born, was captured my entire heart. Never, never, had I felt so entirely complete.

A daughter. The Lord had deemed it right that our first child was a girl. And what a beautiful child she was. We named her Isabel, just like me, like my mother, and my grandmother before her. This young babe would carry on the female tradition of the Trastámara legacy.

She was quick to discover her lungs, cooing gently with her sweet, sonorous voice, her eyes staring into my own, penetrating me, heart and soul. Holding her in my arms, it was as if I beheld the only thing in the world that mattered. Nothing mattered more than my child.

Now, more than ever before, was I determined to secure the throne, her throne. It was up to me to establish a safe future for my child, a future that would be so different than my own childhood.

"King Fernando desires your presence," said the servant, interrupting the moment I savored with my little girl.

The nursemaid came to take little Isabel from me, and the sweet, almost melodious rattle of her cry made it nearly impossible to leave the room. But I was not a country wife, and could not enjoy the pleasures of simply being a mother. There were matters that must be attended to, and my first duty was still to the kingdom.

I straightened the golden trimmed lace of little Isabel's blush silk gown, placed my hand on the bonnet covering the soft golden baby hair atop her head, and kissed my child once more before attending to my husband.

The wooden floor creaked as I entered the room, where I found Fernando waiting.

"Leave us," he commanded, without lifting his head from the pages spread before him. The servant bowed and silently closed the doors behind him.

"Forgive me for disturbing you. I would rather you rested, my dear. We've received news that requires your attention, but I beg you, please sit first."

The birth had been a difficult one, and the recovery slow. Fernando was constantly worried for my health, begging me to rest and heal, so we could start trying again for a son.

He handed a thick scroll to me, and I scanned through its message.

"Juana has been married to the brother of the king of France? But she is still so young, not even ten years of age," I said, horrified. The child was being given in marriage at far too young an age. She most likely hadn't even flowered yet.

Then, the political significance of the act sunk in.

"So then, Enrique plans to create marriage ties with the French."

"Keep reading," Fernando said, his eyes watching for my reaction.

I lowered my head and continued looking over the page.

"What's this? Dis... I've been disinherited?" I said to myself, my voice cracking.

France, the great enemy of Spain, had tied itself to the la Beltraneja. The child once named as illegitimate, Enrique now again claimed as his own.

"He has given a nine-year-old babe into the hands of the French," Fernando said. "Innocence in exchange for the force of armies."

My lips pursed, the way they always did when I concentrated.

"It's a move of desperation. Enrique is willing to do anything to keep me from claiming my sovereign right, even place the French on the Castilian throne. My kinsmen will never stand for it. Castilla y León will never rest with their crown atop a French head."

"The matter of your legitimacy is the present threat," Fernando said. "A public decree was made on behalf of the king just days ago in the Valle de Lozoya. You are no longer heir, nor are you a princess. Enrique has forbidden anyone to treat you as such. The repercussions of this, on our Court, on our child, her future…"

My blood began to boil. "How could he do this? To disinherit me, the last of his family!"

Fernando stood and paced the room.

"It must have been their plan all along, him and Pacheco. They meant to strong-arm you. Either do their bidding or be disinherited. Enrique is the only living male in your family; he has the power to do just that."

"Send for the archbishop. We need him present."

"No. We will handle this ourselves. From this time forward, I want him involved in none of our affairs."

I had seen this break coming. The two men had been increasingly at each other's throats for months. Despite my efforts, they refused to get along.

"We must apprise Archbishop Carrillo of this matter. Even if we don't take his advice, he must be included."

"To what ends? What benefit does it do us to include a man so hungry for control over us? The man only grows more demanding, and I refuse, *refuse,* to be ruled by anyone, especially Carrillo. Face it, Isabel, the archbishop has served his purpose, and can do no more for us. You've outgrown your need for him."

"If it were not for him, I would be married to the king of Portugal, or to another of my brother's choosing. The archbishop has done much for my cause, and I would reward his loyalty."

"Yes, reward him, however it please you, whatever he deserves. Yes, he has done much to ensure your success, but what good is any of it without the papal dispensation. He swore we would have that, and he failed. He failed us in the most essential task he was given.

Everything is worthless without that dispensation, Isabel. *Everything*. He swore that we would have that document, he told us to trust him. But he couldn't complete the one mission that we needed most. And now, you are disinherited and Juana is heir, married to the French and all their military power, who will gladly send their soldiers to our soil to claim the throne in Juana's name. And if that should happen, then it will be *me* who stands before you and the armies of France. It is time you place your trust in me, and end your dependence on Carrillo."

I couldn't discredit the truth in Fernando's words. As much as I wanted to include Carrillo and harness his power in my arsenal against Enrique, I no longer could.

Carrillo had stumbled, he had promised more than he could deliver. And his error could cost us everything. This time, I would depend on none other than myself.

This time, it would be through my own agency that we would be saved.

Chapter XXVI
March 1471

A single tear rolled down Beatriz de Bobadilla's rosy cheek and onto the pale hand that I held, as two old friends prepared to say goodbye. But the time had come, she had to go. Too much had taken place between Enrique's camp and my own, and with her husband Andrés de Cabrera standing staunchly alongside Enrique, it was no longer wise for her to stay here with me.

"I will feel quite alone without your company," I told her, doing my best to smile. "How shall I fair without the encouragement of my dearest friend and wisest counselor?"

"I do worry about leaving you here. Especially now."

She was right to be worried. Never had I found myself in such a vulnerable position.

"I'm not afraid, so you mustn't worry either. The Lord is on my side," I declared without a shadow of a doubt, either in my voice or in my being.

"I know you are not afraid. Nothing has ever shaken the courage of my iron-willed Isabel," she said, hugging me once more as the carriage pulled up behind her. "I'm just sorry to have to leave you here alone to deal with the little bickerings of those two," she added playfully, referring to my husband and the archbishop of Toledo.

"As am I," I laughed. I was relieved that we were saying goodbye on a lighter note.

I had hoped that leaving the home of the archbishop's brother and coming to stay at my husband's family home in Medina de Rioseco would have had more of an effect on Carrillo's insistence to exert his control. People were beginning to call him "el tercer rey," the third king, a moniker that only added to Fernando's frustration.

The rift between Fernando and Carrillo had only intensified with the passing of time. Carrillo felt entitled to a certain level of leverage over us, and expected my husband and me to obey his instructions. He had, after all, been one of the pivotal forces in advancing our cause and protecting me. But Fernando refused to be treated as if he were a child that needed to be guided by his father. He was determined to not let that happen, but insisted that Carrillo be "offered the carrot, not the whip," as he put it.

"Don't worry, all will work itself out, one way or another," Beatriz promised. "Still, I am sorry to have to say goodbye to you."

"Your foremost duty is to your husband. You must return to his side."

Beatriz looked down and smiled softly. "Just thinking of him warms my heart. Yes, I am ready to return to him."

"You are fortunate. Your husband is a wonderful man, greatly respected by so many. It's important that you return to him and to Enrique's Court now, so that you don't tarnish the trust that the king has in your husband."

Beatriz looked up at me, her eyes filling with tears. "I don't know when I will see you again." She inhaled deeply, and her eyes looked up at the sky, searching for an answer that wasn't there. "But before I go, there is something I have for you." Carefully, Beatriz slid an emerald ring, the shape of an octagon, set in a brilliant yellow gold, onto my little finger.

"I have had this since I was a child, and have worn it always. Rarely has it been off my person. This way, I will never be too far from you."

I ran my fingers along the edges of the emerald.

"Beatriz, you will always be with me, no matter the distance."

"And while I am away, I can promise you this. Although in Enrique's Court I may be, it is to you whom I remain loyal. And I intend to serve you still. Few have the ear of the king the way my good husband does. He wields a great deal of influence; I mean to make use of it. And so, even if I am not here with you, I will do everything in my power to help you. I will be your ambassador."

I took both her hands in my own, and did my best to seem confident. "Dear friend," I said, squeezing her hands. "You are a woman with an innate gift — you are a peacemaker. And I have no doubt that you will do everything you can to help me to build the alliances I need. And so, I kiss you farewell with the assurance of peace, knowing that you will be of greater service to me by being at Enrique's Court than by being with me here."

The driver gripped the reigns of the carriage, and the horses began their trot, moving further and further away from me, with my Beatriz inside. I gently ran my finger along the hand-cut edges of the green stone ring and felt my heart sink inside of my chest — the familiar pains of loneliness that plague me every time I must say goodbye. But there was little time to mourn when one of the greatest matters of State awaited me.

Turning on my heel, I headed towards the Privy Council, where my advisors waited. Immediately I felt the tension pervading the space, a tension I was growing more accustomed to.

The presence of such tension had been a constant in my life since the day Enrique pulled my little brother and me from our mother's house. Since the moment I was torn from her arms, I had come to learn how to survive within the rigidity that innately existed within the political. First, the tension I endured within the walls of his Court, a realm where I had no place. Then, the tension of the constant fear I suffered during a civil war in which my brothers faced off against one another. And now, the tension of finding myself at the head of a table of men who all thought themselves better and more capable of fulfilling the role that I alone could fill.

Yes, the presence of anxiety seemed to never leave my side. But now that I recognized it as such, I refused to let it stifle my path. No longer did I try to avoid the feeling of agitation and unrest, I now accepted it as a part of the world I existed in. For, my life was one of neither leisure nor submission, but of action, and to achieve the ends I aimed at, there would be more than a few rules that must change.

Still, the pressure caused my stomach to knot. But the smile on my face remained firm, a mask that revealed none of my true emotions.

"We will not behave too rashly," said Archbishop Carrillo to the others, as if he were leading the council. "The princess must come to the king in a spirit of serenity, of—"

"Serenity at such a time as this?" Fernando interjected. "That is your suggestion?"

"Isabel must appear as if she is in control, and not merely provoked by Enrique's actions," Carrillo insisted. Then, turning to me, he continued in a more leveled tone. "The king is clearly reacting from the offense of your choice to marry without his consent. His pride is injured. Your disobedience to his role as the male authority of your family, now coupled with what he views as your disregard of the agreement, prove your lack of respect for him. You have publicly embarrassed your brother and king." Turning back to Fernando, he said, "Nonetheless, just because the king has declared that Isabel is no longer a princess does not give her leave to behave without propriety. She must still behave in a regal manner."

"What then? Should our sovereign princess, the one true heir to the throne, beg on her knees for forgiveness, for the sake of propriety?" Chacón countered. His nephew, Cárdenas, shook his head in disagreement with the archbishop, while the lawyer sat quietly, absorbing every detail.

"I would sooner wage war on Enrique and his band alike," Fernando said.

"War, you say?" the archbishop scoffed. "Your father has all the forces of Aragón occupied now, does he not? And you mean to wage war now? When we've never found ourselves in a more vulnerable position? Friends abandon us, our foundation of support quakes beneath our feet, and you think of war. Have you no better suggestion?"

"You think you know what is best, but you lead us to yet another blunder," my husband retorted, his voice rising in frustration.

Carrillo stood up, insulted, and glared down at Fernando.

I stared with intent at the large rectangular table before me, then I closed my eyes and listened to this group of men, nobles arguing like hens.

A lone woman surrounded by men, all insisting they knew best, willing to convince her to do their bidding. My mind went back to Enrique's chess set, to that day at Court when Pacheco handed me the chess piece of the queen and deigned to provide me insight into the inner-workings of female honor. That little chess piece, the little wooden queen, surrounded entirely by men, all demanding to exercise their will over her — she alone understood what I felt at this moment in time.

My interaction with my advisors must, naturally, be one of respect, after all, their ego was a matter to contend with. Yet, while I valued their opinions, I was determined that the decisions must ultimately be my own, and must be guided by no other but myself. The chess piece of the queen may have the most limited movements now, but I would see to it that the rules of the game changed – for me, for my daughter, and for every female sovereign to come.

I raised my hand, gesturing for silence.

"My lords, I have specifically chosen each of you to act as my advisors, and with great reason, for there are few whose opinion I esteem more than your own. The archbishop speaks with reason," I said, to which Carrillo arrogantly lifted his chin, thinking I had obediently taken his side. "As you say, King Enrique has, in fact, refused to honor me with a response. He will no doubt continue in his abstinence," I explained, my voice low and stoic. "Now, he takes a drastic course, disinheriting me, and punishing anyone who would recognize me as heir apparent. Furthermore, Pacheco wants nothing more than to incite us to the point where our vision is blurred by our rage, and we react without foresight. He would welcome a war against us, especially now, when we lack the support we once held and will soon again enjoy."

Exhaling slowly, I leaned forward and, one by one, met the eye of each of my advisors.

"It is of my opinion that one must always be prepared to adapt to new circumstances. Too often, one follows along the well-trodden path of their forefathers and predecessors, but their recycled philosophies are outdated, irrelevant. Therefore," I said, turning to Carrillo, "I mean to take a… a less submissive course of action. A final letter will be written."

"*Princesa,* if Enrique has not honored you with a response while you were still heir, what makes you think he will now that you are effectively cut off from any royal privilege?" Carrillo pressed.

"This letter will not be written for the king. I intend it for a different audience."

Silence hung in the room, the men staring, waiting for me to continue.

"You say that propriety on the part of a princess is called for, and most certainly you speak truth. But the focus of our appeal, our audience, is no longer the king. The audience, my lords, is *el pueblo*. It is the public opinion that will turn the tide back into the Isabeline camp and win this war once and for all."

"*El pueblo*? Do you mean the powerless, uneducated peasants and laborers?" he questioned.

"You forget, sir, that the throne rests on the shoulders of the people, both our nobles and the common man. Without their support, the throne is nothing."

"You imply that it is the people who govern a nation?"

"God Himself appoints a king or queen to their office, but what authority does a ruler enjoy if he lacks the support of his people?"

"So, essentially you plan to use this letter as a form of propaganda," Cárdenas said.

"Considering the accusations and threats that Enrique has made, does the princess have another choice?" Fernando said in my support. "When in war, there is no time to pause, and there is no room for pacifism. And make no mistake, we are at war. We must act boldly." He placed his hand over my own, and I knew he understood the strategy behind my recourse was a war waged without arms.

No longer was I fighting solely for myself and the Trastámara inheritance. Now I was a mother. Now I fought for the inheritance of my daughter, and her children, the sovereign rights of my flesh and blood.

"Enrique means to disgrace Isabel as much as he, himself has been disgraced, after all those years of impotence and scandal," Cárdenas exclaimed. "But to gain the people's favor… it is exactly the response we need to check the king. Shrewd, indeed, my lady."

Chacón nodded his head in agreement. "Yes, the public," he said, as if he had been turning over the idea in his head while the others voiced their opinions. "It is *their* support we need. Let the public see Isabel as the princess she is, and Enrique will no longer have a leg to stand on. After all, Enrique drew the battle lines. He meant to disgrace Isabel before the eyes of the public by declaring your marriage as illicit and your child as illegitimate. They must be made to see you as the woman of royal birth who behaves with honor, and who will defend your birthright as the true *infanta*. They must see you as princess of your people."

"Make no mistake, I am fighting for the honor of Castilla, my honor, for I am Castilla. No longer is there room for silence. Now is the time that the king must be confronted," I said, my voice steadily and confidently rising. "This letter will behold all the injustice my brother Alfonso and I endured at the hands of the king and his queen. Let the people see how their king tore children from the arms of their widowed mother. Let them see that he placed children of royal blood into the hands of a venomous, lustful queen, a woman who would have loved nothing more than to steal away my inheritance so that her own bastard daughter, la Beltraneja, could take what is mine by right. Let the public see the reality of what I lived through."

"Hmm, yes, yes you are right," Chacón continued. "Create a contrast. Show yourself as the child of royal blood to Juan II - loving daughter, devoted wife and mother, pious princess. Create a comparison, and the public will do the rest. You will be a princess arrayed in dignity."

"A princess of dignity, yes. But you paint Enrique as a king of injustice. Do we dare risk portraying him as such?" Cárdenas questioned.

"It is a risk that must be taken. This is our one chance, an opportunity we dare not sacrifice. We need the public to grasp the full scale of the mistreatment of the princess," Chacón explained to his nephew. "The king's accusations and his sordid attempts to destroy her reputation must be confronted."

Here, the lawyer spoke. "The king uses law to disinherit Isabel, as he has the right to do up until she is twenty-five years of age," he explained, as if he were reasoning the argument to himself as much as to us. "But your allegations against him must be made known. He demands that the princess abide by a treaty that he himself was the first to dishonor, then was so bold as to treat her with contempt, as if she were a captive. Attempts were made to steal her inheritance, and to force Isabel against her will to marry the king of Portugal. And now, he has married Juana, a princess who only years before had been declared by her own father as illegitimate, to France, thereby placing a Frenchman on our throne... Such actions may prove to be devastating to the future of the kingdom. This, too, must be exposed to the public."

The archbishop finally spoke up. "Your counselor speaks true. The king has made his complaints public, your defense must be made public, as well, particularly that the choice of husband was not made by you alone, but was carefully considered and guided by members of the Castilian nobility, as opposed to Enrique's desperate and thoughtless decision to recognize an illegitimate daughter, declare her as heir, and wed her to France."

"King Enrique intends to portray me as a woman who defies the confines of the Church, who disrespects the authority of the king and the head of my household..." I turned their words of advice over in my head. "Your words are wise, my lords," I finally decided. "I do not wish to shame his Majesty. But the public must be made to understand *my* actions."

"And for that, the opinion of the *pueblo* must be shepherded," Fernando added. "Lead them to question his authority - how can Enrique dare to hold the princess to the promises made in Guisando when he breaks his own accord?"

"But there, you go too far. This letter is meant as a defense, not as an attack," I explained, in disagreement with my own husband, and I sensed Fernando's annoyance. "Enrique is the sovereign king, both mine and yours. I will not allow his sacred rights to be questioned. I aspire only to be heir of the throne, not to take his place."

"And how do you plan to dispel the statement that you did not receive dispensation, but instead fabricated a papal bull?" asked Chacón.

It was the most polemic issue I had to face. Nevertheless, it must be addressed. If I couldn't find a way to explain that my actions were in alignment with the Church, I was essentially declaring myself a fornicator and my child a bastard.

Unshaken, I lifted my chin proudly, refusing to be overcome.

"The Church was involved in my marital decision and vows. I have a clear conscience. My brother is not the judge in this matter, and when the moment arises that I should need to produce such documents, they will be available." The answer was vague, but there was no more that needed to be said. It was beneath me to go more into detail.

The table of advisors debated back and forth for hours about what subjects must be addressed, and how to present them in the most favorable light.

"Finally," I emphasized, just before pen met paper, "I want to make it clear, foremost to the people of Castilla, but also to my brother, that my greatest desire, and that of my husband, is for peace."

"Certainly, my lady. But the phrasing of this is pivotal. Despite our current situation, it must appear as if we are in a position in which we have the resources to defend ourselves, but that we *choose* peace," Archbishop Carrillo interjected. "Let it be made known that the choice of Juana as heir would only lead to more chaos, to more robbery and violence and death — a continuation of Enrique's feeble reign. Instead, to choose Isabel is to choose a future of prosperity, unity, justice."

"Above all," Cárdenas added, "order for our land and peace between brothers."

Indeed, he was right. It was essential that it be understood that this letter was not meant to anger, dishonor or challenge my brother, but instead was written in the name of harmony, virtue and integrity.

"For too long, this country has suffered from the vacillations of my brother's inability to make a decision. The kingdom sees him as a man who is easily manipulated, weak. It must be clear that I, Isabel, will rule with unwavering decisiveness."

"Should it not be worded in a way that portrays myself as the one who ensures justice?" Fernando interjected, looking from me to the others. "After all, I am Isabel's husband, already a declared king of my own lands. Perhaps it would make the public more comfortable to know that it is a male ruler who brings order to the throne."

"No," I answered, surprised to find myself voicing such defiant resolution in speaking to my husband.

Fernando frowned.

"I may be a woman, but it is me who is to rule over Castilla y León. And it will be myself, alone, who administers justice to my people."

Chapter XXVII
July 1471

The candles flickered, casting a soft light onto the small Bible on the desk. Again, I found myself on bended knee before the prie-dieu, whispering to God. My elbows and legs ached, though not as much as before, while at the Court of Enrique, where my prie-dieu was simple and plain, an object inspiring humility before God. The one I now used, made of ornately carved wood with gold detailing, was a wedding gift from Chacón, and was, in fact, used by Fernando and I at our wedding. Perhaps it was only fitting that I should be praying on our wedding prie-dieu now.

For months, my prayers were a repetition of the same monotonous words, begging God to bring my husband home to me, begging God to give me another child. One letter after another had been sent to Fernando, insisting on his return. Castilla had need of him. I needed him. His first duty was here. Every day our financial resources and friends grew more and more scarce, and everyday, I felt the weight of my travails bearing down upon my head.

And yet, here I was again, on my knees before the rising of the sun, clenching a rosary in one hand, and my husband's letter in the other. Fernando did his best to explain and innumerate his reasons why he could not yet return. He willed me to understand, Aragón was at war with France, and with his father in his eighties, Fernando, heir apparent to the kingdom of Aragón, had no choice but to fight. His eloquent words were lost to me. All I saw was his obstinate refusal to come to me when I needed him.

But today, these monotonous prayers for my husband's security and return were unseated by a letter that had recently arrived. The conclave had ended, and with it, a new Pope, Sixtus IV assumed the papal crown.

Today my prayers were for the soul of his holiness, Pope Paulo II, may he rest in peace, and for Pope Sixtus, the newly elected leader, chosen by God for His Church.

Slowly rising, my mind still absent, I paced my way towards my bedchambers.

"Chacón," I said to a servant. "Bring him to my chambers... I would speak to him in private." The servant bowed his head and obeyed.

The hour was still early, any other man's presence within the privacy of my quarters would have been wholly inappropriate, sure to put my husband into a rage. Chacón was an exception.

Once alone, I handed him the letter detailing the events taking place in Rome and the sacred ceremony crowning Sixtus IV as the new head of the Church. Chacón was a man of faith, he would understand the sense of loss I felt at the passing of our holy father. But to my great surprise, he clasped his hands together with a look of elation on his face.

"The Lord smiles upon you, princess," he declared. "We are saved!"

I stared at him, taken aback.

"I'm sure I have no idea what you mean, sir."

"We must send an envoy to the cardinal at once. He is one of us, a cardinal of our own homeland, Rodrigo Borgia of Valencia," he said, speaking to himself, then turned to me. "Cardinal Borgia is a Spaniard, and owes your family a great deal. Why, his family originally came to power within the Catholic Church by the help of your father's favorite, Álvaro de Luna. And his beloved uncle, Pope Calixtus III, God rest his soul, shared many of your values and objectives. It was Borgia, himself, who placed the crown on his Holiness' head. The cardinal is a young, ambitious man, and enjoys a great deal of favor in Rome. We must find a means of garnering his support for our cause."

I understood he meant for us to capitalize on the connection of our shared past.

"You mean to make Cardinal Borgia our man? But he is the same one who previously lent so much support to Pope Paulo, the same pope who refused me my dispensation and instead threw his favor to King Enrique."

"Rome has as thick a political web as any other Court. With a new pope come new loyalties. Enrique may have enjoyed the favor of Pope Paulo, but let us not assume that Cardinal Rodrigo would support Enrique's cause as well, or that he has any intention of continuing to do so."

My hand rested over my mouth, two fingers tapping against my upper lip, while I was in thought.

"All popes have ambitions, objectives they wish to accomplish during their reign. This one will be no different. Even men of the cloth have their appetites and aspirations — initiatives they hate to see unreached," Chacón continued. "Pope Paulo may have, at one time, favored Enrique, but he also had ambitions. He meant to defeat the Muslims in their war against the Faith, and expected more Spanish support than Enrique was willing to lend."

"Enrique's camp was well aware of the Vatican's displeasure at the scant support given by Castilla to aid in their holy fight."

"No doubt, Enrique's actions left them quite disillusioned," Chacón held. "The key here, Isabel, is to seek out what the Vatican most aspires to achieve. For Cardinal Borgia, answering that question is simple. You must remember the war against Islam has, for ages, been the great ambition of Borgia's family."

"I can still recall, when I was just a child," I said, "the great efforts Borgia's uncle, Pope Callixtus, threw behind the war against the Muslim advancement. It was just after the violence of the fall of Constantinople in 1453. Do you remember when he called for support?"

"Yes, and I remember you taking the little money you had and sending it to aid his efforts," Chacón said, with a proud, fatherly smile.

"Pope Callixtus' teachings were powerful, I often think back on many of his words. In fact, it was his efforts that paved the way for Joan of Arc to be recognized as a saint." I pressed against the back of my chair and stood.

"Pope Sixtus, to be sure, will be equally as enthusiastic about the war."

"We will send an emissary. Rome must know that my husband and I are wholly devoted to the papal cause, and that when I am queen, the Vatican can be assured of Castilla's unwavering support of the Pope's crusade."

The coolness of the water ran between the fingers of my outstretched hand as my horse, a white stallion, drank it in. I watched the animal savor the freshness of the water after the thrill of our ride, and my thoughts went to my husband. My hand instinctively reached for my pocket, my nails digging into the paper of the most recent letter he'd sent, my lungs fighting back the desire to cry out in frustration.

Again, he refused to oblige my request for him to return to me. Aragón was at war still, on the brink of overtaking Barcelona. Aragón needed him; he had no choice but to remain.

But there were no limits to Fernando's audacity. With the greatest insistence, my husband dared to suggest that I write to my brother, asking that Enrique name my husband as the king's heir to the throne, forfeiting my own position as heir apparent. Fernando held that our position remained vulnerable due to the anxiety Castilians felt at the thought of their future monarch being a woman, an anxiety that was only magnified by the fact that I gave birth to a daughter instead of a son.

The sound of a horse's hooves pounding hard against the Earth grew louder, interrupting my thoughts.

I counted the hoofs steps. One rider. Within a minute I identified the rider. It was Chacón.

He looked for a long moment at my face, then silently dismounted, tied his horse to a tree, then came and stood next to me. For a long while, he remained quiet, just keeping me company.

"How did you know I was here?" I finally asked, breaking the stillness of silence.

"Because I know you. I've known you your whole life. And when I saw you ride off by yourself after receiving today's mail, I knew something had upset you."

"I just needed a moment to myself," I stated, not wishing to discuss.

"Sometimes, when someone feels most alone, the kindest thing to do is just to be there."

He stared at the water before us, the sunlight sparkling brilliantly against the surface, and waited until I was ready to talk.

"Is it normal for marriage to be such a cause of frustration," I began, half-joking.

"You were too little to remember your parent's marriage, but yes, marriage can be..." he paused, searching for the right words. "Marriage is one of the greatest challenges God has chosen mankind to enjoy."

"But your marriage seems happy, satisfying."

"In many ways it is, but not all the time, and not right from the start. It took years for us to learn how to communicate with love and respect, how to talk in a way that the other would understand what we meant. It takes time for a couple to learn how to become, essentially, one flesh, as they say."

"One flesh," I scoffed with a mixture of contempt and disappointment in my voice. There can be no possibility of becoming one flesh when one is filled with as much ambition as Fernando. "My husband," I said, then, hearing the bitterness in my voice, stopped and checked myself. "My husband wishes to rob me of my birthright, to treat me as nothing more than a queen consort. I have no intention of letting that happen." My voice began to rise despite myself, and rage filled my being. "He means to treat me as if I am any other woman. Apparently, I am but one among the many that Fernando takes liberties with. Does he not know that I am well apprised of his infidelities? His behavior is notorious! Did you hear that he even parades his lover around the battlefield?! They say she dresses herself up, as if she herself is to go into battle." My eyes filled with tears, and I broke down crying. "How could I be so foolish. I knew he was a philanderer before I married him. How could I think that one woman would be enough? How could I dare to think that *I* would be enough?"

Chacón placed his hand gently on my shoulder, like a father comforting his child, and I turned to him and hugged him tightly.

"I know you are hurt. But I assure you, the prince loves you."

"How can you say that? How can he love me, and hurt me like this? How can he love me, and have another woman in his arms as he falls asleep at night?" As soon as I said this out loud, the image of my husband's infidelity filled my mind's eye.

"Men are of a different nature than women, especially men like Fernando. I don't mean to excuse him, but you yourself said you knew how he was before you married him. You are wiser than to think marriage will change a man." Chacón leaned back, breaking our embrace, and wiped the tears from my eyes. "Oh, Isabel, you place too great a value on fidelity. He is a red-blooded Spaniard, a prince and king. Such behavior can only be expected. But it doesn't mean that it is not you who reigns over his heart. You must understand, it is possible for a man to love his wife entirely, and still take a lover."

"But to flaunt his illicit affairs the way he does! To dishonor the vows we made before God, to expose me to such humiliation before the eyes of everyone ... If I would have known he would betray my trust, I would have never let myself open up to him the way I did."

For years, the walls of my heart were rigid. But when I met Fernando, I fell in love. My heart, foolish compass that it was, guided me poorly, promising me that he would protect it, and with this promise, the walls of my heart tumbled down.

"The first fruits of heartbreak are always the most painful. Once you have overcome their sharp stabs, you will realize just how resilient you are."

"His disloyalty is nothing compared to his shameless ambitions. He dares to think that I would step down, and name him as heir. He means to make me submit, as if I am nothing more than a housewife, and not the daughter of Juan II and *infanta* of Castilla y León."

"I know you are hurting, and I understand you are angry, but you must not forget that you love Fernando. There are times that we, all of us, must give grace and forgiveness to others. Even more so when we never receive an apology."

Chacón's dispassionate reasoning forced me to regain control, and soon my thinking gave way to better analyze my husband's actions. I had been begging Fernando to return to me for months. And despite my pleas, he insisted on staying by his father's side to help with the war effort. Why? Fernando knew as much as I did that we needed to try again for a son, that we were vulnerable until the kingdom enjoyed the security of a male heir to one day inherit the throne. And yet, he refused to come to me.

And then it all became clear.

By withholding the possibility of having another child and perhaps giving birth to a son, Fernando was making himself the only option of a male to inherit the throne, even superseding his wife and daughter.

My rage again seethed inside of me, and still, I would not allow Fernando's sin to be my undoing. A fractured marriage, as King Enrique and Queen Juana had learned, was impermissible. I could not allow myself to commit the same error. The public must see Fernando and me as the adoring royal couple. Despite the reality of our marriage being far from ideal, it was imperative that we were perceived as such. All eyes were on us, and I knew this pressure would only grow greater still as our marriage acted as the example for the entire realm. In order to come to rule and exercise power, my husband was an essential piece of the puzzle. Taking hold of my temper, I forced myself to put my bitterness aside, a decision that was not founded in grace and forgiveness, as Chacón might have wished, but instead for necessities sake.

My right to rule was my inheritance, mine alone. I refused to surrender that claim simply because I was a woman. I may not be able to project myself as equivalent to a king, but neither would I allow my husband to act as Head of State to a kingdom that was not his.

There was but one solution: to create a reality. A marriage could be fashioned, perceived as one of unity and equality, of a man and a wife, fulfilling their traditional roles and sacred marital duties. The crown would rest on both of our heads, but it would be the queen alone that maneuvered the pieces of *this* political chessboard.

My jaw set and I gazed into Chacón's eyes. "You are right. I love Fernando, I do. And more importantly, I need him. Our strength is in our unity. And that is exactly what Castilla will see."

Chapter XXVIII
February 1473

Five representatives were dispatched, all hailing from the Vatican, all armed and equipped with the power of the Pope. Rome had sent out envoys to travel throughout Europe, papal bulls in hand, ready to negotiate and absolve whatever issues needed absolving in order to secure support for the Pope's war against the Turks.

Soon, the famous vice chancellor, Rodrigo Borgia, would be arriving on Spanish soil. Archbishop Carrillo successfully arranged for Cardinal Borgia to honor us with his presence at Carrillo's estate in Alcalá de Henares, and as soon as the visit was confirmed, there had been no end to the lavishness in which the archbishop of Toledo planned to welcome him.

Carrillo, a man who typically was thought to be careful with the management of his wealth, willingly spent a small fortune to pay for the preparations and entertainments of the Spanish cardinal, even going to such lengths as to involve himself in every detail of the planning. To properly welcome Cardinal Borgia, Carrillo saw fit that at least ten additional menservants and a handful of kitchen staff would be needed, insisting on new liveries being made for all the staff. He ordered his finest silver flat wear to be laid out, new candles purchased, and his estate to be groomed from top to bottom. Likewise, as the cardinal had gained somewhat of a reputation as... no one would dare call a man of the cloth a hedonist, but he certainly was a man that appreciated life's luxuries, Carrillo made sure to curate an impressive selection of vintage wine and exotic delicacies.

The arrival of his Eminence was as grandiose as Carrillo's preparations. Nobles and villagers from all around gathered in the streets with hat in hand, just to see with their own eyes the Spanish cardinal. Little children sat on father's shoulders, while others wiggled through the crowds to watch the procession.

When the cardinal descended from the horse-drawn carriage, Carrillo, not surprisingly, was the first to welcome him, making a show of kneeling and kissing the ruby cardinal ring. I couldn't recall ever seeing Carrillo so eager to impress, though I could at least guess why. There was opportunity in this alliance, and not merely for the betterment of my cause. Carrillo had always been a man of ambition. Should he gain the favor of Cardinal Borgia, there may be a promotion, even a cardinalship, in his future.

For me as much as for Carrillo, possibility and future lay in the balance, all depending on this one man. If only I could find a moment to speak with him in private. But try as I might, Borgia had little free time, and was very seldom by himself.

There had to be a way. I was determined to find a moment alone, without interruption or distraction, so that I might win him to my cause.

And so I waited, watching for my opportunity. The cardinal's afternoons were nearly entirely occupied with one interview after another. But once the heat of the day broke, the interviews concluded and the cardinal had the habit of taking his rest. Dismissing my ladies, I made my way to the outside rooms where I knew he would be, hoping to find him alone.

I found him in his armchair, silent, as if meditating, his hands opened, palms facing the sky, his eyes closed, his face reaching up towards the heavens. The moment looked so intimate, and the cardinal so pious, I almost turned to leave.

His eyes gently opened and he turned his head towards me, smiling warmly.

"Forgive me," I began, and bowed with deep reverence. "I do hope I am not intruding."

"Princess Isabel, what a pleasant surprise." His voice was lighthearted and charming. "Do come sit. It is rather lovely this time of day, don't you agree? It is during these moments of solitude that

I find my peace. It is peace that sustains and strengths me. This peace is God."

I remained silent, in awe.

"It is kind of you to join me. I was hoping that you would come to me before my time here is complete."

"Thank you, your Eminence. My husband sends you his warmest regards," I began, trying to find how to begin. "He was greatly honored by your visit to his home in Aragón last May, and still regales me with the pleasure he took in conversing with you."

Indeed, Fernando was entirely enthralled by Cardinal Borgia, and it was small wonder why. Borgia was a man of culture and charisma. He could discuss any manner of subjects, from poets and artists to theological debates. He was as much a scholar as a man of the Renaissance, all of which attracted Fernando to him. And like my husband, Borgia was known to have a taste for beautiful women, which had gained the cardinal a salacious reputation.

"My stay in Aragón was one of my most pleasant experiences in all of Spain. It would have been delightful to remain longer. Alas, there is too much to be done in too short a time, and my duty is to Rome. Still, it pleased me well that Fernando troubled himself to arrange an encounter once more, after my having left Aragón. He spoke with great passion and conviction of the matter of Castilian succession. I understand you are satisfied with his Holiness, the Pope's blessing."

"Good cardinal," I said, my words replete with emotion, and I leaned closer to him. "I have sought a private word with you for just this reason. I beg you to accept my gratitude for your great efforts in securing the papal bull for our marriage. The dispensation and support of his Holiness has brought me the greatest relief. I am aware that your efforts were essential in bringing this to fruition, and hope there is some way that I can repay you."

Cardinal Borgia clasped his hands together, and the luxurious red fabric of his robe nearly hid his pale sturdy hands.

"The Pope is aware of your commitment to the Faith. He envisions you as the future of this most Christian nation," he stated with his usual frankness.

I bowed my head in acknowledgment of such a profound compliment.

"I am but a humble servant of his Holiness," I said with deep reverence.

"The Vatican is greatly disturbed by the growing power of the Ottoman Sultan Mehmed. Since the devastation he brought upon Constantinople, Christendom has failed bitterly in its efforts to rebuke the sultan's advances. Have no doubt, the infidel victory has been devastating. Greece, Serbia, Hungary, Anatolia, Austria, all fall victim to this enemy of the Faith. So crushing is his blow that our cities surrender to him before he even begins an attack, and still, he beheads those that don't convert to his faith, then enslaves the rest." His face twisted with disgust. "I cannot tell you how many Christian girls suffer from debauchery in his harems, and how many Christian boys are enlisted into his troops as slave-soldiers. Now, he fashions himself as 'Caesar,' and dares to claim that he will forge his way into Rome to put an end to the Faith."

"Our Lord God will never allow that to happen," I answered impassioned, but a shudder ran down my spine as I envisioned this threat to the Church. The repercussions of the fall of Constantinople continued to plague those of the Christian faith, and after so many defeats at the hands of the Muslims, many Christians feared our Church might be nearing extinction.

The cardinal smiled and nodded his head, steadily maintaining eye contact with me. "Our sources inform us that he plans an attack against Western Europe, and has done much to prepare his navy. Strategically, for the sultan to attack by sea, he will need access to a Mediterranean port. Therefore, the ties between Sultan Mehmed and the Muslim kingdom of Andalucía make Castilla dangerously vulnerable. It is highly probable that your kingdom will soon become his next target as the enemy inches closer to Rome."

"My land is incessantly plagued by their destruction. Each year the Castilians endure violence, raids, and devastation by the Muslims of Granada. As you say, their victims, my own countrymen, are forced into slavery, our noblewomen into their harems. I cannot express how eager I am to assist the Vatican in their efforts in the crusade against Islam."

"And make no mistake," he emphasized, his voice growing solemn, "our holy war against the Islamic threat that proceeds to infiltrate the Spanish Peninsula is nothing short of a Crusade."

"This would never have been possible if our kingdom was united instead of suffering revolts and wasting energy and resources fighting against one another. I wish for it to be known, my husband and I consider it to be the Crown's responsibility to protect our people."

"I have no doubt that you, young princess, do not lack the determination to defend the kingdom better than his Majesty, King Enrique."

This was the sign I had been waiting for, proof that I had Cardinal Borgia's favor, and with him came the support of the Vatican. Once I had won this, there was little more I would need.

"Thank you, father. You can be sure that Fernando and I will bring the kingdom to heel under the unity of our Crown, and once our brave countrymen band together, the infidel will no longer be able to breach our territory."

A servant came forward and poured wine from a pitcher into a cup for the cardinal, then took a few paces back to his place against the wall.

"Nothing grants me more satisfaction than serving the Church," I continued. "And you, Cardinal Borgia, have done more for me than I can ever repay. But there must be something my husband and I can do to thank you." I was eager to discover the desires of the Pope's man. I knew men like Cardinal Borgia, men with enormous power, but never enough. "Certainly, you have personal endeavors."

Borgia did not answer, but stared at me with his steady gaze, a peaceful smile resting on his face, waiting to hear what I might offer.

"Your Eminence, you may be aware of the profound respect I had for your uncle, Pope Callixtus III. His holy devotion to the Church will forever be memorialized in my heart. And my husband and I have been aware of your growing leadership during the past few decades, your support of papal projects such as the construction of the Sistine Chapel and the Vatican Archives. But these will not be remembered as *your* accomplishments. I would imagine you must have desires for your future as well. It would do us great honor to assist such a devoted servant of God in whatever way possible. And so, to support you and to show our loyalty, I would like to offer you provinces in your beloved Valencia. Spain is your *patria;* we give you our unwavering royal friendship."

Leaning forward, Cardinal Borgia spoke with pious intimacy. "Doña Isabel, I am deeply touched by your sentiment. I have spent many years serving in Rome, but yes, Spain will always be my home. But before you can grant gifts such as land holdings, you must secure your position. The Pope's desire, as is mine, is that Spain is at peace. I am burdened by the volatility of its past, and I want to ensure stability for its future. I have spent several months here in the Spanish Peninsula, and the land is overtaken with poverty and crime. Your citizens suffer robbery and violence, and entertain little hope for justice."

"I can promise that Fernando and I share this same desire, a hope for peace in a kingdom ruled with justice."

A smile of approval rested on his face. "Might I offer my suggestion? A few months ago, I met with Pedro Gonzáles de Mendoza, Bishop of Sigüenza. It is *his* support you require in order to realize your ambitions."

"Mendoza?" I replied, skeptically. "But he is one of Enrique's greatest supporters. The bishop comes from a family that is staunchly loyal to Enrique, as they have been to all the kings of

Spain. I fear that he would see any support he were to give me as being unfaithful to his king and a betrayal to his own family legacy."

"It is true, his family takes great pride in their reputation of devotion," he countered. "But one must remember, there is always room for negotiation."

"Forgive me, but I don't see what I could offer him. He has already received the bishopric and enjoys such a degree of power over Enrique that he is known as the 'third king.'"

"Months ago, in September, Bishop Mendoza met with me on behalf of King Enrique. The bishop indeed is eager to serve his king, and came to me seeking the Vatican's support for Enrique's cause. But my loyalty is, of course, to God and to the man God has set apart from all other men to lead His flock: his Holiness, the Pope. Unfortunately, the Pope has found Enrique's energy in his crusade to be lacking. He is displeased with the scandal his behavior has provoked. But I see that you, young Isabel, you have the piety necessary to lead your country closer to God and the wisdom to garner the support from the right people. Before returning to the Vatican, I plan to meet once more with Mendoza." He leaned forward and gave a wink. "I may not be able to solve the great matter of Castilla's succession for you, beautiful Isabel, but I certainly can help set the course in motion."

My thick velvet cape fought back the winter's grizzly chill and I pulled the fur-trimmed hood off, letting my golden locks drape behind me. The air nipped at my nose and cheeks, still I waited outside, as was appropriate, to welcome my husband and his men home for Christmas. The pounding of hooves came to a halt, Fernando in the lead, a pack of men behind him. Swinging his muddy boots over the saddle, my husband leapt with ease to the ground, bending to one knee and kissing my hand. Then, looking into my eyes with that same roguish smile I remembered from the first time I saw him, he stood, took me into his arms and kissed me, there in front of everyone. I kissed him back without hesitation. But my heart still seethed with rage and hurt.

My anger would have to wait until we were alone and away from the prying eyes of the Court, until I could purge myself of all my wrath caused by his ambition, all the heartbreak provoked by his lust. But when we were alone, it no longer mattered if my raised voice sent the tongues of the courtiers wagging. I refused to allow my husband to think he could behave with such disrespect for our marriage.

Finally, once the embers of my rage simmered to a kindle and my tear-stained cheeks dried, Fernando begged my forgiveness. He swore that he would never lack such discretion again. I wanted to slap him, to make him swear that he would never betray me with another woman again, but such an oath from a man like Fernando was an oath that would soon be broken. He offered discretion, and I knew that this was the most I could expect of him. He was a king, and a king of Spain. He would be no different than all the others like him, kings that sired their heirs off queens and sired their bastards off lovers. I must accept that he may not love me the way I wanted to be loved, but he did, in fact, love me.

But now? Now we must try for another child, and I wanted the child to be born of the love between two parents and not merely a sense of duty to one's husband and nation.

Anger soon gave way to passionate embrace, and in that moment, my pride and hurt no longer mattered. All I wanted was him — his touch, his taste, his lips.

My husband was home, but soon would be away once more. I refused to allow this short moment in time we shared together to be lost. Such a choice was made not for love of him, but for love of myself. Anger, forgiveness, rage, hurt — the ugly faces of all those emotions were cloaked in darkness and forgotten, at least for this one fleeting hour of marital bliss.

Feeling the warmth of his rugged skin against mine, relaxing in the security of his outstretched arms, breathing in his masculine scent, it was as if I could let go of everything for the first time. No longer must I be the princess, the warrior, the heir. When I was with my husband, I could simply be a woman.

"You are even more beautiful than the last time I say you," he said as he gently ran the back of his fingers along the curve of my back.

I brushed the long locks of rose gold curls over my shoulder and, resting my head on my hands, I turned to face him. "Your memory betrays you. You've been away too long."

"Anytime away from you is too long." He kissed my shoulder, then leaned back against the pillows with his hands supporting his neck. "The poem by Don Manrique reached me while I was still in Aragón."

The works by Gómez Manrique, the leading poet of our Court, had gained a great deal of notoriety, but I knew that the poem my husband referred to was the one in which Manrique portrayed the deep sense of solitude I felt without my husband, and the lack of joy of life's pleasures when he was absent.

"I would that I could stay," he continued.

"You have a duty to your father. No one understands that more than me. If I did not, I would refuse you leave."

He sighed deeply. "If I could but be everywhere at once, here with you and there, leading the battle…I do not wish to leave my home without its owner."

Traditionally, the role of the husband was to lead his household, but because of the war in Aragón, the heavy weight of the responsibilities fell to me. For some time now, it was me, and not my husband, who must negotiate, respond and react. The burden was crushing at first, but soon I learned to adapt. Still, it was not wise to appear as though his household were run at the hands of his wife, and efforts were made to give Fernando opportunity to lead, even if only for appearance sake.

"Before you set off again, we really must come to a decision on what to do with Cardinal Borgia's suggestion," I began, presenting him with the Mendoza dilemma. "I fear I have no choice but to obey the cardinal, but really I don't see how it could be possible. House Mendoza places great weight on their legacy of loyalty to the kings of Castilla. It's doubtful they would ever defy king Enrique."

"Then don't make him," he replied, as if it were the simplest thing in the world. I stared back at him, and he laughed at the seriousness in my expression. "The trick is, avoid making Pedro Mendoza feel as if he must choose between you and the king. It's nothing more than a matter of presentation. Mendoza can still be entirely loyal to his king. Their House can continue in their tradition of loyalty to the Crown while supporting you as the next in line to the throne."

"Hmm. And how do you suggest I bring him under my banner? What have I to offer that Enrique hasn't already given?"

"Exactly the question to ask. You're right, the Mendoza family has lands and wealth, the king has seen to that. But what is it that they do not have, that would not only bring glory to the individual, but to his entire family?" My husband's dark eyes stared intently at me. "Greatness. Glory. Give them prestige like they've never tasted. Present the Mendozas with the cardinalate of Castilla. Make Pedro Mendoza a prince of the Church. Then, I can promise you, they will serve under your banner."

I shook my head. "My love, I could not make that offer. Such a privilege should be given to Archbishop Carrillo. A cardinalship would be a natural progression to his career, and I mean to reward him for his years of loyalty to me. I couldn't possibly take that away from the archbishop."

He shifted his position. "That man has taken advantage of us when we needed him most."

"I admit, he is a man of great ambition, but he also serves to his best capacity."

Fernando lowered his chin and looked up at me. "It's more than ambition Isabel, it's avarice. Everything he does, he does to feed his own greed. He means to rule us, just as Álvaro de Luna and Juan Pacheco ruled every man in your family, from your father to your brothers. And I have no intention of letting that happen."

I stood up, pacing the floor and gathering my thoughts. Years ago, I had sworn that Pacheco would be the last of the favorites. But now, I came to discover just how much control I had placed in the hands of this courtier who was slowly evolving into a favorite in his own right. The power he exercised needed to be brindled, and yet how could I dare abandon him after so many years of loyalty?

"Carrillo has been devoted to my cause, to my brother King Alfonso's cause, since the beginning."

"But you must ask yourself, how much more can he do for us? He has served his purpose. You have outgrown him. But Mendoza? The support of Bishop Mendoza brings with it the support of his entire House — one of the most powerful families in all of Spain. Obey Cardinal Borgia's advice," he proposed, and kissed my neck. "You will not regret it."

I knew my husband was right. And yet I felt deeply conflicted knowing that I was going to disappoint a man who had done so much to ensure my safety and success.

Fernando turned on his side and looked into my eyes. "Consider the man that we know Bishop Mendoza to be," he argued, tackling the issue from another angle. "His reputation of piety and kindness proceeds him. A cardinal must not be chosen merely based on which of our subjects we deem to honor, but who can best serve his flock. A cardinal must be both a shepherd to the people and a prince of the Church, and will one day be among the college who elect the pope. Such an honored ecclesiastical role must not be underestimated. It would be unwise for us to place such power into the hands of the Archbishop of Toledo. You and I both know the man who will best serve both you and your kingdom to be Mendoza."

Spring, 1473

Again, Fernando was gone. Again, his father needed him. The war in Aragón raged on, his banner men called, and their prince answered.

Again, I found myself alone, with nothing but my youthful shoulders to help me bear the weight of responsibility. My husband could see how these burdens bore down on me, and more than once voiced his concern for leaving me in "a house without an owner," as he phrased it. But time passed, I grew accustomed to managing on my own, and was soon beginning to see that our house was not without an owner. The owner of the house was, in fact, me.

For nearly two years my husband had been absent, only returning to Castilla for brief interludes. His father's war seemed to drag on and on, pulling my husband away from Castilla when I needed him here. It was useless to complain, I told myself. There was much work to be done, and I needed to continue to press forward.

Meanwhile, the environment in Castilla had gone from bad to worse. Looting, rape, violence, and theft broke out in various towns and cities throughout the kingdom. The citizens called for justice, but no one knew what that meant anymore.

Beatriz de Bobadilla and I were in the habit of sending correspondences to one another each week. It was a small comfort that made the world feel not quite so lonely. One of Beatriz' letters had just arrived. She told of the recent weddings, baptisms, the card games played, the change in dress by the ladies of Court, and other events and incidents that took place at the Alcázar, where her husband, Andrés de Cabrera, held the esteemed position of treasurer. Cabrera was growing increasingly concerned with the state he found Segovia to be in. Most recently, her husband discovered merchants using counterfeit currency. The merchants claimed that they knew no better than any other man that the money was false. Still, the citizens were outraged and rioting ensued. The town shouted for the king to return the land to lawfulness and rectitude.

To make matters worse, the countryside was split by religious strife. The Jewish converts to Christianity, known as *conversos,* endured one violent encounter after another at the hands of the Christians. Again, no justice served, no punishment rendered. Without a ruler to establish authority, the people took matters into their own hands. Another pillar of stability wobbled and fell, replaced by anarchy. The last few shreds of the good Castilians faith in the authority of their king withered away.

The favor I had secured with Cardinal Borgia afforded me greater confidence in my own abilities. But I still had much terrain to traverse before my position was secure. Borgia's counsel was wise, and I had little doubt that Mendoza and his clan would back my cause soon enough. But even this achievement wasn't enough.

One more man was needed, Andrés de Cabrera, the husband of Beatriz de Bobadilla. But gaining his support would be an even greater feat than it had been to bring Bishop Mendoza to my side. Cabrera was a man of great integrity, a loyalist to Enrique through and through. Enrique more than valued Cabrera, he treated him with respect. He treated him as a friend.

My mind scanned through the men who could act as envoys to treat with Cabrera. That required careful consideration. An envoy's poor presentation, an ill-stated word perceived as an insult, any number of things could displease Cabrera, resulting in the failure of the mission. And failure was unacceptable. To achieve my purpose of redeeming our kingdom through reuniting our family, Cabrera was an imperative piece. Once Enrique realized that I had the support of the Vatican and the most powerful families in the realm, he would have no choice but to relent. Or so I hoped.

The dealings with Andrés de Cabrera could only be entrusted to someone who was both worthy of my confidence and Cabrera's esteem. There was but one man who came to mind: Alonso de

Quintenilla. He was sent for immediately, with orders to bring Cabrera into our camp, whatever the cost.

Meanwhile, there was still more work to be done. Despite Enrique's efforts of undermining my honor, he had done me the service of making my name one of the most discussed subjects in Christiandom. This attention would be put to good use.

Lavish entertainment was a cradle to diplomacy, and I wished to forge and foster better political relations. Dignitaries were invited and royals dined, all honored guests within our walls. Our Court was young, charming, and cultured, leaving both diplomats and princes enchanted. No stone was left unturned, even those that might be considered enemies were desired as friends. I even wrote to King Louis XI, despite the war between France and my husband's kingdom of Aragón, and offered the hand of my young daughter, Isabel, to the *dauphin*, Charles.

I wrote and wrote and continued to write.

One by one, the ink of my quill stretched its reach like a spider's web into the hands of one nobleman after another. Perhaps their reception of my endeavors would be hesitant, even cold, at first. Such was expected. After all, my younger brother Alfonso had nearly dethroned the seated king, and as far as Enrique was concerned, I was illegitimate, not even a princess. Perhaps they feared that communication with me might reap the displeasure of the king. I understood that many of these men hesitated before responding to me. And still, I wrote, intending for nothing more than that these first letters would serve as a means of breaking down the stigma against me.

One by one, the letters were sent, and one by one, I waited patiently for their response. And slowly, one by one, the nobles wrote back, just as I knew they would.

Certain members of the nobility required more assuaging than others. That was fine. All I asked was an opportunity to dispel concerns against me.

Some were surprised to find that they were, essentially, being pursued by a princess instead of by my husband. Fernando had not the authority to bestow the gifts of land and titles. Such were the rights that I alone was entitled to, as was in accordance with the marital agreement between my husband and myself. Once the promise of land, titles, and future reward for their loyalty was given, they were appeased. Either way, they came around, nearly every last one.

Yes, the eyes of the Castilians were fixed on me. And what did they find? The image of a sovereign in her own right, one that could engage in foreign policy as easily as domestic affairs, that was ingrained in the affairs of the people, that sought to form ties amongst the nobles and heal our fractured realm.

"Señor Alonso de Quintenilla," the servant announced.

"*Doña Princesa,*" he said with respect and solemnity, then leaned forward and bowed. Quintenilla, among my most devoted subjects, had been at my side for years. Nevertheless, he always insisted on treating me with reserve and respect, reminding me that I was the master and he the vassal.

"It is good to see an old friend." I stood and walked towards him to greet him, then reached out both of my hands to take his in my own.

"I hope not too old," he chuckled jovially. "Though I do admit, I am getting a touch grey around the ears."

"Please, sit," I invited, and motioned to the seat before me. "We have much to celebrate. You are deserving of the highest of congratulations. You did exceedingly well."

Señor Quintenilla gently bowed his head in acknowledgment. "It may have taken several months and many trips to fair Segovia, but I am quite pleased that Señor Cabrera finally saw the light."

"Your service in this matter has been invaluable. Fernando and I feel much relieved that this is now complete. The negotiations may have taken longer than expected, but I am certainly glad that you arrived in Segovia when you did."

"As am I. Time was essential in order to execute this mission properly. For, not only do we now have Andrés de Cabrera in our camp, but most of the Court is coming around as well, and I dare say it is only a matter of time before the king, himself, comes to see reason."

"How is my brother, the king?"

"Unfortunately, my lady, his Grace seems… weathered. At times he looked as if he had surrendered the last of himself, and life could simply do with him as it willed. Ruling a nation that finds itself constantly in the midst of religious and economic upheaval is taking its toll on his Majesty."

I shook my head, sorry for the sadness that I knew Enrique felt.

"I'm sorry that my brother has had to endure all of this. Such will mar the memory of his reign."

"Indeed, the entire Court is saying just that. In fact, not long after my arrival, it seemed that the courtiers immediately recognized me as 'the princess' envoy' and privately sought me out to discuss what your plans are and where you stand on matters of religious conflict. Many are calling you the 'redeemer of Castilla.' They say you are sent from God to save our kingdom from ruin."

This was not the first time I had heard the nickname bestowed upon me. The title of "redeemer of Castilla" was spreading throughout the country and even into neighboring lands. The realm saw her wounds and knew she needed the healing of redemption, but such redemption would only come through first bleeding out and purging the nation of its impurity.

"The religious strife is a problem that is only growing more worrisome," I said in agreement.

"Just so. Andrés de Cabrera was of the same mind. This violence has left the man quite shaken. Though he has a reputation as a man of integrity and piety, he is still a *converso*, and fears that since his family has only been a member of the Catholic faith for less than a century, he will fall victim to the hands of violence. With the brutality against the hundreds of *conversos* in Córdoba in March, followed by the assaults against the *conversos* in Sevilla, he was devastated to see that the king failed to bring the perpetrators to justice. Cabrera, as well as the others, recognizes that you have distinguished yourself from Enrique in this sense. Not once have you wavered in your resolve. When you say you will do something, your words are not in vain. They applaud your decision to honor your brother as sole ruler, your resolve for peace, your feminine virtue and grace. You, young princess Isabel, have won the heart of your people."

I stood up and clasped my hands. "How can I thank you enough. Just as I promised Señor Cabrera the marquisate de Moya, I promise that your efforts will be remembered. Simply name your reward."

Chapter XXIX
Spring 1473

By the end of the spring of 1473, I was to witness the enormously important procession in which Mendoza was given the cardinalship. After the solemn morning Mass service, the march of little children all dressed in white, followed by the priests dressed in black made their way through the streets as the Segovians stood in a crowded row, waving their hats in their hands. Behind them came the freshly titled Cardinal Pedro Mendoza. I saw to it that Beatriz de Bobadilla's husband, Andrés de Cabrera, enjoyed the honor of carrying the hat that was to be placed on the cardinal's head. It would be among the first of the ways in which I would pay him recognition.

After the ceremony, we attended the festivities in honor of Cardinal Mendoza, hosted by his relatives. House Mendoza was renowned for their immense wealth, and no expense was spared to observe the enormous privilege that their entire family would enjoy to have one of their own named as cardinal. The entertainments were sumptuous; the Mendoza's could clearly give a lesson in entertainment.

The day was warm and the aroma of blooming flowers filled the air. I thought about my husband's advice to choose Pedro Mendoza as cardinal instead of Carrillo. The choice may have cost me the future support of Carrillo, but as I looked at the man that stood before me, wearing his red hat and robes with solemnity and pride, and the gold *zuccetti* ring on his hand representing his allegiance to the Pope, I knew that I had made the right decision. This was the man who truly sought to serve God and kingdom first, and that was the advisor I would need most by my side in the coming days.

Beatriz took my hand and placed it in the crook of her elbow. "I cannot express how proud I was to see my husband present Mendoza with the cardinal's hat. This will be a moment that will always be remembered with great fondness. I thank you."

I warmly squeezed her hand back.

"It is a pleasure to be able to show my appreciation to your husband. After all, he has done me great honor by pledging his loyalty to me. If there is thanks to be said, it is from me to your husband, and even more so to you."

"To me?" she asked, surprised.

"Naturally. I know that you were relentless in championing my cause while at Enrique's Court."

"You are too kind. My efforts were but little — for me, it is the most natural thing in the world to speak of your virtue and honor. Of that, you have no need to thank me."

"Oh, but I do. You have had a greater impact than you imagine. So much so, that I received a royal invitation."

Beatriz stopped and turned to me, her doe-like brown eyes widening with excitement. "An invitation? For what?"

"An invitation from my brother. His Majesty desires that I join him in December to celebrate Christmas together. And I believe I have you, dear sister, to thank for it," I said, patting her hand as we slowly walked. "A little bird told me that you pulled the king aside and gave him somewhat of an ear lashing. Pray tell me what in the world happened." I couldn't help but sound as intrigued as a girl; just the thought of the scene made me wish I were a fly on the wall.

Beatriz laughed and gently sighed. "Oh, well I must admit, the rumor is true, though I should never have spoken to the king so harshly. But I just couldn't take it any longer. More and more courtiers have been speaking to Enrique on your behalf, and Pacheco couldn't bear it. He did what he always does, and was pouring lies into your brother's ear about you. And I will not have anyone speaking ill of you. I won't bear it."

"That awful man. He cannot endure the thought of competition, and anyone that the king might have a relationship with other than him, he sees as exactly that, as competition."

"The marqués is insufferable, and that is exactly what I told his Majesty. I told him that Pacheco has brought nothing but trouble to him, to his courtiers and to his kingdom, that he is an abominable and base being who lacks all sense of morality. I told your brother that most of his Court, including my husband, has endured repeated offenses, and that Pacheco is responsible for isolating the king from the people closest to him." Her voice turned gentle and reflective. "He looked so broken, as if he were going to crack under my scolding. I reminded the king that he is not alone, that he has a sister who loves him and needs him, a sister who has wanted nothing from him but peace. I told him that, for the good of his people and for the good of himself, he needed to make amends with you and let these old wounds heal."

Once I overcame my astonishment at the exchange between Beatriz and my brother, I threw my head back and laughed out loud.

"Oh, Beatriz! You leave me quite amazed. I have never known you to be a woman with such an outspoken opinion. You have always been nothing but calm discretion."

"If you had been in that Court, Isabel, you would have understood why I behaved the way I did." Beatriz' genuine sentiment of protectiveness over me warmed my heart.

"Your reaction was quite appropriate. If my brother hadn't received such a response from a woman that wields such respect in his Court, he would still be under the manipulative hand of Pacheco, and I would not have received that invitation."

"So, now that you have my husband, Cardinal Mendoza, and Cardinal Borgia, what will you do next?"

"Prepare."

"The Master of Horse will bring round the mare," the servant announced.

I gave a slight nod and smiled in acknowledgment, then turned and paced towards Chacón, carrying my little girl in my arms.

"*Mamá* will be gone for a very short time, darling, but I will miss you every moment. Just remember, you are in my heart, *mi corazón*," I said, gently tapping her heart.

"*Corrra-thón*," she repeated in her sweet baby voice, pointing to her heart.

"Yes, my love, that's right. And I am in yours, and there is nowhere you will go that I won't be with you," I promised, then handed baby Isabel to Chacón. I forced a smile on my face and looked away, fearing that I would lose my composure and break down in tears.

"Don't worry, she will be well looked after," he said, reassuringly.

"Thank you. I know she is in the best of hands with you," I replied, and placed my hand affectionately on his rosy cheek.

Fernando interlaced his fingers between my own. "There is no need for me to tell you not to worry. I know I married a strong woman," he said and leaned in to kiss me. His lips were warm and soft against my own. My husband had only been back from Aragón a short while and already we had to say another goodbye, but this time it was me leaving, and not him.

"I will be safe," I promised, though there was no way either of us could know for sure if I would return home to my family safely. My husband and I both worried that my brother, reputed for his mercurial ways, would change his mind at any moment.

Turning, I took a step away to mount my horse, but his hand pulled me back. He held me against his chest, his fingers gently caressing my scalp.

"I won't be far from you, my love," he whispered. I looked up at his face, his soulful eyes and dark lashes, and kissed him. "And will come as soon as you call on me."

I smiled through the tears that started to cloud my eyes, and tapped my finger on my heart, just like I did with our baby, for it was there, in my heart, that he, too, would always be.

"It's time," Beatriz de Bobadilla said from atop her horse, alongside Gonzálo Fernández de Córdoba. "We must make haste."

"*Princesa*, welcome to Segovia," announced Andrés de Cabrera in his warm, yet formal voice. "You are most welcome here."

Gonzálo lifted me from my horse and set me on the ground and I walked towards Cabrera.

"I did not expect to enjoy such an honor as to have the treasurer of Segovia welcome me at the city gates," I replied, and reached out both hands to him.

"It would be too great an injustice to welcome the princess of Castilla y León with nothing more than standard procedure. Ah, and you have returned to me the jewel of the kingdom," he said, and as he hugged his wife Beatriz, I noticed how she seemed to relax in his embrace, as if she had finally come home. It was clear that these two courtiers had truly found love within marriage, a rare gift in the world we lived in. Turning towards me, Cabrera continued. "I have no doubt that you must be exhausted. The king is thrilled to have you here and has prepared rooms for you in the Alcázar. Might I lead you there now, that you might enjoy a moment of repose after your journey?"

Señor Cabrera led Beatriz, Gonzálo and me through the hallways of high reaching ceilings ornamented with artwork and gilded in gold and stained-glass windows, then through the Hall of the Galley, built in the XIV century by Queen Catherine of Lancaster. As we passed through, I knew there was something unique about this room. Its Islamic *mudéjar* aesthetic captivated my brother, but as for me, the room was especially pleasing because of the Eucharist prayer inscribed near the ceiling.

Señor Cabrera opened the widely set, thick wooden door to our chambers.

"Please, rest after your journey. The king will be back from his hunt in a few hours time, and I will send for you when he returns," he said, then bowed and shut the door behind him.

The rooms were elegant and tasteful, and it was evident that King Enrique had been personally involved in the décor. Large luxurious tapestries and silver candelabras hung from the ceiling and my brother had even seen to bringing in a *prie-dieu* for prayer.

Gonzálo, my one means of protection, waited just outside, as Beatriz helped me to change from my riding clothes.

"Please, let's hurry. My brother won't be gone much longer, I'm sure, and I want to be waiting for him before he arrives."

"Don't worry, Isabel. All will be well," Beatriz answered, doing her best to use a calm tone, helping to settle my nerves.

I inhaled deeply, then slowly released the air.

"Four years have passed since we last saw each other. So much has transpired. I don't know how he will react to seeing me," I told her, grateful that I had her there with me.

"Remember, he sent the invitation to you. Your presence here is desired and welcomed. He wants to see you as much as you want to see him. It's time for both of you to put the past behind you."

Beatriz helped me dress, lacing up the back of the emerald green gown and arranging the cloth of gold skirts underneath. Outside the door, I could hear the soft clanking noise of Gonzálo de Córdoba's sword against its sheath. Although I trusted that my brother had the best intentions, both Fernando and I were much relieved to have Gonzálo to defend and protect me, though I knew it made my husband uncomfortable that he, himself wasn't here, should I need to be protected. Despite Fernando's slight jealousy of Gonzálo, he was nevertheless relieved by his presence here with me, knowing that Gonzálo was, by far, the most accomplished swordsman in all the kingdom, and that he was invariably loyal to me. Should the need arise, we had no doubt that Gonzálo de Córdoba would fight to the death to protect me.

As Beatriz slipped the pointed toe shoes onto my feet, my thoughts of the memories Gonzálo and I had shared all those years ago brought a smile to my lips. Soldier and friend, the man proved his worth, first to Alfonso, then to me. During the war, when every day brought the fear that it might be the day I lost my younger brother, my heart was comforted to know that my little brother was fiercely and loyally protected by the finest swordsman in all Castilla.

The years passed, friends and allies came and went, but Gonzálo de Córdoba and I only grew closer. Many of my fondest memories were with him, many of my most enlightening conversations made with him. The boy, now a man, made a study of the philosophies of Aristotle or Cicero, and not merely for his own pleasure. He knew how I relished intellectual debates, how much I treasured reading the works of great minds of our past. Growing up, Gonzálo took pleasure in making me gifts of manuscripts of their works, and more recently in presenting me with works in Latin.

The language of Latin was, of course, fundamental to a ruler's education. But as a child with two brothers, no one expected that I might one day come to rule. Thus, there was no need for me to acquire an education in Latin. But now it had become essential. Gonzálo's gift of books and poems in Latin strengthened my abilities in the language more every day, and soon I found myself quite proficient, even bringing in a tutor for our little Isabel. The ability to converse in Latin would prepare both my daughter and me for diplomacy in the years to come.

Just like Beatriz and Andrés de Cabrera, Gonzálo's allegiance to my cause, his single-minded devotion that spanned back even before he ever knew I would rule, would be rewarded. Once I was queen, I would see to it that he received the titles and lands that a gentleman and noble *caballero* of his caliber was worthy of. For, not only was he a great warrior and polished courtier, but he was a man of letters. And despite Beatriz' comments that he was in love with me, I promised myself that I would find him a suitable match, a wife of noble, old Castilian blood, who would love him and support him the way a man of his stature deserved.

A knock came at the door, and I knew it was a servant sent by Andrés de Cabrera.

"My lady, his Majesty, the king has arrived."

The servant led the way, with Gonzálo a step ahead of me, and Beatriz walking several paces behind me, emphasizing my dignified rank. Again, we passed through the magnificent hallways and corridors, and the warmth of the sun's gentle rays streamed in as the sun began to set, leaving an impression of divine creation that I would not soon forget.

The finely carved wooden doors sat before me as the servant entered to announce my arrival. My heart began to race, imagining what I would encounter — the hundreds of eyes that would come to rest on me, ready to judge, waiting for my reaction to the king, and his reaction to me. But I couldn't allow myself to reveal any nervousness. I was the princess and heir apparent to the throne. I must appear as noble and composed as my title. Inhaling slowly, I willed myself to take control of my countenance, to hide unwanted emotions with that familiar veil of confidence and authority, and proudly lifting my chin, I entered the Throne Room.

"Your Royal Highness," I said with lowered eyes, and performed a deep and respectful bow. When I rose, I was shocked. Hardly a soul was to be found. The space was nearly empty.

The king, his face unreadable, signaled for me to approach. He stood, and walked towards me.

"Sister." The word cracked as he spoke. It was all he said, and then he embraced me. We stayed like that for a long time, and in that moment I could feel all the tension and anger of the past dissipate away. "Follow me."

The king led me into a private room.

"My honored king and beloved brother, I come before you today to swear to you my solemn vow of loyalty," I began, speaking the sincere promise I had prepared for this encounter.

But there was so much I wanted to express, and the gentle, vulnerable look in Enrique's eyes moved me, reaching through my chest into my heart, forcing the emotion to take hold of my tongue, forcing my heart to spill out the words they had coveted for so many years. I wanted so badly for my brother to know how much I cared about him, how I wished to please him.

"My husband, Prince Fernando and I, desire to serve you with the greatest humility. We want for nothing more than to obey your wishes. I beg you, good king, to look at us with grace, to think about the many benefits that marriage to Fernando, King of Sicily and Prince of Aragón, means for the future of your kingdom. My purpose was never to insult you, my brother, my lord and king. For any insult I have caused, I beg your pardon."

The walls of ice surrounding his heart began to melt. He knew as well as I did that my words were rooted in profound and utter sincerity.

"Let us be forever united as one family," he said softly. His countenance changed, becoming both regal and familial. "Segovia welcomes you with open arms, as do I."

"It is with the greatest of pleasure that I am here." As I rested in his arms and discovered the tenderness of his embrace, I felt certain that the pain of the past had closed its door, and once again I had a brother.

"And I hope your husband is soon to join us. Did he not accompany you?"

"No, I was accompanied by Doña Beatriz de Bobadilla and Señor Gonzálo Fernández de Córdoba. But my husband would be delighted to receive an invitation to Segovia. He is anxious to meet his king."

"Excellent. It's settled, then," Enrique replied, clapping his hands together. "Tonight is an evening to be celebrated and you shall be the guest of honor. And tomorrow, we will enjoy a more private reception. Your good friends and mine, Señor Andrés de Cabrera and his wife, have prepared a special evening to celebrate your arrival. I do hope your Fernando will join us for the occasion."

"As you wish, your Highness."

Beatriz' practiced hands gave one final adjustment to the hem of my amethyst-purple silk gown, and before entering the grand ballroom, I ran my fingers over the sapphire and ruby Maltese cross pendant fastened onto the fabric. In every corner of the room, one could find the romantic golden hew of the candles warming the space. Their gentle flickering light danced on the walls, leading one's eyes to the ornate artwork painted on the ballroom ceiling, highlighting the sophistication of the palace. The musicians played from the patios above and courtiers danced before the eyes of the king. Meanwhile, servants passed between the courtiers, carrying trays of exotic delicacies and wines from Portugal, France, and Spain.

"Cava?" Andrés to Cabrera offered his wife a glass of sparkling wine from the northern region of Spain.

"My favorite, thank you, darling," she said, and tenderly stroked his face before taking the crystal glass.

"*Princesa*?" he offered, gesturing to the wine.

"Thank you, but no," I replied.

Gonzálo de Córdoba enjoyed a glass of red wine from the region of Rioja. Closing my eyes, I breathed in the aroma of the wine's notes of cherry and vanilla.

"Watch the nobles. Observe how each one comes before the king and bows, begging for him to acknowledge them," Gonzálo whispered to me, coming just close enough so that I alone could hear.

I nodded my head once.

"I will make you a wager. I will bet you that the same men who stand before the king will also make their way to you."

"A few will come, surely. But I doubt *all* of them will pay me such a compliment. There are still those who resist me."

"No, my lady. None will resist you. Some are wise, others opportunistic, but every one of the nobles will come before you. Every last one."

The king left his chair and sat down next to the musicians.

"Isabel," he called out to me. "Will you dance for me, and I will play for you, like before?"

Giving a slight bow, I stepped away from the crowd into an open space. One of the musicians handed the king his *guitarra*, and coming to the center of the room, I held my gown in my hands and curtsied before him. Then he began to play.

As he plucked the strings of the instrument, I sensed the eyes of every one of the courtiers penetrate into me. Nevertheless, I centered my focus onto the music, moving my body in unison with the rhythm of the song.

The courtiers knew as well as I that this moment was more significant than a mere dance and song. It was a moment replete with symbolism. It was a manifestation being made by the king that I was firmly established in his favor.

The next day was spent enjoying the leisures of Segovia. His Grace and I rode side by side through the valleys and plains of the countryside, just the two of us. And we talked, reminisced and laughed. The world, as I knew it, was changing.

My handmaiden began unlacing my gown to prepare me for bed.

"I can manage that," my husband said, dismissing the servant for the evening.

"You looked ravishing tonight," Fernando said to me. He continued to undress me, brushing my hair to one side and kissing my neck slowly. "I couldn't wait to be alone with you."

"Did you not enjoy the private reception? Beatriz and Andrés organized it especially for you."

He pressed his face into my hair, breathing me in. "It was elegant and intimate. The perfect environment for me to make your brother's acquaintance. Still, I prefer being here, with you. You've been away too long. Tonight, I will have you for myself. Our daughter needs a brother. It is well-time we tried."

The shuffling of feet and a pounding knock on the front door interrupted us.

"Apologies for the intrusion, but it's the king," Andrés de Cabrera said, nearly breathless. "He is ill."

"Take me to him," I said. Fernando re-laced my gown, his hands nimbler than my own handmaidens. Without a moment to waste, my husband and I fell in behind Cabrera. Andrés led us and we scurried through the hallways that weaved through the Alcázar and into a secret passageway.

"No one must know of the king's health," he whispered, then continued, leading us through a narrow hall of cold stone flooring and low ceiling that twisted in different directions. Finally, Cabrera showed us to the king's chambers, then turned and took his leave.

"Your Grace," I began, harkening towards my brother.

"Out!" Pacheco's voice bellowed. "Get out of here, you and your illegitimate husband."

I stared at him in shock.

"You dare to speak to the princess in such a manner," Fernando shot back and placed his hand on his sword.

"Your wife will be spoken to as I see fit. This is her doing. She poisoned the king."

I looked at my brother's face. It was ashen, and his skin looked dull, even lifeless. By the look of his skin, he very well could have been poisoned, but not by me. Never by me.

Enrique turned and looked at me, his eyes as hard as ice. Pacheco had turned him on me, I knew.

"Brother," I said, imploring him to look into my eyes and see the truth. "Brother, I would never…"

Enrique turned his face to Pacheco, refusing to honor me with a reply. "I would rest now."

"Of course, your Majesty," he answered, then turned his glare on me.

I refused to acknowledge Pacheco. My obedience was to my brother, never to the loathsome creature who damaged every person he ever encountered.

"As you wish, your Highness," I said to my brother, and bowed before exiting.

Fernando and I said not a word until we were safely inside the privacy of our chambers.

"Do you think this is Pacheco's doing?" I whispered. "Could Pacheco have used poison to harm Enrique, just as he did with my little brother?"

Fernando gave no answer, but instead his fingers were busy clasping together his riding vest.

"Dress quickly. We will not be sleeping here. I mean for us to leave tonight." Fernando placed his dagger inside its sheath. "Segovia is too dangerous for us to stay."

"I will remain. I must hear what the doctor's diagnosis is."

"And if it turns out that the king has indeed been poisoned? What then? Isabel, come to your senses. We must leave, and leave now. It's not safe here for us. If it is determined that the king has been poisoned, it will be you they blame."

"No. Fernando, I will not leave."

"And risk imprisonment, or worse? Isabel, be reasonable. Let us return to Sepulveda, where we have the strength of an army."

Fernando had a point. We had little to protect us here, and could easily be framed as the scapegoat to a royal murder attempt. But if we left now, it would seem as if we were trying to flee.

"Impossible. We will stay. To remain is a declaration of our innocence. Trust me, we must hold our ground. My presence here maintains my control. I will not be overcome by Pacheco, not this time. I've worked too hard to earn the trust of the nobles of my brother's Court. If we leave Segovia now, we will never take it back."

Fernando could see that I was digging my heels in. It was decided. I would remain.

"And our daughter? Should we continue to leave her under the supervision of the Buendía family and Cardinal Mendoza?"

"No, she is safest with us. Send for her to be brought here. Our family will all be together. Our strength is in our unity."

We stayed put, never leaving the Alcázar. Instead, it was the king who willed to leave, abandoning his beloved city and returning to his palace in Madrid. I sensed Pacheco's hand in this. The man was determined to separate my brother and me any way he could. I wrote, inquiring about his health, sharing endearing anecdotes about my little daughter Isabel, how she was growing so fast, and sent miniatures of her sweet, angelic face. I hoped he would read these letters and remember that he had a family who loved him.

Instead, he remained silent. Pacheco kept his abusive grip firmly on my brother, filling the king's mind with suspicion, isolating Enrique from anyone who posed as a rival for his royal attention.

Nevertheless, I pressed forward, my ever-moving quill becoming my weapon. My correspondence with the nobles across Castilla y León continued, our network of communication throughout the kingdom growing stronger and steadier by the day. With each letter, I came to better understand the fears and endeavors of my countrymen, and they discovered in me a leader of unceasing dedication.

I pulled the fur stole tightly around my shoulders and sat by the crackling fire. Fall of 1474 had come and gone, and winter was fast approaching. The days were shorter and colder. And I missed my husband.

Every night I kissed my daughter goodnight and lay in bed alone, wondering when my husband would return. Again, the war in Aragón pulled him away, and again, my husband obliged the call. He was quick to obey his father, the king of Aragón, and rush off to the adventures of battle, the camaraderie of the soldiers and the flirtations of the mistresses and prostitutes that were ubiquitous in the camps during times of war. But he neglected his duty to me, his wife, and his duty to Castilla. We needed another child, an heir. And yet, here I found myself every night, alone in the cold, silk sheets.

"My lady," the servant said, presenting me with the silver tray that carried several letters.

I leafed through the pile, searching for the one letter I had been anxiously waiting for, my husband's response. I grabbed the letter opener, and in my eagerness, I accidentally pricked myself. Blood welled up over the tip of my finger and dripped onto the edge of the page. I knew my mother would have called this a bad omen, but I brushed it aside.

My eyes scanned through his words. At such a moment, I cared little for whatever he had written. Anyway, I would read it again in more detail later. At this moment, there was but one thing that mattered: how quickly Fernando could return to me.

My lips curled into a frown, and I closed the letter.

"Doña Sophia," I called out to my handmaid. "Ready my things. I will be leaving at once."

"Before the arrival of Prince Fernando?"

"Yes," I said, annoyed at her questioning. "And have them bring round the carriage. Do hurry, there is no time to lose."

The pages of his letter crumpled in my fist.

How dare he refuse my call. I made him aware of my need for him, and still he defied me, even at a time when his presence was as imperative for the future of our family as it now was.

Allies at the Court in Madrid had kept me apprised of my brother's condition. His health never fully recovered after that night in January. Once word reached me that Enrique's condition was growing more alarming, I sent for Fernando. Should the king die, Fernando and I would need to move quickly to establish our position as the true and rightful rulers, before any of Juana la Beltraneja's supporters interfered.

But my husband was obstinate, arguing that there was no purpose in his returning just yet. My brother, he reasoned, was healthier than he was made out to be. Enrique was an active man, enjoying riding and hunting at his leisure. And he was so young, only forty-six years old. Fernando had no doubt that the king would recover. He assured me that this was nothing more than a false alarm and he could not separate himself from the Aragonese war, not now, when they needed his leadership most.

But since the death of Juan Pacheco, the Marqués de Villena, in the beginning of October, many of my friends at Court noticed a sharp decline in the health of the king, most likely a result of the loss of his friend and advisor. Previously he might feel woozy after a long day of riding, but now he couldn't even get out of bed.

I feared that my brother's time was limited, and I needed to get to him. If his time had truly come, I needed to say goodbye.

"The king will see you now," the servant announced.

I nodded my head in acknowledgment and allowed the servant to lead me in. He stopped and turned towards me before entering.

"The doctor already left," the servant said. "They have bled him, perhaps more than they should have. He is weak, and his condition is unstable, passing in and out of consciousness."

I understood the servant was trying to prepare me for what I was about to see.

"Has the priest come?" I asked.

"He will be here shortly. Your brother wishes to see you first."

"Of course," I said, placing a gold coin into his hand, then entered the royal chambers.

There he lay, the king of Castilla y León, curled up on his side in his oversized feather bed, the cold shadow of death at the door. For a moment I couldn't move, standing in shock at the realization of the possibility of the death of a king. Laying there in the fetal position, he looked as fragile as a baby that was removed too soon from his mother's belly. Just then, he turned his face towards me.

"Isabel, is that you?" His voice was weak, barely audible.

"Yes, your Grace. I am here."

"Sister, I am glad you came."

A sigh of relief escaped me. I wasn't sure how he would welcome me, but from that one word, calling me "sister," I knew he, too, wanted me there.

He turned over on his back, and struggled to push himself up.

"Here, allow me to help you, Sire," I offered, and stuffed two feather pillows behind his back. "Is that better?"

"Hmm, yes," he replied, allowing me close to his royal person. His skin looked grayish and smelled of death. "It's always a gift to enjoy the company of a young beauty doting on me, particularly when it is a woman as lovely as you," he smiled weakly.

I reached out to him and he patted the top of my palm, then rested my hand over his.

"I feel as if we are but two roses, grown from the same root. But my last petal is about to shed, and I am staring at the rose that is yet priming to bloom."

I couldn't image what it must be like to feel the approach of death and to look at the one that would soon take his place.

He looked away, smiling to himself. It was a sad smile.

"Isabel, you have fought with great resilience for the day you would take the crown that now rests on my head. But to fight for the crown is profoundly different than to bear the burden of a king. The country blames me for many wrongs. No matter how hard I tried to love my people well, they were never appeased. To rule is to accept that a great portion of your countrymen will always be dissatisfied... and disloyal. I know you think you will govern this country better than I did, and truly I hope you do."

His cough interrupted him, and he began to choke. I brought a bowl over to him and he spit up a dark reddish-purple blood.

The king looked up at me, his eyes penetrating and sad. "You have no idea how lonely it is for the one who bears the crown atop his head."

I stared back at him, unsettled. It was true, there were few things in life as lonely as being king, and inevitably, that task was soon to fall onto my shoulders. The only thing lonelier was the way we were all expected to pretend.

To pretend. Yes, that was it — what it was that made us all feel so lonely. A performance to portray, by all of us, courtiers, royals, the clergy, maiden and whore, soldier and farmer - all of us had our part. So many rules on how each of us was to behave. What was appropriate, what was vulgar, what was dignified and what was base. Somehow, I would have to find my way through the labyrinth of rules and codes of propriety if I intended on surviving this world that willed to swallow me whole, just as it did my brothers.

"Hush," was all I said, hoping to calm him, and dipping the towel into cool water, I wiped the cold beads of sweat off his forehead.

"They compare you to Mother Mary. They say you are the Redeemer, sent by God to restore Castilla y León and heal the nation. But you, too, may find that one day you will need forgiveness from your subjects for nothing more than doing what you thought best for your kingdom."

"I know you did your very best. History's remembrance of its sovereigns, all of its sovereigns, is rarely forgiving." There was nothing more to say.

"Isabel, before you go, pray for me."

The bells on every church in the city of Segovia began to ring.

"The king is dead," the street criers shouted out to the citizens.

But I already knew. At this point, my web of informants had slowly spread to different reaches all throughout the kingdom, and my best sources were planted at the Court of Enrique. Word of the king's passing had reached me hours ago. And I was prepared. After visiting my brother, there was no doubt in my mind that his time was soon to end.

Despite my letter to Fernando informing him of my brother's condition, my husband did not return. And I didn't press him further. My husband had been made aware that as soon as the king died, we would be declared. If he failed to present himself for such a monumental moment, that was not my concern.

No, my concern was to seize the moment, before I lost my chance.

"A shawl, your Majesty?" Beatriz de Bobadilla offered. "The Mass being said for Enrique is to take place early this morning. It will be frightfully cold."

"No, thank you." This December morning was frigid, and a thin layer of ice was frozen over the cobblestone streets that I would soon be proceeding through. "Let me endure the chill. I want to feel every part of this day."

Beatriz fitted the midnight black silk gown over my shoulders and draped the black lace veil atop my head, tucking in the golden waves of my hair.

The Mass in remembrance of my brother was solemn, almost poetic in its poignancy. The streets were filled with the citizens of Segovia, my brother's most cherished city, every one of them respectfully dressed in black. As I made my way between the rows of onlookers, my countrymen bowed their head and removed their caps.

After Mass, my entourage and I slowly proceeded through the streets, then returned to the royal bedchamber of the Alcázar, the rooms that previously belonged to my brother.

"Quickly," Beatriz said, signaling with her finger to three of my ladies-in-waiting to come help undress me while a fourth helped her bring my coronation gown out of the royal wardrobe. Now all of them attended to me, carefully fastening the brilliant white gown onto my body. Then Beatriz opened the silver jewelry case. Inside, protected by a bed of velvet, rested the diamond necklace with matching bracelet and earrings.

"Magnificent," I whispered, gently running my fingertips along the stones of the necklace. One of the ladies-in-waiting held the case as Beatriz lifted the necklace and positioned it on my neck just above my bodice, like a collar.

"Magnificent, indeed," Beatriz replied. "It's a work of perfection. Worthy of a ruler just as magnificent." She secured the clasp behind my neck. "The necklace is just shy of one hundred diamonds, ranging in different sizes. And the cross pendant hanging from the center holds an emerald that is nearly five carats."

"It's exquisite, unlike anything I've ever seen."

"And very appropriate for an occasion as prodigious as today." She hugged me. "Today we celebrate you. Your victory has come."

"Your Highness," a servant announced, "Señor Gutierre de Cárdenas and Señor Diego de Valera have arrived."

"Let them come."

The men entered and bowed before me. I studied them carefully, pleased that they had dressed for the occasion.

Diego de Valera had years of experience as a historian. Before serving in my Court, he had served in that of my father and later my brother, Enrique IV. It was essential to have him here documenting this juncture in history.

"Don Valera," I said to my court chronicler. "I am pleased to see that you have brought your papers with you. You may begin your work immediately. But I require that you present these observations to me as soon as you are finished. Whatever does not receive my approval must be burned."

"Certainly, madam. When will your husband be arriving? It appears as if the procession is about to begin, and we are lacking a king," the chronicler pointed out. His soft, almost childlike voice always irked me. Despite the friendly intonation of his voice, I was aware of the criticism in his statement.

"The king is currently performing his duty in Aragón. Nevertheless, the procession will, indeed, begin momentarily."

Valera nodded in acknowledgment, but his disapproval was palpable. My historian was a man that prized protocol nearly above all else, and it did not sit right with him that the royal procession would be led by a woman unaccompanied by her husband.

"Your Majesty," Chacón interrupted, returning to the matter at hand. "The procession will be as follows: behind the men bearing the Trastámara coat of arms will be Cárdenas," he said, gesturing to his nephew beside him, "then you will come, carried atop a white horse, to the Church of San Miguel. Behind you will walk Andrés de Cabrera and Beatriz de Bobadilla, then the bishop of Segovia, and finally, Segovia's city officials, nobles and members of the clergy. Once you swear your oath to the Church and to the people, all will then pledge their allegiance to you, and finally, Andrés de Cabrera will hand you the keys to the Alcázar and its treasury."

"Excellent. Well done, sir. One final thing: my daughter, Isabel. She is to be presented before the crowd as my successor. It must be understood that the right to rule passes from myself as queen to my daughter. As it is, Castilla must grow accustomed to a female ruler."

"Of course," Chacón answered, knowing that this was not merely a request, but a royal command.

"The street callers, they are clear on what to cry out as I pass?" I asked, turning to Gutierre de Cárdenas.

"Yes, your Highness. I was explicit in the exact verbiage they must use during your procession through the streets, before you receive your oath of loyalty.

"*Castilla, Castilla, Castilla, for our queen and lady, Queen Isabel, and for King Fernando, her legitimate husband.*"

I suspected that Señor Valera was among the faction of Castilians who still viewed my husband as not merely king consort who had acquired his royal position through marriage, but instead as the true regent. Despite the specifications detailed in our legally binding marital agreement, many expected that once wed, Fernando would be granted the authority to rule because he was male. They would soon find themselves availed of this misunderstanding.

"Very good," I said, smiling to Señor Cárdenas. "Doña Beatriz, would you please…"

Beatriz de Bobadilla stepped away, then returned with a large rectangular case made of elm burl wood. She unhinged the clasp and lifted the lid to reveal a majestic, unsheathed sword with five crosses.

With the sight of such a magnificent sword, the memory of Joan of Arc flashed before my eyes. Joan of Arc had been an inspiration to me since my earliest memories of life — a woman with the heart of a man who fearlessly served her country and her God. I thought of her leading her troops in battle. She, too, carried a sword with five crosses. And though she wielded the sword, it was solely used to lead and inspire, never to kill.

"There will be no scepter carried today," I announced.

Señor Valera's eyes widened disapprovingly. He was not pleased that I was breaking with the tradition of holding the orb and cross.

No matter. Soon enough he would come around. Soon enough, they all would.

For those who felt any apprehension about a woman taking the throne, what they were about to see was sure to only stir more displeasure. I could endure the disapproval. Lions don't concern themselves with the opinions of sheep.

Valera, along with the others, would pay witness to the procession that passed through the plaza to the church once more. This moment had been carefully orchestrated for months, and I well knew that the onlookers would understand the symbolic importance of what they were about to witness: a resplendent woman bathed in sparkling white, being led forth by a man bearing an unsheathed sword – a representation of the purification of the land. They would bend the knee, and I would be proclaimed queen.

"Señor Cárdenas," I said, my voice resounding with august solemnity, and lifted the heavy sword out of its encasement. "You are to walk before me, carrying the sword in your right hand. Hold it high, for all of Spain to see that the age of corruption, lawlessness, and immorality has reached its end. Beginning today, I, Isabel, will deliver my kingdom into peace, unity, and faith."

CPSIA information can be obtained
at www.ICGtesting.com
Printed in the USA
BVHW080227221219
567281BV00001B/11/P

9 781945 181733